REUNION AT GREYSTONE MANOR

—

Bonnie Vanak

HARLEQUIN

ROMANTIC
SUSPENSE

HARLEQUIN®
ROMANTIC SUSPENSE™

Recycling programs
for this product may
not exist in your area.

ISBN-13: 978-1-335-73809-7

Reunion at Greystone Manor

Copyright © 2022 by Bonnie Vanak

For questions and comments about the quality of this book, please contact us at CustomerService@Harlequin.com.

Harlequin Enterprises ULC
22 Adelaide St. West, 41st Floor
Toronto, Ontario M5H 4E3, Canada
www.Harlequin.com

Printed in U.S.A.

Dear Reader,

Spooky old houses always held fascination for me. When I set out to write *Reunion at Greystone Manor*, I had vivid memories of my childhood home in New Jersey. My brother and I swore our basement was haunted. I certainly thought it so when I heard an ominous thud on the basement steps one night while my parents were out. I was terrified until I discovered the noise was made by a potato falling out of the sack kept on the landing. Scared of a falling potato!

Scary sounds are the least of hero Roarke Calhoun's problems with Greystone Manor. Considered the town's bad boy when he was growing up, the FBI agent has vowed to never return to his childhood home until the death of Livi, his eccentric great-aunt, forces him back to claim the rambling mansion she left him. Roarke hopes to avoid Megan Robinson, the woman who broke his heart, but discovers he must work with her to sell Greystone Manor.

It won't be easy, for Roarke and Megan must deal with deep feelings that never died. Roarke's protective streak surfaces when he saves Megan from a dangerous trap set in the house. They discover there could be treasure hidden in the manor, and someone will stop at nothing—not even murder—to obtain it.

I hope you enjoy *Reunion at Greystone Manor*. Thank you for reading my books!

Bonnie Vanak

He checked out the room, with its dormer windows overlooking the front lawn, and then gestured for Meg to enter. She made a face as she saw the dolls.

Roarke agreed. "I always hated these damn dolls. But the mannequins are worse."

Meg shivered as well. "This room always gave me the creeps. It's why I hated coming up here to store her things. But she insisted on putting them in this room to keep them safe."

He paused in crossing the room. "Someone wanted to steal her belongings?"

"I got the feeling that's why she really wanted the valuable items moved. But then after she said that, she laughed and said she was a pack rat with an active imagination and should just give everything away."

The chest sat under the center dormer window. But it wasn't the wooden chest that drew his attention. Roarke stared at the window. "Someone's been here recently."

Meg gasped. "I've never seen that before!"

The lettering on the window was backwards, but he could clearly read the two words that made his blood run cold.

Help me.

New York Times and *USA TODAY* bestselling author **Bonnie Vanak** is passionate about romance novels and telling stories. A former newspaper reporter, she worked as a journalist for a large international charity for several years, traveling to countries such as Haiti to report on poor living conditions. Bonnie lives in Florida with her husband, Frank, and is a member of Romance Writers of America. She loves to hear from readers. She can be reached through her website, bonnievanak.com.

Books by Bonnie Vanak

Harlequin Romantic Suspense

Rescue from Darkness
Reunion at Greystone Manor

Colton 911: Chicago

Colton 911: Under Suspicion

The Coltons of Red Ridge

His Forgotten Colton Fiancée

SOS Agency

Navy SEAL Seduction
Shielded by the Cowboy SEAL
Navy SEAL Protector

Visit the Author Profile page at Harlequin.com

For Tonya Langley, a warm and caring fellow dog lover who kept me centered over the past two years. Thank you for your compassion, strength, empathy and your love for dogs!

Prologue

The stars overhead burst with light, pinpricks of sparkles in the night sky. So beautiful. If only they could remain here forever, away from everyone who threatened their love.

She could dream. But at seventeen, Megan Robinson had already discovered that dreams and plans always changed.

"Cold?" Roarke asked softly, pulling her into his arms again.

"Not with you."

Never with him, Roarke Calhoun, the boy who fired her blood, made her feel alive and thrilled the way no one else ever had.

It didn't matter that it was Michigan and the temperatures dropped down to the fifties even on summer nights. No way was she cold around Roarke, when he heated her from the inside out. Roarke was the most exciting boy she'd ever dated. Her past dates were as dull as the merry-go-round, while Roarke was the roller coaster. With his handsome looks, vivid green eyes and rugged swagger, he was the guy all the girls in school secretly wanted.

The guy all their dads dreaded.

They'd just finished making love, tangling together on the blanket outside the caretaker's cottage on his great-aunt Lavinia's estate. Meg was relieved she had started birth control. Her own father would not take her to the doctor, so Roarke's great-aunt Livi had, cautioning Meg with a good dose of practicality. Meg was grateful to her.

He tunneled his long fingers through her hair. "Princess, we have to talk. About us, and that damn fire."

Meg turned her face away. She didn't want to talk about her father meeting with Livi inside the mansion. Or think about how everyone in town thought Roarke had set the fire that burned down the Kinkaids' lake house.

Gently, he turned her face back to him. "We can't stay out here forever, sweetheart. We have to face reality."

"You're innocent," she burst out. "They weren't able to prove anything."

Roarke sighed, and the sound made him seem older than his eighteen years. "No proof, but in the eyes of everyone, I did it. Everyone in school knows I hate Deke Kinkaid and his family."

Indignation shot through her. "His dad foreclosed on your house and kicked you out. You have a perfect right to hate him. That's understandable."

He rubbed his cheek against the top of her head. "Ah, princess, I love you and your fierce defense of me. You're my entire world."

Meg snuggled closer. "And you're mine. Nothing can touch us, Roarke."

"I have to get the hell out of this town. I'm joining the Navy. I graduated and no one can tell me what to do with my life. If I stay here, I'll turn into the criminal everyone thinks I am."

She felt a jolt of pride and alarm. "You're enlisting?"

He nodded. "I've been reading about the Navy SEALs. I'm going to be one, Meg. Make you proud of me."

She nuzzled his neck. "I'm already proud of you, Roarke. You can be anything you want to. You're smart and courageous and I've never met anyone as determined as you."

"You're pretty special yourself. Never let anyone tell you otherwise. Not even that father of yours. Make your own path, Meg. Not his." He sighed again. "If Mom had lived and my father hadn't been such a jerk, maybe things would have been different for me. Too many bad breaks."

It wasn't fair. Roarke's father had divorced his mother when Roarke was only three in order to marry his wealthy mistress and move to Chicago. He'd provided little financial assistance to his son, focusing on his new family. His mother had died a year ago, turning his entire world upside down. If not for his great-aunt Livi, he'd be homeless.

"I can't bear it if you leave. I want to go with you."

A light laugh. "Princess, you've got another year of high school. I'm not ruining your life any more than I've already ruined it."

"You could never ruin my life!"

"Yeah, you're the only one who would say that. Wait for me. I love you." He picked up her hand and kissed it in a courtly gesture. "I want to marry you, Meg Robinson. Be my wife."

She flung her arms around him and kissed him deeply. Laughing, he kissed her back. "I'd better get you inside. You're shivering and I plan to take good care of my wife."

They dressed and followed the stone pathway winding back to the main house. Meg clutched his hand for support as much as comfort.

She knew what lay ahead. Her father would be furious by their disappearance and reappearance, and confronting him about their future plans wouldn't be easy. Professor Albert Robinson didn't like Roarke. Only her father's friendship with Roarke's great-aunt had saved Meg. Every Tuesday the professor came over to argue and debate history and literature with Livi, who had given a generous endowment to his department.

Meg knew she was in trouble from the moment they entered the library where her father and Livi sat in chairs by the fire. A cheerful fire crackled in the hearth, and Livi's silver service sat on the teak table between them, along with two floral teacups. So elegant and refined. Warm.

Not as icy as her father's gray gaze as he and Livi looked up and saw them.

With a rueful look, Roarke plucked a stray twig from her hair.

"You've been sleeping together. This time you've gone too far, Roarke Calhoun," he blustered.

"Now, Albert," Livi chided. "Meg is…"

She waved a hand. "Here. I'm right here. So is Roarke. I love him, Dad. He's asked me to marry him and wait for him."

"You're having sex!"

"Yes, we are." She drew in a breath. "And I'm on birth control so you don't have to worry about me getting pregnant. This is my life and I want Roarke as my future husband."

Roarke squeezed her hand. "That's right, sir. I'm headed out to join the Navy. I'm going to be a Navy SEAL. I have it in me. I've asked Meg to wait for me. I know she's young, but we love each other."

Her heart sank as her father ignored Roarke and turned to Livi. As if she and Roarke were invisible. As if her opinion didn't count.

"Do you approve of this?" he asked Livi.

Livi threw up her hands. "Albert, dear, let's hear them out."

"Hear them out." Her father's jaw turned rigid. "You're going to stick up for him again like you did when they arrested him for arson."

"Nothing came of it," Livi said calmly. "He was innocent."

"His class ring was found in the ashes."

Roarke's jaw tightened. Meg's heart raced. She could see the fury in his eyes.

He dropped Meg's hand and stepped forward. "I am innocent. How many times do I have to tell you? My class ring was stolen weeks ago. Someone set me up."

Her father snorted. "We can only go by evidence. There's still the matter of a witness who saw a man of your height, wearing a leather jacket just like yours, who ran from the scene and took off on a motorcycle just like you have."

"And the charges were dropped because the evidence was circumstantial. Are you kidding me? You're labeling me an arsonist and I didn't do it, dammit!" Roarke raked a hand through his shoulder-length hair.

Meg's father narrowed his eyes. "Do not yell at me, young man."

Livi's eyes filled with pity. "I'm sorry, dear. The Kinkaids' insurance company paid out, but everyone still thinks you had something to do with it over that fight you had with Deke last month."

Her throat closing, Meg felt the same helplessness Roarke must have felt. The fight was partly her fault, as Deke had asked her out. When she'd told him she was exclusively dating Roarke, Deke had confronted Roarke and taunted him.

Roarke punched him in the face. Deke tried to fight back, but though he was taller and more muscled, Roarke had stamina. He never quit. Meg knew that resolve would gain him a space with the elite Navy SEALs.

Maybe *then* people would finally respect *that wild Calhoun boy*.

"Although that black eye and swollen jaw did improve Deke's looks," Livi mused, winking at them.

Usually Livi's good humor could coax Roarke from a bad mood. Not this time.

"Let them think whatever they wish. I don't care. I'm gone." He turned to Meg. "Meg, promise you'll come to me when I get my leave. We'll work something out."

Her father marched over to Meg, but his words were for Roarke.

"You're a bad influence, Roarke Calhoun. Meg has great plans. She's going to college to become a teacher. She plans to stay here in Cooper Falls and make something of herself. She's not going to become the wife of a jailbird, and end up broke and homeless on the street."

"For goodness' sake, Albert, broke and homeless? I would never allow that to happen," Livi cried out. "Can't we discuss this calmly and leave the dramatics for your classroom?"

Her father ignored Livi. "You're not what I want for my daughter. Look at you. You dress like, like a hoodlum."

Green gaze stormy, Roarke plucked at the hem of his brown leather jacket. "I ride a bike. Leather protects my skin."

"And I'm protecting Meg." He turned to Livi. "Meg is seventeen! He's ruining her."

"He's not ruining her." Livi heaved an exasperated sigh. "She's young, but she is smart and knows her own mind. They're in love, Albert. As much in love as you were with Linda, God rest her soul. Roarke is ready for new adventures and to begin his life. Do you really believe keeping

Meg here in this town, with the same experiences and same friends, will expand her horizons?"

Hope flared inside Meg. Maybe there was a chance.

Then her father turned to her, and she saw the same desperation and sorrow in his eyes she'd glimpsed since her mother died when she was twelve.

"Meg, I want what's best for you, honey. You're too young for any kind of commitment. You're my world and…" His voice cracked. "I can't bear for you to leave. I can't lose you like I lost your mother. You're all I have. I love you."

"Dad…" She couldn't speak. Guilt filled her.

Roarke put his hands on her shoulders and turned her toward him. "Meg, promise me you'll wait for me. Promise me you'll marry me when you turn eighteen. We'll make it work out. Promise to be there for me. I need you."

Her mouth opened and closed as she felt suffocated by the pressure of parent and lover. She could not speak, could not even manage a nod, only wonder in abject misery how she could have everything she'd ever dreamed of having.

"Roarke…" His name came out as a whisper, almost a prayer.

The light died from his eyes. "Yeah, I see. I'll write you, Meg. Email you. If you want me to be in your life, you'll write me back."

He hugged his aunt. "Goodbye, Livi. Love you. I'll be in touch. Thanks for everything."

With a snort, he stormed away, banging the front door behind him. Meg ran to the door, everything in her heart bursting out, everything she had wanted to say and could not.

She tried to speak, call out the words, but they drowned in the roar of his Harley as he sped off into the night.

Into the darkness and out of her life.

Chapter 1

He had never planned for a moment like this, but life had a quirky way of hurling him into the unknown.

Roarke Calhoun dragged in a deep breath. *Stay strong, stay brave, stay sane.* The mantra that kept him alive and fighting through two tours as a Navy SEAL ran through his mind like a silent prayer.

Heart racing, he remained still, listening to the sounds in the inky night. The darkness remained eerily silent, but for insects humming in the nearby trees.

In the distance a dog barked. He braced himself. The bark might warn of intruders. Certainly he didn't want anyone knowing he was back in town. Nope, not Roarke Calhoun, the bad boy everyone thought would end up in prison.

He approached the railroad tracks dividing the poor side of town, his side, from the wealthier inhabitants. Movement caught his eye in the dim sodium streetlights, followed by an earsplitting yelp of distress.

Roarke ground to a halt, his heart racing. A small dog,

caught on the tracks. In the distance, he heard an ominous whistle.

Train coming. One of those long freights.

After dropping his duffel bag, he raced to the tracks. A thin rope ringed the dog's neck, the end of which was looped around a railroad spike pounded into the tracks. The dog howled louder, struggling to get free.

The train chugged closer. Little time to waste.

Training kicked in as he analyzed the sitch. Knots too tight. The dog growled, frantic to be free.

"Easy, boy," he soothed in a low tone, avoiding the dog's snapping jaws.

Roarke flipped out his pocketknife, unfolded it and sawed through the cord. But the rain-soaked rope was tough. Cursing, he worked faster, the dog quiet now as if it realized its savior was trying to help.

If I don't get this rope cut, we're both goners.

He breathed deep and focused, using his training to remain calm and detached as the train barreled toward them, the freight's headlamp now glaring only a few hundred feet away. The engineer blew the horn and the brakes squealed.

Not enough to stop.

Finally! Roarke tossed the knife aside, tugged at the rope, which broke. Wrapping both arms around the freed dog, he pivoted, dropped and rolled away from the track seconds before the locomotive roared past.

Beneath him, the dog squirmed, but not much, as if the mutt realized how close he'd come to death. The grind and squeal of brakes sounded, and he sat up, still clutching the dog.

"You okay?" the engineer yelled, running toward him.

"Yeah." He released the wriggling mutt. "He almost bought it. Who the hell would tie a dog to the tracks?"

"Don't know." The engineer scratched his head, frowning. "Lots of odd things happening these days in Cooper Falls. Well, if you're okay, I have a schedule."

Nodding brusquely, he watched the man race back to the engine's cab, and with a blast of the whistle and a jerk of cars, the freight moved forward again.

The dog wagged its tail and whined. Roarke scratched its ears. Small dog, weighing about twenty pounds, definitely a mixed breed.

"You got a home? Who did this to you?" he murmured.

Seemed like good ole Cooper Falls hadn't changed. People still tossed mongrels aside. He'd been one of those mongrels. But an innocent dog? It infuriated him.

Roarke fetched his pack, and fished inside for the honey-and-oat granola bars he always carried. He opened two and tossed them to the dog, who gobbled them down.

Sighing, he picked up the rope and loosened it around the dog's neck. "Starved and left for dead. Come on, fella. Better days are ahead."

The local pet shelter wasn't far. He couldn't leave the dog here in the open, but he couldn't take him, either.

A short time later, he left the dog outside the dark building. A kind soul had left a doghouse inside a pen filled with straw, along with a bowl of water and a sign that said to drop off strays and pets and they would take care of them when they opened in the morning. With a final pat to the dog's head, he headed back toward his destination.

Didn't take long.

Gravel crunched beneath his boots as he advanced. The black duffel hung heavy on his shoulder, but he didn't pause to adjust it. The sooner he accomplished his mission, the sooner he could be home in Washington, DC, again, safe and entrenched in his comfort zone at the FBI.

Eyes trained to see in the dark could make out the target

ahead. Innocent looking enough, but it had brought him back to this hellhole of a town.

The hellhole he'd thought he'd forever abandoned.

Roarke stopped. Listened again. Nothing.

Nothing except his own rapid heartbeat. Sweat streamed down his back, despite the cool breeze ruffling his hair.

Gradually the black night retreated, allowing him to see the target details. Milky white cataract glass windows stared blindly back at him. White paint peeling in strips. Porch steps sagging.

An air of abandonment and disuse.

All his now. Greystone Manor.

He'd inherited this mess, a mess that could turn into a jewel with elbow grease and repairs. *Thanks, Aunt Lavinia.* He felt a rush of gratitude and grief. Selling this monster of a mansion could save his stepniece's life.

Roarke would face enemy fire, and worse, for Holly. "Welcome back home," he muttered.

Welcome back to Cooper Falls, Michigan, his birthplace.

With a resolute sigh, he strode up the steps, careful to navigate the third from the top. It had always creaked, and now looked splintered. Like his damn lost hopes.

No use getting melancholy.

After using the key Lavinia's attorney had mailed, he entered the house and flipped on the hall light. Elk antlers from the overhead chandelier cast eerie shadows on the floor. As a boy, he'd spent many happy hours stalking and shooting the antlers with his BB gun.

Lavinia had helped, wearing her safari pith helmet acquired in Africa as she shouted out encouragement. Every week, the town electrician replaced light bulbs in the fixture broken from his poor aim.

"You'll get better, my boy," Lavinia had assured him.

"You couldn't hit water if you fell into my pool, but you'll get better."

Last week at the FBI's shooting range, he'd scored perfect marks. All head shots.

Livi had been right.

"Hey, Livi, where you hiding?" he called.

Habit, but this time no answer, but for the wind knocking against the dirty windows.

Grief bunched in his guts. No more Livi to open her arms and hug him tight and tell him to ignore the bullies who teased him about being poor. No more Livi to tell him stories about her world travels, or patch up his cuts when he'd gotten into yet another fight at school.

No more Livi's strong voice lecturing him that even if his father was a loser, that didn't mean he needed to follow in his footsteps.

My sister failed with her son, your father, dear boy, but you, Roarke, you're going places and you'll be someone someday. Don't screw up your life because of your worthless father.

No more Livi to gently clasp his rough hand in her paperthin one, and tell him when his mother died that hearts could be broken, but they got mended, too.

Roarke swallowed past the sudden thickness in his throat.

This place had been a refuge in the past, the one house he knew he'd never wear out his welcome. No matter what he'd done, Lavinia had always forgiven him. Even that one time when he'd stolen a car. *Her* car—a classic '69 Shelby Mustang.

Oh, she'd forgiven him, but she'd also let him spend the night in jail. Refused to bail him out to teach him a lesson. And then Megan had posted bond for him.

Roarke went still, memories thick in his mind. Megan

Robinson, the sweetest, kindest girl ever to call Cooper Falls home.

The only good thing besides Livi in his sorry young life after Mom died.

Megan Robinson, the girl who'd broken his heart.

He glanced around. Though it was old and needed work, the mansion should sell for a good price. Roarke planned to give the proceeds from the sale to fund his stepniece's transplant surgery. Holly was growing sicker by the day.

The house looked the same, frozen in time. The library where he'd spent many hours reading had to be the same. Roarke headed there.

Something crunched beneath his left engineer boot.

What the…

Grimacing, he pulled his boot free and bent down to examine the cause. Roofing nails sticking through a board attached to the floor. The hardwood floor had warped here, and maybe someone repaired it the wrong way.

Or perhaps not. Anyone scampering barefoot through the house would meet with a nasty surprise.

Unease rippled through him as he glanced around and listened. Nothing.

But someone had clearly been here, though Lavinia's lawyer had assured him the house had been locked and closed since his aunt died two weeks ago.

Tomorrow he'd investigate further to see if any more *surprises* awaited him.

Snapping on lights, he went through the downstairs, checking windows and the back door leading out of the kitchen to ensure they were locked and secured. As a kid, he'd been both fascinated and scared by this old house, especially the basement with its sinister, dark corners. Lavinia knew of his fear and had added more lighting to assure young Roarke nothing could creep up the stairs and harm him.

Now he made sure the door to the basement was closed.

The flight from DC had been long. Yawning, he picked up his duffel, locked the front door and started to trudge upstairs.

Examining each step for anything else unexpected.

He looked at every board in the hallway. Nothing. It could have been left by a careless worker. Lavinia had tried remodeling before she grew weak and needed assistance.

Maybe.

After he changed the sheets on Lavinia's stately king-size bed, undressed and climbed into the four-poster, Roarke lay there, staring at the shadows dancing on the ceiling from the moon-dappled oak trees. And then he heard something other than the wind.

It sounded as if it came from the attic.

Stupid. He was alone.

There were no such things as ghosts.

But it was a long time before he finally fell asleep.

Chapter 2

If the termites stopped holding hands, the house, and all her hopes, would surely collapse.

Megan Robinson stared at Greystone Manor, the once-elegant mansion formerly owned by Lavinia Carlson Tremaine Walker, Cooper Fall's wealthiest and most eccentric citizen. The outside needed work. Oh, no, that was like saying that Moby Dick was a big fish.

The bright September sunshine showed paint peeling in long strips off the porch railing and columns, and the windows hadn't been cleaned since disco went out of style.

Who cared what it looked like outside, as long as treasures remained within?

"Thanks, Lavinia," she said aloud before tears burned her eyes.

She didn't pause to wipe them, only let them flow. The hollow in her chest ached harder.

Megan tried to clear the lump in her throat. Crying wouldn't bring Livi back, wouldn't fill the air with Livi's infectious, carefree laughter.

You're only thirty, Meggie, Livi had told her, her paper-thin hand clutching Megan's. *You need to experience all life has to offer.*

I miss you, Livi.

She couldn't bring herself to think about the mysterious circumstances surrounding Livi's death. The sheriff had closed the investigation.

You sure you want to spend time here, after what happened?

Time was running out. The sooner she got started on the inventory, the sooner she could leave the house. Meg didn't know who had inherited the mansion. Probably the historical society divas, who itched to restore the house to its former glory.

After quietly sliding the key into the lock, she strode inside, overcome with reverence and awe for the once-grand majesty of the finest home in all of Cooper Falls.

Built in 1898 and fully restored over the years to include modern plumbing and electric. Original hardwood floors. The red-and-white Oriental rug in the entryway was a little faded, but lovely. That elk chandelier... She shook her head, awash in fond memories. And a favorite piece—an original 1938 Philco radio in a polished wood cabinet. Megan touched a knob, remembering how she used to dance in the hallway when Livi turned it to her favorite station. The smell of lemon polish hung in the air, indicating the last time Megan helped Livi dust the banister they both loved to slide down in their younger years.

A shiver snaked down her spine. Every time she'd been here previously, the house had come alive with Lavinia's braying laughter and vibrant personality.

Now it seemed...haunted.

Silly. Haunted by what? It was only a house.

A house tainted by death...

Megan left her purse in the entry hall and stepped into the living room to the right, overcome with memories. Someone, the real estate agent, perhaps, had removed the white sheets covering the furniture.

A cloud of dust wafted upward as Megan plopped onto an overstuffed chair. She sneezed and her eyes watered. Maybe allergies. Or more tears.

"Oh, Livi," she whispered to the sofa. "Why did you have to die?"

No answer, but for the wind whistling down the chimney, stirring up another cloud of dust. The house hummed with an undercurrent of sad energy.

Maybe her own sad energy. But Livi wouldn't want her to be sad. Only carry on after her absence.

You need to experience all life has to offer.

Livi had actually given her the entire mansion's contents. She and Livi had talked about getting appraisals for everything and then selling the valuables, splitting the proceeds with Megan.

Livi knew Megan had struggled to keep her father's bookstore afloat since his death four months ago.

Megan raked her gaze over the living room, with its assortment of cluttered shelves.

Maybe there were enough valuable antiques to sell at auction and pay for the back rent and the rent increase that the bookstore soon faced, but going through each room would take…

"Too long." She clenched her fists and fought the knot of fear rising in her stomach.

Not only would she lose her father's beloved bookstore, but the apartment above it as well. Homeless, alone and broke was so not what she'd anticipated for the approaching winter.

Get out of this town and pursue your dream!

Livi's voice kept echoing in her mind, thick as the memories. Maybe Livi was right. Time to leave the small-town life for Washington, DC, and take a chance on life.

And then she remembered her last trip to the nation's capital.

Megan wandered over to the ancient grand piano in the corner. An array of faded pictures peppered the dusty instrument. Only two held her interest. She picked up the photo of a young laughing Roarke Calhoun, arms around Lavinia as they both smirked at the camera. Lavinia was gray-haired, but the spark in her eyes still gleamed, and age had not yet caught up with the town's beloved matriarch.

The second photo looked more recent. Roarke, his long hair clipped short, his steely green gaze staring into the lens. Instead of jeans and a T-shirt, he wore a powder blue shirt, red tie and dark business suit. The Federal Bureau of Investigation backdrop hinted how far he'd come. So elegant and charming. Her heart skipped a beat. Even his photo still held the power to draw her in, mesmerize her with desire. Her friends in high school had teased her into asking him for a date—Roarke, the baddest boy in school, and the cutest. All the girls had had a secret crush on him.

Meg had it the worst. She had kissed him on that date, expecting him to take it a step further.

He hadn't. They'd stayed up all night talking. Her crazy teenage desire had turned into something deeper that night when she'd looked past his leanly muscled body, soulful green eyes and firm mouth and saw glimpses of the man beneath.

A fist clenched her heart as she stared at Roarke. Familiar longing, desire and anger rushed through her.

Seeing Roarke again meant shattering her heart into little pieces all over. He was gone for good.

Megan set the photo facedown.

It wasn't supposed to be like this. Roarke had been her world once. And yet he'd left and never looked back. Megan had counted on him to be a spring, coil and then snap back. Not project himself out of her life for good. Or shatter all her hopes and dreams five years ago when she saw him with another woman.

Go stuff yourself, Roarke Calhoun, wherever you are.

Her phone buzzed. Megan glanced at the text message and her stomach clenched. Another reminder from Deke Kinkaid about the back rent on her apartment. He'd been texting her all week.

She'd negotiated with him for more time. The sooner she got to work cataloging these items, the sooner she could contact an auction house and appraiser.

She took her tablet out of her purse to begin working. This was going to be like trying to catalog the Smithsonian.

One area at a time. Megan headed for the sleek black piano, made a note.

"One grand piano, worth maybe $50,000 if it's in good shape… Five photos of a lying jerk known as Roarke Calhoun…worthless," she muttered aloud.

A board creaked overhead.

Blood froze in her veins. Megan went still. Could be a real estate agent, but no voices warned of visitors, the door had been locked and no car had been in the driveway when she'd parked.

Old houses were known for housing vagrants.

Maybe this vagrant carried a weapon.

She didn't have anything. Her frantic gaze whipped around. Against a bookshelf rested a wooden Māori taiaha spear Lavinia acquired in New Zealand. It slid into her trembling hands.

She licked her dry lips and crept toward the staircase,

spear clutched tight. The comforting, dusty shelves of the bookstore seemed like a safe haven.

Not this sprawling mansion with its old memories and clutter, where a killer could break inside and hide, lurking in the corridor so he could slaughter her just like the scared woman in a mystery novel…

Megan advanced, her cell phone ready to dial 9-11.

It could be a cat or a wild animal that had climbed into the house from a broken window.

More likely it was a man. Maybe a seven-foot tall man with a sinister weapon of his own, ready to kill the stupid woman who came here alone, unarmed…

Megan reached the upstairs landing. A light shone from the bathroom at the hallway's end. Water dripped. Someone had made themselves home here and showered.

A clean vagrant, perhaps.

Tiptoeing down the green shag carpeting, she clutched the spear. Outside the bathroom, she held it in both hands, the deadly tip outward.

"Come out and show yourself before I call Sheriff Doyle. This is private property and you are trespassing," Megan ordered.

A man stepped into the hallway, silhouetted in the dark hallway by the bathroom's bright light behind him.

"You're holding that wrong," a deep voice informed her. "It's not a broomstick. It's an ancient weapon."

Megan blinked, her fear turning to shock.

Now she could see more clearly the man with a yellow bath towel knotted around his lean waist. Water dripped onto the wooden floor from his strong, sinewy arms. Dark hair slicked back, green eyes first dancing with amusement and then turning guarded. Just like the man himself.

Roarke Calhoun, once the man of her dreams…now the nightmare from her past.

Chapter 3

"Roarke?"

He nodded, wetting his suddenly dry lips. Nothing could prepare him for this.

Not even with all the training he'd experienced, the times as both a SEAL and later an FBI agent when he'd had to remain cool in situations fraught with danger.

No physical danger here, only his ex-girlfriend Megan, with her shiny ash brown hair tumbling past her slender shoulders, her deep blue eyes wide. Nope, no danger here.

But damn, his heart sure warned it might explode as sweat joined the droplets of water sliding down his back. All the longings and yearnings of the past rushed to his head, making him dizzy, along with the familiar desire she always roused in him.

No other woman had ever come close to making him burn for her.

No other woman had ever come close to shattering his heart, either.

Once they couldn't wait to see each other after school;

they'd rush into each other's arms and sneak off for hot and heavy necking sessions. And then later, when he took her virginity in the back of his aunt's '69 Shelby, their hot breaths fogging the windows…

He drew in another deep, steadying breath.

"How did you get in here?" She glanced around. "I didn't see a car out front."

"Rideshare from the airport."

He didn't mention how the driver dropped him off a long distance from the house so no one could see him coming. Or about his adventure with the pup and train.

Keeping a firm grip on the towel around his hips, Roarke stared at Megan. She'd gained weight and it suited her. A blue floral dress with short sleeves flowed over the lush curves of her body, reminding him of what he'd once held tight…and then lost. Her pixie haircut had grown out past her shoulders. He glanced down at her bare legs. Still shapely and long.

Never considered a beauty, Megan was more striking than attractive. It wasn't her looks that had drawn him close when they were younger, but her down-to-earth personality and stubborn streak in sticking up for the underdog. In this case, him.

Five years had passed since they'd last seen each other and damn, she remained as alluring to him and as spunky. Except for the shadows in her eyes. Then he remembered what Lavinia had told him about Al Robinson. That must have hurt. Her mother had died when Megan was twelve and she and her father were quite close.

"I'm sorry about your dad."

She blinked. "Uh, thanks. How did you know… Oh, Lavinia."

"She kept me updated on everything going on in town."

A faint smile pushed aside the shadows. "She still knew

everyone else's business. Especially mine. She was Dad's favorite customer at the bookstore."

"I remember how they used to argue about history. Livi always said your dad had the classical training of a professor, but she had the world experience to prove him wrong."

The smile bloomed, and a spark entered her eyes. "Dad did enjoy debating with her."

"Even when they were arguing about us."

Suspicion flared in her blue eyes. She didn't lower the spear, but held it outright as if wanting to poke him hard. "Why are you here?"

"Could ask the same of you." Except she wasn't the one standing dripping in the hallway, clad only in a towel. He wondered if he let the towel drop, would she scurry away?

Or worse, look mighty interested.

Bad idea. The currents of sexual energy still sizzled between them like water in a heated frying pan. He'd been burned once before. No desire to do so again.

"I inherited the entire contents of Greystone Manor," she informed him in a voice colder than the Arctic.

He blinked, stunned at the news. "I inherited the manor. According to her will, I also inherited everything else that goes with it."

Megan blinked and lost her confident look. "It can't be true. Not that you'd know. You never returned here to visit. Did you even know she'd talked about going into assisted living?"

His stomach clenched as he gave her a level look. No one had told him, especially not his proud aunt. "No."

"She was so lonely. My father saw more of her than you did—her own nephew. Dad was the one who made sure she visited the doctor because Livi was so proud and didn't want to admit she was getting older."

He couldn't argue that point. Roarke pushed aside the

guilt. Livi had understood how his work as an agent for the FBI took him on the road.

But he wished he'd known she was sick. He would have flown here and cared for her.

And that was the paradox of Lavinia Carlson Tremaine Walker, married twice, widowed once, divorced once. Childless, she'd treated Roarke like the son she'd never birthed. But pride prevented her from reaching out to him and letting Roarke know she needed him.

She'd always said they were too much alike—independent and stubborn.

"I didn't know she was sick, Megan." He pushed a hand through his wet hair. "No one told me about her funeral, dammit."

A delicate flush tinted her cheeks. "I'm sorry you didn't know about the funeral, Roarke. Livi's attorney stated she wanted a quick burial, none of the fuss and bother."

That niggling prick of instinct kicked up again. "Who buried her?"

Megan bit her lip. "Her attorney took care of everything, including the funeral home arrangements. It was a small private burial in the town cemetery. Livi wanted to be buried next to her first husband, whom she loved. They had bought a plot together."

"I know," he told her, irritated. "I already visited." It was almost as tough as when his mother died. Seeing the headstone carved with Livi's name had made the loss hit home.

"We barely knew she was gone before the service happened. The way Livi wanted it."

His great-aunt always hated funerals and mourning. Yet it wasn't enough. Funerals were for the living, and he needed that closure.

Roarke stared at her mouth, the kick in his gut warning the old chemistry hadn't died. He still wanted her as much as he had when he was eighteen. He cleared his throat and focused on the spear in her hands.

"Let me get dressed and we'll talk." He wasn't about to argue half naked.

Maybe do something else half naked… Something they both had excelled at. Hot passion, tangling between the sheets.

That ship had sailed into the night when he'd climbed onto his Harley and roared off toward the East Coast. All the letters and cards he'd sent to her after he'd joined the Navy had been stamped Return to Sender.

His phone calls went to a disconnected number. Even his emails were never answered… Until Megan's final one.

Megan couldn't have made it clearer she no longer wanted him in her life.

She didn't move, but at least lowered the spear. "I think this is best resolved with Lavinia's attorney. He has the latest version of her will."

Roarke shrugged. "Suit yourself. I'll meet you downtown at his office."

"I'd offer you a ride, but I'm sure you can fend for yourself. I suggest you wear something appropriate for business."

That snippy voice, a reminder of all the others in this blasted town who'd looked down their noses at him, finally snapped his control. Roarke dropped the towel.

"Will this suffice?"

The shocked look on her face made him grin, but the unmistakable flare of pure desire hinted she hadn't forgotten what they'd shared. He wrapped the towel around his waist again and went to dress before he did something they would both regret.

When he finally emerged downstairs in a navy suit,

starched blue shirt and striped tie, he'd controlled himself. Megan stood in the entryway, jingling a set of keys.

"I'm sorry I acted like a jerk upstairs." She sighed. "Usually I'm not that rude. It's just… I never expected you to be here."

He leaned against the banister. "It's been a long time. Guess I'm kind of a shock."

Her gaze roved around the hallway, flitting like a hummingbird. "Shock is a good way to put it. No one warned me you'd returned."

"I planned it that way." He rolled a shoulder, muscles knotting with tension. "I didn't exactly want anyone to know I was back. Some people wouldn't be happy I'm here."

"That was a long time ago, Roarke. They've forgotten any of your, ah, former transgressions."

Did you?

Roarke gazed at the sandals covering her feet. Conventional pink toenails. Once she'd leaned toward wilder colors. He glanced at her face, the freckles she never tried to cover now hidden behind a layer of cosmetics. Another change. She looked much more stylish and sophisticated.

Once they'd been together, wild and free.

Until he talked of leaving the cage that entrapped him in this town, and she chose to remain behind the bars.

"At least you weren't wearing pointed shoes," he drawled.

At her frown, he added, "When you kicked my ass upstairs. Pointed shoes would have hurt like hell."

A pink blush tinted her cheeks. So pretty. Desire kicked him again, low in the gut. He steeled himself against it, mentally recalling all the letters he'd written to her while in the Navy that she never answered.

"Again, my apologies. Shall we go? You can ride with me."

So polite and distant. *Yeah, thanks. Do me a solid, Meg.*

Instead he headed outside with her, pausing only to lock the door behind them. A white-and-black dog barked and rushed up the steps. Tail wagging, he jumped on Megan. Roarke recoiled. What the hell?

"Hey, boy, where have you been?" Megan pointed to the ground. "Down."

The dog sat, grinning at her.

"He's your dog?" Roarke asked. "I rescued him last night."

"Rescued?" Megan patted the dog's head. "From what? Rigor was staying at Sid Harris's farm. He must have escaped."

"Right onto the train tracks." Roarke fisted his hands. "Someone tied him up there and left him there for a freight to run over. Seems like things haven't changed in Cooper Falls. They're still bad to strays in this town."

Megan's eyes widened. "What?" she shrieked.

At least she hadn't lost her love of animals and that righteous indignation for them. It was another painful reminder of things they had in common.

"I don't know, princess. This is your town, not mine. I rescued him and then left him outside the shelter for the night. Maybe you should find a more secure pen for your dog so he won't run away again."

She crouched down, hugged Rigor, who squirmed. "Stop accusing me, Roarke. Rigor was Livi's dog and she gave him to Sid until Sid could find him a good home. She had planned to go into assisted living and they don't allow dogs at the home."

It made no sense. Livi had never been a dog lover. Oh, she'd supported rescue organizations, but she traveled too much to own a pet.

"How long did she have him?"

"Not long." Megan's voice dropped. "Livi was lonely living in this big house…and afraid."

"So she got a dog as a companion."

"Not just as a companion. Defense. Rigor is pretty protective of those he likes, and he barks a lot at strangers." Her expression grew troubled. "What kind of person ties a dog to the railroad tracks?"

The kind of person who doesn't like dogs. Or this particular dog. But why? Because they dislike the dog or because it belonged to Livi?

Rigor's tongue lolled out as the dog grinned at him, as if he knew Roarke was thinking about him.

A little tickle started on the nape of his neck. There it was again, the gut instinct that had served him well as a SEAL in Afghanistan, and then later as a new member of the FBI.

"Why was Livi afraid? Who, or what, was scaring her?" He gave her the hard stare reserved for interrogating suspects. "How exactly did my aunt die, Meg?"

Her gaze shot away as her hand paused in petting Rigor. "It was sudden."

"You know," he said softly. "What's going on around here that you don't want to tell me?"

Standing up, she brushed off her hands. "We'll have to leave him in the house. We'll talk on the way to the attorney's. I don't want to be late."

She found an old bowl in the kitchen, filled it with fresh water for the dog and brought it into the room where Roarke always felt most comfortable—Livi's library, where she'd liked to read. The crimson walls, white inlaid bookshelves, plush leather sofa, gooseneck lamps and big picture window overlooking the backyard were bright and welcoming. A windowed alcove featured two chairs side by side. Whimsical Livi with her odd sense of humor had placed an old-fashioned safe between them, and added a brass table lamp for reading.

Books are a treasure more than money, Livi once declared.

The dog curled up on the rug before the sofa and gave a contented sigh. Roarke scratched him behind the ears. He glanced at Meg.

"His name is Rigor?"

Meg grinned. "Rigor Mortis. Livi liked the name. He's good at one trick."

She pointed at the dog. "Rigor, play dead."

The dog rolled over, his limbs stiff in the air. Roarke laughed. "Livi always had a peculiar sense of humor. Most people don't know what rigor mortis is."

Meg smiled and that smile, it struck him right in the chest. He missed her smile, how it lit up her face, made her incandescent as if her smile could wipe away all the darkness in his world.

"Livi didn't until she started reading up on what you do, and what happens to a person after death. It was macabre, but she was so proud of you. She wanted to know exactly what you do in your job, Roarke. It was her way of keeping close to you." She snapped her fingers and the dog rolled over and sat up.

Guilt flickered through him. *I should have come home sooner.*

A frown touched her face as she gazed around the room. "That's odd. I swore Livi kept the Chinese porcelain vase on that bookshelf. It's quite valuable. And now it's gone."

"Maybe she moved things around."

Meg's frown deepened. "Livi loved that vase and how it caught the afternoon sunlight in this room."

They went outside. There, Roarke received another surprise. Megan's vehicle.

The bright red Jeep seemed as out of place with Megan as the dog was with Livi. This was a vehicle suited for adventurous souls.

He buckled his seat belt after climbing into the passenger seat. "When did you get this?"

She tossed her purse in the back and climbed inside. "Two years ago. Dad wanted a vehicle that could go four-wheeling in the mud."

Another shock. The stately professor Albert Robinson, scholar of history and literature? The same man who'd peered over the tops of his glasses with a severe frown when Roarke pulled up on his Harley to take Megan on a date?

"Why? Archeological finds? Or discovering the lost youth he never had?"

Megan bit her lip. "Bucket list. Though I didn't know it at the time."

Cursing silently, he wished he'd stuck to another rideshare. Or could manage to keep his damn mouth shut.

He turned. "Let's start over. I'm Roarke Calhoun. Nice to meet you, Megan Robinson."

Her palm was slim and warm encased in his big paw. Roarke held it for a minute longer than necessary as they shook hands. "You always did have the softest hands."

Then, because he could no more resist touching his mouth to her skin than he could resist a delicious warm brandy on a cold night, he turned her hand over, kissed her palm. One small slight kiss pressed to her skin. Beneath his lips, her hand trembled.

Glancing up, he saw a mixture of longing and anger on her face. Roarke drew away as if he'd kissed a red-hot burner. "Let's go."

How stupid could he get? He hadn't come to Cooper Falls to reacquaint himself with Megan. Fix up the manor, put it on the market and then leave. When it sold, the money would go to his stepbrother to fund Holly's transplant surgery.

As they drove toward town, Megan chattered about everything except what he needed to know. His ex pointed out new construction along Route 10, the neat, cozy homes taking over farmland, how the Millers decided to hold fast to their farm and raise ostriches. Her words tumbled over each other like socks in a dryer as he drummed his fingers on his thigh.

When they reached Main Street, he finally interrupted. Roarke held up one hand. "It's all right, Megan. You don't need to play tour guide. I have no intention of sticking around."

Was that relief or regret in her eyes? Relief, probably.

Didn't matter.

"Why was Livi scared and wanting protection?"

Megan bit her bottom lip. Nerves. He knew this gesture. She'd done it several times in the past, like right before they'd made love…

"Livi was having issues with the house. I can't say more than that. Not right now."

"Was she sick? Her attorney didn't say."

"No. Livi was getting older, a little more frail, too. I think she feared living alone and having an accident, no one to find her."

Fresh air might help ease the stifling atmosphere in the vehicle. Roarke rolled down a window and pulled in a deep breath. They drove past Swenson's Ice Cream Shoppe, where two older women sat at the bistro tables, enjoying cones. They glanced at the Jeep, saw him and he swore their eyes bugged out of their faces. Roarke lifted a hand in greeting.

Helga Carnes and Elaine Hillstrom. Oh, yeah, they recognized him, judging from the dual frowns.

"That will get tongues wagging," Megan muttered. "They still blame you for setting off stink bombs at the fall PTA festival."

He smirked. "I did."

"I know. I covered for you."

Turning away before he got charmed by her smile again, he studied the sweep of colorful flowers in the window boxes of businesses. "Are they still teaching fourth grade?"

Not that he gave two flying figs about those biddies, but he hated the idea of his misdeeds affecting his stepniece in school. Cooper Falls did not forgive the past and sometimes the sins of the fathers, and the uncles, fell upon the next generation.

"They retired last year."

At least he could feel thankful for that news. Holly wouldn't have to live with the shadow of his tainted past in school.

It wasn't about him, but Holly. Not even his stepbrother, who'd gotten his grandparents' adulation, unlike Roarke and his mother.

Roarke had lived in a rundown two-bedroom house on the wrong side of the tracks and the entire town looked down their noses at them, while Chet, his stepbrother, was put on a pillar.

It didn't matter now.

And the sooner he could get the issue of the manor's ownership out of the way, fix up the place and sell it, the better.

Without the temptation of Megan Robinson at his side.

He still had the power to fire her blood. But she wasn't seventeen anymore, and this time she knew better than to listen to her body's demands.

What they'd shared had simply been pure teenage desire,

extinguished when all the letters and emails she'd sent to him had gone unanswered.

Megan pulled into the manor driveway and shut off the engine. Keys jingled in her hand, despite her inner mantra to calm her nerves.

Why had Lavinia done this?

The meeting at the attorney's office had not gone as she'd anticipated. Megan jumped out of the Jeep and headed into the house. Roarke had remained at the attorney's. The lawyer had promised to drive him to the rental car agency, although Meg didn't know why. Lavinia's attorney had given Roarke possession of another inheritance—Lavinia's classic 1969 Shelby Mustang, housed in the detached garage. He should have all the transportation he needed.

A furious blush heated her face. He did love that car. So did she. Fast and furious, it had the personality of Roarke himself. One wild joyride with Roarke had ended in passion as Megan lost her virginity to him in the back seat. Her arms snaking around his neck, the tender way he'd kissed her senseless...

Even now she grew weak recalling the physical side of their relationship.

But he had moved on long ago, shattering her heart and steeling her resolve to never again fall in love with a man who adored adventure and adrenaline rushes more than he cared for her.

And yet seeing him again ignited all those old feelings, the delicious anticipation curling low in her belly, her lady parts sitting up and saying, *Why, hello there!* With his startling green eyes, shock of dark hair now cut short and charming grin that had coaxed the clothing right off her years ago, Roarke had had no trouble getting dates back in high school.

Yet he'd wanted her. Only her. A lump formed at the back of her throat. But not enough.

Back at the attorney's office, Roarke had told her to wait for him before entering Livi's house, but she didn't listen to him anymore.

What they'd discovered at the attorney's: Lavinia's will gave them equal access to the mansion. Megan was to have the contents of the house. Roarke had inherited the house and could sell it if he wished.

Maybe she'd get lucky and it would sell quickly. Then her ex would return to wherever he called home these days.

The sunny day had soured, along with her mood. Rain misted the air outside. Megan shivered. Clouds scuttled across the sky, blocking the sun. They were in for a good old-fashioned downpour soon.

Wait for Roarke? She'd rather wait for the apocalypse.

Once inside she set her purse on a side table, regret filling her. Selling Livi's belongings felt like selling her soul. Livi loved history and antiques as much as Meg did. But Roarke's great-aunt had made it clear she wanted Megan to part with the past and start over.

Sell everything, her personal letter had stated. *Don't let the past drag you down, honey.*

She paced, reminding herself of all the times she'd paced in her own apartment above the bookstore, waiting for Roarke to pull up outside on his Harley. Hoping Dad would remain asleep because she hated the judgmental look on his face.

Megan drifted her fingers over the elegant table, tracing a heart in the dust. Sure, there'd been other boys who wanted to date her. But Roarke was exciting, dangerous, and every time she was near him, her heart leaped. His kisses made her female thermostat soar upward, and when he put his hands on her the first time…

But that was all in the past. The sooner she could inventory the contents and auction them, the faster she'd be free of Greystone Manor and Roarke Calhoun. Best to start now.

She let Rigor outside, where he bounded around the backyard, ignoring the light rainfall and barking at the squirrels in the trees. Greystone Manor claimed more than twenty acres, much of it forested. Rigor, an outdoor dog, felt right at home in the expansive yard. Livi had even built him a doghouse under the shade of a giant oak.

Minutes later, pad in hand, she looked over the formal dining room.

This was going to take forever—and she needed cash now. Most of all, she needed to keep this from Roarke. Maybe he had broken her heart all those years ago, but she had her pride and couldn't let him know she was broke.

Megan went into the library.

A lump clogged her throat as she swept a hand over the bookshelves, remembering Livi's high-pitched voice as she'd argued in this room with her father, both of them opinionated and intelligent. How she'd enjoyed those intellectual debates!

Now they were both gone, voices forever silenced.

Megan wiped away the tears and studied the room with its elegant antiques. Livi's family had owned a few fine pieces of antique furniture. She loved the Queen Anne walnut secretary with its twin doors, fold-down desk and drawers. She opened the desktop and the drawers. Livi had stuffed everything in here, from napkins for a bridal shower from twenty years ago to old receipts from the 1970s. It would take forever to clean out this one piece.

She glanced at her cell phone, realizing she needed to check her email.

Using her phone, she scrolled through the messages on the bookstore's email address. Most of the clients knew she'd reduced hours to deal with Lavinia's house. There were a few good wishes, inquiries about rare books and then one message that caught her eye.

Heard you inherited the contents of Greystone Manor. The old lady had a collection of rare tapestries in the base-ment. Will pay top dollar for them if you sell. Email me back. A. Smith.

Megan pondered the message. Lavinia used to have a collection of handwoven tapestries. Maybe she told some-one about them. Certainly Lavinia liked discussing her life and the items she'd acquired in her world travels.

The basement had always been spooky, but after Roarke had nightmares about monsters hiding there, Lavinia in-stalled bright lighting.

The light switch at the top of the stairs didn't work. There was one at the bottom as well. Roarke would have to fix that. Darkness loomed before her.

Maybe she should wait.

Maybe if she waited for Roarke, she'd be waiting for-ever. If this customer was wanting to purchase the tapestries now, a good price would help pay for the rental increase and the money she owed.

Finding a flashlight in this place would take forever. Using the flashlight app on her cell phone, she descended.

Halfway down, the front door slammed. "Megan?"

Roarke. Terrific. She turned. "In the basement," she yelled.

As he descended the stairs, Megan turned to take the next step.

There was no next step. A scream ripped from her throat as Megan lost her balance and started to fall.

Roarke caught her before she tumbled into the blackness. Mouth dry, she stared into his grim expression.

"I told you to wait."

Chapter 4

Snug in his embrace, she couldn't help but inhale his scent. Faint spicy cologne, damp hair and pure masculinity. For a moment she shot back to the past, when they'd skipped the school dance and held their own private dance by the lake, she in Roarke's arms as they twirled to the music on his car radio. Nothing bothered them back then. Not even the fact that Roarke was suspended and couldn't attend the school dance.

Roarke gently untangled from her and lifted her by the waist, setting her on the step above him. She'd forgotten how strong he was.

"Thanks," she said, wishing her voice remained as steady as his hands.

His green gaze swept over her. "You okay?"

He brushed back a lock of hair from her face. Rain had dampened his dark hair, droplets clinging to his lean cheeks.

She nodded, unnerved by his touch almost as much as the recent mishap.

A circle of light peered into the inky blackness as he shone his cell phone light down the stairs. Or rather where the stairs had been.

"Stay here."

Not that she had any desire to explore further. Megan watched as he jumped off the last step onto the concrete.

"The two bottom steps are gone," he told her.

"Wood rot." *Please tell me I'm right.*

Roarke ran a hand over the last step. "Sawed off."

Her heart raced as she clung to the banister with sweaty palms. Then again, whoever had removed the last steps might have sabotaged the banister as well. "Please, let's get out of here."

When they cleared the steps and were in the hallway, Megan rubbed her hands against her dress as she told him about the message from the customer interested in the tapestries.

"They would fetch a good price for someone who collects."

Roarke frowned. "Wouldn't it be prudent to inventory everything and then sell at auction?"

Megan's stomach roiled. "Probably, but I just want this over with, okay?"

Admitting she was broke, and in debt, was not what she'd anticipated when she thought about seeing Roarke again.

In her fantasies, she'd be twenty pounds thinner, driving a sports car and living a life of great adventure. Not teetering on the edge past thirty, desperate to pay bills.

His gaze darkened. "Look, Megan, I know I've been an ass since I got here…"

"And then some," she muttered.

"But there's something going on here I don't like and we need to work together. So when I tell you to wait for me, wait. This house… Something feels wrong here."

So it wasn't only her who'd felt the odd vibe. "It does. Why would someone saw off the stairs?"

"Whoever sent you that email wanting the tapestries. They wanted you to go downstairs and break your neck."

His blunt words sent her stomach doing somersaults. "To hurt me? Why?"

Roarke's expression turned grim. "I don't know. Let me see that email."

After she handed over her phone, he frowned. "No full name, no phone number. I'll run a trace on this later."

"You can track an email?"

"I work for the FBI. We can do all sorts of things." He handed back her phone. "I'll need to access your email to forward this."

For a moment she hesitated. Trust Roarke?

"I don't know…"

He sighed. "Our lab has the best techs, Megan. I promise I'll forward it right to them. You can change your password after if you're afraid I'll get into your email again."

Or your pants, his intense green gaze hinted.

Maybe that smoldering look was her imagination. Surely Roarke didn't want her anymore. He'd made that clear with his final exit.

She pulled out her cell and texted him the website address and the password.

"Who would saw off these steps? No one else but the attorney had a key," she mused aloud.

"And the Realtor, but Martha James wouldn't do this any more than she'd walk down Main Street naked."

As she stared, he smiled. "That's a joke, princess. Meant to bring a little blood back to those pretty cheeks of yours."

Joking, when she could have tumbled into the darkness and broken her neck? "Your sense of humor has grown more peculiar over the years."

"Wow, I forgot."

As she tilted her head at him, Roarke added, "How pretty you are when you get angry."

As she sputtered with indignation, his smile grew wider. "Guess I can still do it to you."

Mirth danced in his green eyes, sparking memories of when they'd been together and how he'd teased her into a good humor when her grades had fallen and Dad had scolded.

Or kissed her into an even better one. Megan stared at the contours of his firm lips, remembering how he'd kissed his way across her body, no fumbling boy, but a barely eighteen-year-old with a man's expert touch...

"Do what?" she finally asked. *And don't say turn me into a ball of female hormones because I will never admit that to you. Especially you.*

"Talk you off a ledge when you're scared."

It worked. But didn't solve the more pressing concern. Feeling the beginnings of a headache, Megan pressed a finger to her temple. "Who would deliberately saw off basement steps? And why? Was it meant for Lavinia?"

"I don't know." Roarke narrowed his eyes. "Someone else has been here, and this isn't the first booby trap."

After he finished telling her about the board with the nails, Megan's hopes fell. "Someone clearly doesn't want us here."

"Or the both of us. I inherited the house, a well-known fact in town, according to the driver who picked me up at the jetport." His gaze scanned the hallway. "Not that I expected everyone to greet the prodigal son with open arms, but this is taking the town's dislike to a deeper level of hell."

She forgot her earlier anger. "Roarke, not everyone in town hates you."

"Could fool me."

"You never gave them a chance."

The scowl marring his handsome face spoke of old wounds never healed. "They never gave me a chance. Or my mom. Everyone whispered about her behind my back, to my face, it never seemed to end."

"Not everyone." Megan put a hand on his jacket sleeve. "Not me, and others at school."

The level look he shot her sent a shiver down her spine. Roarke hadn't been one to mess with when he was younger, and now that he was a grown, muscled man…

She'd never feared him, only feared the consequences he'd bring upon himself. Prison…or worse.

"School? Right. So if I had so many champions, why didn't any of them help remove the Son of the Town Whore someone painted on my house?"

He'd never told her about that incident.

Meg felt a lurch of regret. What other hurtful things had he kept from her back then? "I didn't know. I'm sorry."

He shrugged. "I painted over it. I don't need your pity, princess."

Irritated, she threw out her hands. "It's not pity. It's stating a fact. I'm sorry they were narrow-minded, cruel people. But don't judge the entire town based on them."

Then he fisted his hands and drew a deep breath. "Forget it. I'm calling the Realtor and getting a list of every person who had a key. You should probably leave now. You can return tomorrow to do inventory only if I'm here with you."

A soft chime at the front door tore her attention away. Two figures showed in the round frosted glass in the double doors.

"Aw, damn." Roarke jammed a hand through his short hair. "Looks like the welcoming committee. They left a voice mail saying they were coming over."

Her heart sank as he opened the door. Too soon. Way too soon for them to come over.

On the porch, stood Mr. and Mrs. William Henry Hodges, III. Roarke's paternal grandparents.

This was so not going to be her day.

Or his.

His grandparents picked a hell of time for a family reunion.

Roarke didn't want to invite them inside. Especially now, with Megan here, making his past come charging back like a freight train determined to run him down. The meeting with the attorney had been troubling. The man had given him a letter Livi wrote, with strict orders to open it in Megan's presence.

He wanted to honor his great-aunt's wishes, but what the hell could she have written?

The grands stared at him in weighty silence. Raindrops gleamed on the shiny black Rolls-Royce sitting in the driveway. The rain had ceased, but the day had grown chilly, and definitely much more so with the people on the front porch.

The chauffeur sat at the wheel. New guy. He wondered what happened to Andy, the old chauffeur. Andy had always been nicer to him than his own grandparents.

"Aren't you going to ask us inside, Roarke?" his grandmother asked.

Leaving the door open, he stepped aside.

They breezed into the house as if they owned it. And why not? Abigail, his grandmother, had grown up here. He suspected it irked her that her sister had inherited the mansion. Her sister, Lavinia, who'd had adventures, traveled the world, married twice and divorced once. Her sister who had treated Roarke like her own grandson, and hadn't cared that Moira legally changed her name and his to Calhoun so her son wouldn't have his father's last name.

Unlike his grandparents, who'd turned him away from their front door when he was only ten and brought his grandmother a bouquet of wildflowers to try to win her acceptance.

No wonder four years later, he'd slashed the tires on their Bentley. Well, they had driven him past the breaking point with that insult to his mother. If not for Livi's loving kindness, he would have stayed in juvie.

He gestured to the waiting chauffeur. "He doesn't have to wait in the car. He can come inside."

Abigail sniffed. "This is family business, Roarke. It will not take long. He may wait in the car."

As his grandfather frowned, Megan glanced at them. "Roarke, your grandparents came here in the rain to talk with you."

"Who invited them?"

"I did," she said, her gaze defiant. "I figured they should see you, seeing it's been years."

Was everyone around here against him? Turning his back, he went outside, knocked at the car window.

The driver rolled down the window. "Yes, sir?"

"What's your name?"

"Benson Miller, Mr. Calhoun. I'm the new driver and I help out around the house. I just started working for your grandparents a few months ago. Do you need anything?"

Livi wouldn't let her servant sit in the car. He decided he'd do what she would. "Come in the house and get some coffee."

"Thank you, Mr. Calhoun!"

"Call me Roarke."

Soon Benson was stomping his feet at the outdoor mat and walking quickly past toward the kitchen.

He escorted his grandparents into the living room. They could damn well remove their own coats. "I'll be right back," he told them.

He put the coffee on to drip, left Benson sitting there in the kitchen and then headed back into the living room. Hopefully his grandparents wouldn't start wandering around the house to argue about what family heirlooms should belong to Abigail. Who knew what other traps existed in this house?

Steeling himself, he sat on the overstuffed chair facing the sofa, where they perched like two bookends.

"I'm making coffee." Not exactly an invite, but old habits and manners drilled into him by Livi died hard.

Even if his grandparents had never offered his mother a drop of coffee, or anything else. His mother, whom they treated like dirt.

"We do not plan to stay long." Abigail exchanged looks with her husband. "We heard you were back in town and came to see for ourselves. Since you did not attend the funeral."

Guilt and grief mixed together, laced with anger. He gave his grandparents a pointed look. "I was working a case and no one told me."

"We know."

Was that an actual guilty look from his stiff-lipped grandmother? He stared. "Who told you?"

More exchanged glances. His grandfather, William, who'd always let his wife do most of the talking, finally spoke up. "Lavinia's attorney informed us he called the FBI and they directed him to Kyle Anderson, your supervisor. Mr. Anderson informed us you were trying to find a missing child."

Kyle, former partner and friend, would be his supervisor as soon as he left Cooper Falls and headed to his home in DC. He couldn't wait to return.

But not now. All his plans to leave the house in the care of the Realtor and contractors sailed out the window. No way would he leave Megan here alone. Not until he found out what was going on and who'd set those traps.

"I didn't get the news Livi died until after the funeral. Why didn't you tell me?"

His stately grandmother, who seldom showed emotion, fiddled with her hands in her lap. Roarke leaned forward. "Why?"

Abigail sighed. "You know my sister, Roarke. She gave explicit instructions for a quick funeral and burial."

"The funeral could have waited." He struggled with his emotions. "Livi was family."

"Her last wishes had to be honored, Roarke."

Someone should have told him. Someone should have given him a heads-up how bad things had gotten with Livi. No one had.

"I didn't even know she'd been sick."

"Nor did we. Lavinia never told us," his grandmother said.

They barely spoke to each other, more like it.

Abigail glanced at her husband. "You're here now, Roarke, and that is what matters. We wanted to invite you to dinner tomorrow night. That is, if you plan to stay in town and do not have plans."

If the woman had stood up and kicked him in the shins, he couldn't have been more stunned. "I am staying for a while. Plans, right now, I can't say."

She actually did smile at him. "Very well. Seven o'clock at the country club. We can have Benson pick you up or you may meet us at the entrance."

Typical of the woman to assume he'd be eager to join

them for dinner. At a loss for words, he licked his lips. The desperate little boy eager for acceptance who'd had their front door slammed in his face wanted to cry out, *Sure, I'd love to have dinner with you.*

The teenager who'd slashed the tires on their Bentley wanted to tell them exactly where they could stick their invitation.

Megan came into the living room, a smile on her face. She'd heard.

"I think dinner with your grandparents would be lovely, Roarke. So much has changed and you should get reacquainted."

Like hell, he would. He'd rather get reacquainted with a land mine, which his grandparents were, considering how they'd treated his mother in the past. They blamed Moira for ruining their precious son's life.

Their precious son, his father, who dumped his mother and never bothered with child support. The day Roarke showed up on his doorstep, Mark Hodges had slammed the door in his face. His own father refused to see him.

"I can't."

The terse words had disappointment shadowing their faces. "Perhaps the day after. We should talk, Roarke," Abigail said.

"I'm busy all week. In fact, I'll be busy the whole time I'm here."

He left the room, Meg's gasp following him.

In the kitchen, Benson had helped himself to the freshly made coffee and sat sipping, looking at his phone. Meg practically sputtered with anger as she traipsed on his heels to the sink.

"That was incredibly rude," she said in a low voice. "They're trying to be nice to you."

"Why do you care?" He turned and met her, eye to eye.

"Did they do something to win you over, like offer to put you in their will as well?"

Blood drained from her face. He saw the clear stamp of hurt in her blue eyes. Roarke inwardly cursed. "Megan, I'm sorry… I didn't mean that."

"Of course you did," she said, her expression growing neutral. "You always spoke what was on your mind, so why be different now and learn some manners?"

Ouch. He actually winced as she stormed out of the kitchen. He glanced at Benson, grinned.

"Tough one, that Megan," the driver murmured. "I like women with fire and spirit."

Roarke's irritation grew. "Coffee break is over," he announced, taking the mug and tossing it into the sink. "Get the car started. They're leaving soon."

The driver had the grace to look abashed. "Roarke, I'm sorry…"

"Mr. Calhoun. Go," he directed.

The driver slunk out of the kitchen.

Could this day get worse? He found out it could when he walked into the living room and saw his grandparents walking around the room, picking up items and setting them down. Megan was nowhere in sight.

Distaste filled him. He leaned against the doorjamb. "Searching for valuables?"

William turned. "Lavinia had indicated to us that she wished us to take her father's Greek statue if anything ever happened to her. It's valuable and has been in the family for years."

Roarke blinked. Surely the old man was jesting. "You mean the one of the naked Psyche and the winged Cupid, the replica of the famous Canova statue at the Louvre?"

His grandfather shuffled his feet, looked away. "Precisely."

He stared at his prudish grandfather as if William had confessed to an affair with a randy stripper named Buffy. He rubbed the back of his neck. The old man hated that statue. It made him vastly uncomfortable, which was why Livi always displayed it in the parlor and then held high tea there, seating William as close as possible to the reproduction.

His aunt had taken particular delight in seeing William sweat.

Abigail smiled at Roarke. "It had particular meaning for us, being that it was in the family for a long time. Lavinia said she put it away, along with some other items, when she finally began cleaning out the house."

Another surprise. Usually he liked surprises. Pleasant ones. "Why was Livi cleaning out the house? Did she plan to sell it?"

"She had mentioned it." Abigail folded and unfolded her hands again. "She didn't want to be alone here any longer and expressed the desire to live in an assisted living center, where nurses could keep an eye on her. My sister was getting up there in years, Roarke. She was eighty-two."

But Livi was a young eighty-two. Last time he'd talked with her, Livi'd had plans for a few months in Europe, perhaps sailing the Rhône River. Her heart was strong and she was healthy.

Roarke nodded. "Thank you for your time. I don't want to take up any more of it. I'll search for the statue right away and I'll be in touch."

He closed the door and leaned against it, wishing suddenly Lavinia had left the house to his grandparents. Or Megan. Or the entire state of Michigan. This was too tough.

Too emotional.

He turned to see Megan standing before him. Too weary to argue anymore, he held up a hand.

"I'm sorry, Roarke. I shouldn't have interfered, but Abigail told me she needed to see you and they *have* changed. They're not the same."

"I wish I could believe it," he said quietly.

Her gaze looked solemn. "I remember what wretches they were to you, Roarke. But that was in the past and they're older and want to get to know you again."

He spread out his hands, unable to voice the tumult of emotions. "They never did forgive me for slashing their tires."

Megan's expression turned impish. "Oh, they forgave you, after I told Livi what they did to you. Only because Livi threatened to cut off your grandmother's allowance."

Feeling as if someone sucker punched him, Roarke took a deep breath. "Say what? My grandmother has money. And how would you know?"

A guilty glance away. "Livi and I grew quite close after you left, Roarke. She confided in me that Abigail received money from the family trust Livi was in charge of dispensing."

"Is that why William was interested in that statue? Money?"

Meg shook her head. "I had it appraised for her a few months ago. It's a good replica, hardly worth more than four-hundred dollars. There has to be a reason why they want it. There are other objects that would bring in more cash. The silver coin collection is probably worth a few thousand at least. She had uncirculated Morgan silver dollars."

His ex glanced at the ceiling. "Livi had me store some belongings in the attic when she began clearing out the house."

"Why was she clearing out her stuff?"

Meg pushed back at the long fall of her hair. "Over the past couple of months, your aunt began acting rather odd and started moving things into the attic. Livi said the attic was a safe spot."

Roarke gazed around. "Safe from what?"

"I don't know. It happened not long after the party Livi hosted. After, Livi didn't want any visitors, except for me. She asked me to install a lock on the attic door."

Someone at that party had rattled his aunt. He mentioned it. "Who was there?"

Meg sighed. "Everyone, it seemed. If Livi felt threatened, I didn't see it. But I didn't stay long because I had a client who wanted a shipment of rare books the next morning."

"Let's look in the attic. And then maybe my cell phone will die if we find the statue, and I'll be unable to call them."

Meg gave a little laugh. "You're bad, Roarke Calhoun."

He wished he could be bad again, because the Roarke of the past would have stormed out the door and never returned, not caring about a little girl in need of a kidney transplant. "If that statue is valuable, it's best we find it now. Do you have a key to the attic lock or do I need to find bolt cutters?"

Going to her purse, she fished out a set of keys hanging from a key chain with a silver heart. "It's the smaller one."

The attic was on the third floor, accessed through narrow steps from a doorway on the second floor. A handrail showed signs of wear, but was sturdy enough and the steps weren't steep. He could see his aunt going up and down these stairs with a fair amount of ease.

Roarke unlocked the door. For a moment he hesitated. "I'll go first and make sure there are no more traps."

A few minutes later he called her upstairs.

The attic had been renovated back in the 1970s, with shag carpeting and wood paneled walls, divided into three sizable rooms, all with plenty of lighting. Closets had been built into the walls. Livi had added a heating and cooling unit as well to make it livable, but the main purpose of the attic was storage.

Except when he was staying with her, hiding from the world.

The entry point had boxes and trunks lined against the walls. More stuff. Roarke walked into the second room. His refuge. The twin bed shoved against the wall still remained, along with a boy-sized desk with a dusty banker's lamp, wooden chest of drawers, a closet and a box filled with toys. He knelt on the carpeting, opened the box, his throat tight. How many happy hours had he spent here, playing with toy soldiers or his cars, forgetting about the names he'd been called in school or the fact his teachers ignored the bullying?

Livi had offered him refuge.

Meg touched his shoulder. He glanced up, blinked away the memories.

"If you want any of Livi's things, or your old toys, let me know."

He shook his head. He didn't care if Megan sold everything. Lavinia had given him a few precious items while she lived, and the most priceless was the time she'd spent with a lonely, angry boy in desperate need to know he was loved.

But Megan, as always, had that deep perception, as if reading every one of his thoughts. "If we find anything you want to keep, Roarke, I mean it, it's yours. She meant so much to you and she was your family."

Instead of answering, he opened the closet door. Clothes, lots of clothes, an old vacuum that had probably been popular in the 1970s and three paintings done with chunky acrylic paint. He frowned. They weren't bad, but certainly not valuable.

"She was into art classes. Chased the boredom away," Meg told him. She leaned over and touched the painting with the oversized yellow-and-white daisies.

The delicious scent of her floral perfume made his head swim with memories. All good ones—Megan in his arms in the back seat of the Shelby...her eager mouth on his lips...

They'd been fumbling teenagers, awkward in their passion, but it felt real and made him burn.

Not teenagers anymore. Roarke closed the door on the closet and the memory. Meg reached around him and yanked the door open.

She removed a jacket from a hanger. "Remember this? It's yours, Roarke."

The brown leather felt soft and supple beneath his fingers as he touched the jacket. He'd worked as a mechanic's helper after school one summer when things were tight. Then his mother found a better job and to celebrate they bought the jacket Roarke had wanted.

He'd wanted it because it was expensive, and the preppy kids in school all had one. He'd desperately wanted to look as if he fit in, and the day he and his mom bought it, Roarke felt like a prince.

Except the jacket backfired on him. By the time he'd been able to afford the jacket, it had gone out of style and the preppy rich kids were wearing denim jackets. Whispers started in school that he rode with a motorcycle gang. The jacket only cemented his bad rep instead of lifting him up socially.

Instead of tossing it aside, knowing how much his mom had had to pay for his heart's desire, he'd worn it proudly to reinforce the stereotype. Only he'd added to his rep through vandalism and breaking the law.

Only Livi had saved his butt, reeling him back in from a life in jail.

He handed her back the jacket. "Give it away. Sell it. I don't care."

Sighing, she draped the jacket over a chair.

"The next room is where Livi asked me to store the things she wanted locked away."

Roarke dusted off his hands. "I'll go first."

But the door leading to the third room in the attic was locked.

"Got a key for this?" he asked.

Meg's eyes widened. "This wasn't locked last time I was up here. Livi never said anything about locking this door."

"I'll be right back. Livi used to keep paper clips in her office desk."

He was back in the attic a few minutes later, carrying two paper clips. In less than a minute, the tumblers clicked and the door unlocked. Meg raised her pretty silk brows.

"Is that what they teach you at the FBI?"

"Not precisely." He grinned. "I learned to pick locks when I was a kid. Livi taught me. One of her ex-lovers was a jewel thief."

The door opened on a well-oiled hush. Roarke flipped on the light switch. A single light bulb flickered on. He wished this room had as much lighting as the others because the two dozen mannequins stored here would creep out the hardiest soul. He didn't scare easily, but these dolls were downright eerie. Most of them were dressed in period clothing, including an antique mannequin dressed in a flapper costume, complete with a cloche hat.

He motioned for Meg to stay away as he crossed the room. Unlike the other two rooms, this room was bare-bones, with exposed rafters and a solid floor instead of carpet. Boxes upon boxes were shoved into the corners. Livi was a borderline hoarder. She hated throwing anything away. He opened one book, sifted through photo albums of pictures taken before she was born.

He carefully replaced the album and shut the box lid.

Then there was the doll collection, row after row of dolls kept behind the glass walls of a law bookcase, staring out into the attic.

He checked out the room, with its dormer windows overlooking the front lawn, and then gestured for Meg to enter. She made a face as she saw the dolls.

Roarke agreed. "I always hated these damn dolls. But the mannequins are worse."

Meg shivered as well. "This room always gave me the creeps. It's why I hated coming up here to store her things. But she insisted on putting them in this room to keep them safe."

He paused in crossing the room. "Someone wanted to steal her belongings?"

"I got the feeling that's why she really wanted the valuable items moved. But then after she said that, she laughed and said she was a pack rat and should just give everything away and her imagination ran away with her."

The chest sat under the center dormer window. But it wasn't the wooden chest that drew his attention. Roarke stared at the window. "Someone's been here recently."

Meg gasped. "I've never seen that before!"

The lettering on the window was backward, but he could clearly read the two words that made his blood run cold.

Help me.

Chapter 5

The lettering was legible, but shaky. He studied the dust surrounding the letters. Thick, the window grimy, but clean lettering.

"Whoever wrote this did it recently. The writing's fresh." He glanced at Meg. "You certain no one's been here since Livi passed?"

"I don't know. All I can say is no one was here when she was alive, except me, and I didn't write that." Meg shook her head. "Can you find out who wrote that?"

"I'd have to dust for fingerprints, but just in looking at this, someone wrote this with a glove." He glanced around.

One mannequin wore a winter coat with a fake fur collar and a wool ski hat, and its hands were covered in brown leather gloves. He examined the mittens. The right glove's pointer finger was covered in dust.

"Here's the culprit… Whoever did this used this glove to write this." He rubbed his neck. "I could send this out for DNA, but I doubt the lab would find anything."

"The only person with the key to the attic was me and

Livi had a spare key she kept hidden. But why would she write this? Her peculiar sense of humor?"

"Nothing funny about this," he said grimly. "It's not one of her famous pranks."

Meg hugged herself, shuddered again. "This room feels so haunted. It's one reason Livi disliked coming up here. She told me old stories about the house and how it was rumored a servant who lived up here had a torrid love affair with the man of the house, and killed herself when he refused to leave his wife."

"One of Livi's tall tales?" He examined the window closer. It had a clear view of anyone coming up the drive. "I used to hide up here for hours, but Livi knew where I was."

"Let's open that chest."

The chest was unlocked, another odd thing, considering the locked door and the locked attic. Roarke knelt on the floorboards and watched as Meg shuffled through the items.

"The coin collection isn't here. Just old clothing. And this…" She lifted out the Cupid and Psyche statue.

Meg examined the bottom. "This is an inexpensive replica. Auction houses put serial numbers on the bottom of items that they sell, and this one doesn't have that. Looks like she could have purchased it at a thrift store. Or her father bought it in New York on one of his business trips. Your grandfather mentioned it had been in the family for years."

Suspicion filled him. Roarke turned the statue over again, probing at the felt-covered bottom. "Unless the old man was losing his mind…there's no reason to want this statue."

Meg held out her hands. "May I?"

"I don't think this statue, or this model, was covered with felt. The felt may have been added on…" She peeled back the fabric and a wide smile touched her mouth. "Ah-ha! Got it."

Roarke studied the statue's bottom and the secret compartment she'd uncovered. Meg set down the hidden panel. "Trap door, secured by magnets. It's an old trick."

The compartment was empty.

"It's a good place to hide money, but too small to hide much money." Roarke probed the inside of the statue.

"Maybe that's a good thing. Someone may have been looking for it," she mused.

Awareness snapped through him. "Megan, what's going on that you're not telling me? The full story?"

She bent her head, studying her feet. Roarke reached over, and with his hand, lifted her chin to meet his gaze.

"What happened, Meg? What aren't you telling me about my great-aunt?"

She didn't jerk away from his touch, but neither did she lean into it as she once had.

"I promised her I'd be there for her, Roarke. And I failed her."

"You were there for her more than anyone else."

Certainly more than me. He quashed that thought, needing answers, not hot emotion.

"It wasn't enough. She grew so afraid, Roarke. So very afraid she never left her house, not in the last month."

What the hell...

"Why? Was she growing senile? Too frail to be alone?"

"No. Livi didn't tell you because she didn't want you worrying about her. She was sharp as ever and quite capable." Megan drew a deep breath and did draw away, swallowing hard.

He had the feeling this was going to be bad. Quite bad. "Then what?"

"Livi rescued the dog because she was afraid. No, she was terrified."

"Of what?" He nearly shouted the answer, then calmed himself.

"Someone was trying to kill her."

She had to get out of here. The air in the attic seemed too stifling, too suffocating. Meg headed for the stairs, trailed by Roarke. He'd looked as if she'd punched him in the stomach.

When they reached the kitchen, she poured herself a glass of water and drank heavily, wiping her forehead with a shaky hand. Roarke wouldn't let this go. She was glad he finally knew, because carrying this kind of secret had been hell.

But she'd promised his great-aunt to keep her mouth shut.

"Water?" she asked, reaching for another glass in the cabinet.

"No. Answers, Meg. Who would kill Livi and why?"

Although she'd expected worry, concern and questions, this low quiet tone and the glitter in his clear green eyes made it clear he'd barely checked his rage. Livi meant the world to Roarke. Had he known his great-aunt was in trouble, he'd have dropped everything and rushed back home.

That level of family loyalty had won her heart years ago. It was the same reason Lavinia had made Megan promise not to tell Roarke what had happened.

"I don't know. There were a few incidents. That was the real reason why she thought about going into an assisted living facility. Not because she couldn't live alone, but she'd be surrounded by people 24/7."

"Tell me everything. Now."

"Outside. I need air."

On the expansive back porch, he sat in one of the wicker rockers. Too nervous to sit, Meg leaned against the railing. She pushed a lock behind one ear, her throat tight, her stomach clenching.

"About four months ago, shortly after Dad died, Livi and I became quite close. She hired me to help her around the house, doing small chores. I think she knew I felt lost after Dad died and needed a little extra money to help pay the funeral expenses." Megan bit her lip. "I loved her for it, especially when she assured me she needed the extra help. But then things changed. I came to her house one night with groceries. Marched through the door only to find her pointing a shotgun in my face."

Roarke's mouth opened. "What the hell?"

"That's what I said." She gave a breathless laugh. "Thankfully, it wasn't loaded. After we both calmed down, because you should have heard me scream, Livi told me she'd heard something outside. And she was certain someone had been inside the house. In fact, it wasn't the first time."

She told him about the four separate incidents. The first seemed harmless—a childish prank of someone soaping her back windows and writing WASH ME.

The second was not childish. Someone kept phoning the house and hanging up when Livi answered.

The third was more ominous. Livi had dozed off in the library while reading, and when she woke up, there was a fire in the hearth and an empty cup of tea on the table beside her. As if someone had been there, sipped tea and left.

Livi never drank tea, only kept it on hand for visitors. After that incident, Livi got Rigor and the guns.

The fourth was the worst.

Megan watched his face as she told him how Livi had

almost been run over by a car one night when she was out in town, crossing the street.

"She'd gone into town. She was walking to her car and someone nearly hit her. She thought it was on purpose. Livi was pretty shaken."

Roarke's green gaze sharpened. "When?"

"About a month before she died. All she saw was a dark vehicle. She turned into a total hermit and refused to leave the house. That's when I started buying all her supplies and dropping them off for her and Rigor."

Roarke's expression darkened, as if he wanted to track down the culprit and deal him a little justice of his own.

"Did she call the sheriff?"

Guilt flickered through her. Maybe she should have done more, convinced Roarke's great-aunt that law enforcement was needed. Megan stared at her hands.

"No, because Livi asked me not to. There was no proof. Even I had trouble believing her. I couldn't help but wonder if she was imagining some things. You know, getting older wasn't easy for Livi. She had so much pride and backbone."

Roarke blew out a breath and she could feel his incandescent rage. He didn't need to raise his voice, only lower it.

"Why the hell didn't someone tell me what was going on? I would have been here in a heartbeat. She should have called me instead of getting a dog or a gun."

"Livi made me promise to keep this from you. She knew the stress of your job."

He stood, and began to pace. "You didn't think, Megan, that perhaps with the resources of the FBI at my disposal, I could have found out who was trying to kill my great-aunt?"

"I promised."

His mouth tightened as she turned to look at him. "Dammit, Megan, you should have notified me, called the sheriff, something!"

"Don't blame me." Megan felt her own temper rise. "I tried to help her. Livi ordered me to keep it quiet. She didn't want anyone worrying about her, especially you. She always said your work came first because you rescued children who were missing."

Roarke fell silent, stared at the blue lake waters in the distance. Finally he shook his head. "I'm sorry. I know how stubborn she was. I'm just frustrated."

It couldn't be easy for him to learn his loving aunt had been threatened. Megan's voice softened. "She used to talk about you all the time. Livi was so proud of you."

"She was the only one who ever told me so, made me feel I wasn't a total failure."

His gaze flicked to her. "Except you, until the day I left Cooper Falls."

Let's not go there, please. Megan changed the subject. "I asked Livi if she wanted me to move in with her, until we could sort things out and see exactly what was happening, but she refused. I think it wasn't that she didn't want me as a roommate, but she feared something bad might happen to me as well. That's when she made plans to move into an assisted living center, as much as she hated it."

Roarke quietly swore and fisted his hands. "I would have moved mountains to find out what the hell was going on."

She understood his anger and frustration, for she'd had some of her own when his aunt had refused help. The sheer helplessness had been the worst. It was only when she'd coaxed Livi into moving out, and helping her find a good place to live, that Megan felt a modicum of relief.

"For all she did for others, Livi never wanted to depend

on anyone. You know how she was," she said, trying to reassure Roarke.

He didn't look convinced. She almost laughed, because with that determined line denting his forehead, he looked remarkably like his great-aunt when her mind was made up.

Meg took a deep breath. None of this was humorous.

"I need to get out of here. I'll go to the hardware store, get new locks. I don't want you here alone while I'm gone. I mean it, Meg."

"I have plenty of errands, so that's not a problem. But what about Rigor?"

He looked at the dog, who had followed them outside. "Is he an outdoor dog?"

Meg pointed to the doghouse by the rose garden. "He likes it outside, as long as you leave fresh water."

"Fine. Get him fresh water and leave him outside. I don't want him in the house alone, either. He might get into trouble and he was Livi's dog and I need to take care of him."

Roarke glanced at his cell.

"Excuse me," he told her. "I have to call Chet."

Roarke left his stepbrother a voice mail, letting him know he'd arrived and was staying at Livi's house.

The sooner he could sell the house and leave, the better for both of them. He would cut his ties and leave.

Just like he had years ago. No more emotional involvement. But she knew Roarke Calhoun.

He would not rest until he found out exactly what happened to his great-aunt.

Chapter 6

Chet and Nancy lived on the outskirts of town in a modest housing development far from the luxurious residences bordering the lakefront. Roarke took his time driving there, trying to collect his thoughts.

Someone tried to kill Livi. And now his beloved great-aunt was dead.

Meg had been tight-lipped. It bothered him that she knew more about Livi's problems than he did.

Roarke's fingers tightened on the steering wheel. One thing at a time. First, the visit with Chet.

Funny how life was. Once he'd wanted nothing to do with his stepbrother, Chet, and his family. Resentment had always lingered because Chet was the darling of his wealthy grandparents. Chet's parents were acceptable and could do no wrong, like their son.

Unlike Roarke, who could do nothing right.

And then two years ago, Chet and Nancy came with Holly, their only daughter, to DC. Not a social visit, but to Walter Reed Hospital to inquire about a kidney transplant for Holly.

Fallen leaves littered the roadside as he drove to Chet's house. The tree-lined streets were well-kept, but this was an older neighborhood with smaller homes and signs of kids with bikes strewn on driveways and basketball hoops attached to houses. Chet and Nancy lived in a two-story Colonial. Chet had texted him the address.

The house was painted light blue, and a child's pink bicycle with training wheels sat on the front porch, parked to one side.

He had never been here before. Roarke parked on the street. He walked up the cracked stoop leading to the house, climbed the steps as if heading for his own execution, took a deep breath and knocked.

The door opened immediately. His stepbrother stood there, and Chet's appearance shook Roarke to the bone. Never had he seen Chet look anything less than tidy. But his brown hair was longer, messy, his T-shirt was rumpled and there were stains on his jeans.

"Thanks for coming. Holly can't wait to see you. She's talked of nothing else for days but *Unca Roarke* visiting."

All his own concerns melted away. Roarke stepped inside and closed the door, his hand on Chet's shoulder. "What's wrong? You look like hell."

"Holly. She's…not doing well." Chet's shoulders sagged, and Roarke realized how much weight he'd lost since he'd seen him two years ago.

Then he straightened and smiled, but the smile didn't reach his eyes. "Come on in. Nancy and Holly are in the back."

They walked through a living room where stacks of laundry sat folded on the sofa. Toys were neatly stacked off to the side. Not a good sign.

They went into the kitchen, where things were not so neat. Dishes were piled in the sink, and pots with food still in them sat on the range. Roarke's Spidey sense warned things were quite bad for the house to get this disorganized.

A set of French doors led onto the porch. Chet hesitated before opening one.

"She gets colder more easily. With the kidney disease, it's harder for her body to regulate its temperature. But the back porch is her favorite place to stay, so I enclosed it and installed a little heater."

Roarke's heart skipped a beat. A month ago, before Livi died, she'd warned him Holly was growing sicker. But he hadn't realized how sick.

"The transplant... Have you entered her into the national database?" Roarke asked.

"I'm a match." A grudging laugh, followed by Chet shaking his head. "So there's no need to search for a donor. But the money, that's the problem. Going to cost more than $250,000 and that doesn't include the antirejection meds she'll need for life."

"Insurance?"

Chet shook his head. "The policy I have doesn't cover it. I'm fighting with them. They don't see it as necessary surgery. They want to keep her on dialysis. I even swallowed my pride and asked my father, you know, the one we share in common? I called him, on my dime, in Rome."

He tensed, anticipating his stepbrother's next words.

Red suffused Chet's face. "He was in Rome with his thirty-year-old bride, wife number four. Told me good luck, but his last wife took all his money in the divorce. His new wife had all the money and she wouldn't take kindly to him spending it on a grandchild of his second marriage."

"Sorry." Roarke meant it. "Not exactly father of the year."

"My mom has tried to do what she can, she and her new husband. They've given all they can, but it's not enough."

"What about William and Abigail?"

A disgusted snort. "Right."

It made no sense. Chet was their grandparents' favorite. "Why not?"

A bitter laugh. "I asked a month ago, right before the town fundraiser. They said we'll see. Guess Nancy being the daughter of a waitress and an auto mechanic didn't sit well with the grands."

Roarke's chest tightened. He never felt close to his stepbrother, never even really made contact with his family until Chet brought them to DC and practically begged him to have dinner with them. Feeling guilty for ignoring Chet all the years since he'd left, Roarke had invited them over to his apartment for a simple meal.

Holly had won him over instantly with her sweetness, cheerful nature and endless curiosity.

Maybe he'd misjudged Chet all these years. He felt a deep sympathy for Chet and his family, who could have benefited from their grandparents' generosity, if they had chosen to share it to save Holly.

"Come on." Chet opened the door.

Holly and her mother were seated at a round table near a window. Holly glanced up, and her expression became radiant. "Unca Roarke!"

"Whoa, Holly Berry, don't get up." Roarke rushed over as she struggled to stand. He bent down and engulfed her in a hug. "Hello, ladybug, good to see you."

He smiled to cover his shock. Disease had stricken her, taking its ugly toll. She was too thin now, her once-bright blue eyes shadowed and her arms nearly like matchsticks. The thick blond curls had grown dull and her cheeks hollow. But her smile was still the same.

Roarke wanted to tickle her ribs, but she seemed too frail. He eased off his grip, worried he might break her.

Holly reached up and hugged him again, as if to prove him wrong.

Nancy, a pretty petite woman, had cut her own blond hair short. Strain showed on her features as she gestured to a seat at the table. "Please, Roarke. Sit a while. It's been too long. How are you?"

"Good. I'm sorry I've been absent. Lots of cases."

"Your work is so important." Nancy bit her lip. "I don't know how you can handle the heartbreak working with parents who…"

Her voice trailed off. Roarke turned to Holly, knowing Nancy didn't want her daughter to see her tears.

"So, ladybug, have you been studying hard? Your dad told me you left school, but you've been keeping up with classes remotely."

"Trying to." Holly pointed to the laptop. "I fell behind in history, but Meg's been tutoring me."

He blinked back his surprise. "She has? I thought she'd be busy with the bookstore."

"Oh, she is, but Meg's the best. She stops by after the bookstore closes."

Chet took the other empty seat at the table. "Meg got her this laptop. The one we had was old and the internet connection unstable. Meg tutors Holly for free, four nights a week for an hour. I understand you've seen her?"

That last question was asked casually, though his stepbrother's eyes were bright with interest. Even Nancy turned to him, the lingering sorrow gone from her expression.

He hesitated. Everyone in town must know by now. Cooper Falls was a small town and gossip spread like wildfire.

"Unca Roarke? Do you like Meg?"

Bright, inquisitive Holly. "As much as you like steamed broccoli." Roarke snorted.

Holly's smile drooped. She plucked at the hem of her

T-shirt. The garment seemed to swallow her. "I know it's rude. I'm sorry. I get bored sitting here at home all day and none of my friends come to visit anymore. I like visitors and knowing what's going on in their lives."

Roarke swallowed hard. At only seven years old, Holly was living vicariously through other people. Sure he wasn't thrilled about seeing Meg again, but that was his issue, not his stepniece's. "Well, feel free to ask me anything. I *did* like Meg. We had a relationship and we're now going to be working together at Livi's house."

Nancy and Chet exchanged glances. "Roarke, sit a spell with her. Nancy and I have to go over some paperwork. We'll be back in a few minutes."

When they left the room, he asked Holly about her schoolwork and her hobbies. Holly showed him a photo on her cell phone of a painting of the lake, where birds flew over the water and the sunlight sparkled.

"Wow." He whistled. "You did this?"

She beamed. "I was the best student in Mrs. Dixon's art class until I had to leave school. Are you going to be in town long? Please say you'll stay a while. I want you to see my painting in real life. Meg's organized an art exhibit with the library next month and they selected my painting to display."

He sighed. "I'm sorry, ladybug. I have to get back to DC. I'm only here for as long as it takes to clean up Livi's house and put it on the market to sell."

His stepniece stared at the table. "It's okay, Unca Roarke. I understand."

He patted her arm. "Tell you what. I can get time off at Christmas and return for a visit then."

"If I'm here."

A chill raced down his spine. "What are you talking

about, Holly? I know the dialysis is rough, hon, but you're not going to die."

"You sound like the doctors and Mom and Dad." She glanced up at him. "Can I show you something?"

At his nod, she rolled up her sleeve. The marks on her arm made his blood run cold. "That was before the doctors put a port in me for dialysis."

"When you get the transplant, you won't need it." He hoped he sounded encouraging.

Looking too cynical for her young years, Holly shook her head. "It's probably not going to happen. I know Mom and Dad keep telling me I will get the transplant, so I go along with it. But it's getting worse, Unca Roarke. I don't want Mom and Dad to get upset and they get real upset when I talk to them about dying. I've kind of given up on hoping the transplant will come through and I don't know how much longer I can take dialysis. I feel like my body is wearing out. I'm so tired all the time."

Stricken, he rubbed his chin. He smiled at her, fighting the terrible feeling in his gut.

"Tell me about Washington and your job, Unca Roarke. Did you find any missing children? Daddy says that's what you do all the time now."

A lump formed in his throat as he thought about Sonia, so much like Holly. So hopeful and cute...

Her body found in a ditch as she clutched her doll, Sonia's pretty blue gaze staring at the sky.

Don't go there.

He told her about a case with a better ending—Anna, a kidnapped girl who turned out to be the granddaughter of wealthy foreigners.

"She's now living with her mom and grandparents in Chile. Very happy. She wrote us a letter recently, thanking us for finding her and bringing her back to her mom."

Holly clapped her hands. "You're my hero, Unca Roarke!"

"Hey, I thought I was your hero," her father joked from the doorway.

Holly frowned as her parents entered the room. "Can I have two heroes?"

"Of course, honey. You can have as many as you like," Nancy told her, wiping her eyes as she gazed at her daughter.

How many times had he worked on a case with missing kids, seeing the parents' devastation when he and Kyle informed them their child had been found dead? He understood the grief but had never come up close and personal to it.

He glanced at his cell phone. "Sorry, I have to go. But I'll be back."

Dropping a kiss on Holly's cheek, he gave a playful tug to her hair, noting again with dismay it was dull and lackluster. The disease, he supposed. "Make sure you study hard, ladybug. You need anything, call me while I'm in town."

An impish grin touched her thin mouth. "Or I'll tell Meg and ask her to ask you."

Roarke shook his head with a mock scowl. "Matchmaker."

"Someone has to find you a girlfriend, Unca Roarke. You're too busy saving kids to find one yourself."

He laughed, said goodbye to Nancy and left the room. Chet followed him to the living room and the front door.

Roarke rubbed the tense muscles in his neck. "Damn, Chet, I'm sorry, I didn't realize how bad she was. She's such a brave kid."

His stepbrother nodded, his expression tight. "That's our Holly. Brave. But not healthy. She's running out of time. I've gone over and over the figures. My job doesn't cover everything, even with dozens of new clients and contracts. Nancy quit her job at the bank when Holly got too sick to attend school."

Roarke knew his stepbrother worked as a salesman, but had been taking more time off lately to help with Holly's medical appointments and dialysis.

Chet waved a paper at him. "We were tallying the figures from the fundraiser the town held recently for Holly. They raised $25,000. It was amazing, but we don't know how to raise more. We need much more."

Roarke whistled, surprised at the generosity of the townspeople. Then again, he had a sour view of the town based on his childhood. "It's a good start."

"Better than a good start. After the fundraiser, someone donated $100,000 to the fund. Anonymously. Really raised our hopes. But still, we need more. The kidney transplant is the most expensive item. The antirejection drugs Holly will have to be on for the rest of her life will cost about $14,000 a year, and insurance…"

"Won't cover them." He did some quick calculations. "Sounds like half a million dollars would come in handy."

"Sure." Chet snorted. "Know anyone who would happen to have it lying around and want to save a kid's life?"

"Me."

Chet blinked. "Are you… What? Is the FBI paying that great of a salary these days?"

Roarke's mouth quirked upward. "Not exactly. But I did inherit Livi's house and the property. I figure after selling it, the money can go to Holly."

His stepbrother stared at him, and something flickered in his dark eyes. Roarke had seen it before in parents whose children went missing and heard they could still be alive. Hope.

Chet blinked a couple of times. "You'd...you'd do that for me? For Holly?"

"I can't think of a better way to spend half a million dollars."

"Are you a saint?" Chet laughed a little, and shook his head. "Or am I dreaming? What happened to you, Roarke? I mean, we were never close. In fact, you refused to call me family up until a couple of years ago."

His chest tightened. "I know we never were on the best of terms, and I was a downright...jerk...to you when you were younger, but this is your daughter's life."

Moisture glistened in Chet's eyes. "Roarke, I don't know what to say. Thank you seems trite in light of what you propose. But sell Aunt Livi's house?"

"It's worth a lot, the last remaining homestead on the lake, with acres of prime real estate. Developers will be fighting to buy it after it's listed."

The light died in Chet's eyes. Roarke frowned. "What's wrong?"

"You can't sell it to a developer," he said flatly.

"Why not?"

"Deed restrictions. The house isn't zoned for multifamily. Livi went before the town council to get zoning approval, but the historical society put up a fight. I helped Livi with the paperwork when she wanted to sell an acre by the lake to a developer. That was before Holly's health started to decline."

Roarke's anger flared. Damn those biddies at the historical society. "You can fight them."

"It takes time," he burst out. "Holly doesn't have that kind of time."

He was a firm believer in the impossible, especially when it came to vulnerable children. Holly had to have that operation. "We'll figure out the details later. I can't believe Livi left me the house to sell knowing it couldn't be sold. Someone will want it. She left the contents of the house to Megan, with the stipulation I can't sell the house until Megan clears it out and does whatever she wishes with Aunt Livi's stuff."

Chet whistled. "Wow. Everything in that grand old house to Megan...your ex-girlfriend? That has to sting."

Not as much as he'd expected. Roarke shrugged. "I don't care about what's in the house. My life isn't here anymore. Sooner I can list the house and get it sold, sooner I can return to DC."

"Right. Got to get back to saving those kids. Too bad, though. Would love for you to stick around, see the results of your generosity." Chet's expression hinted of mirth. "Maybe rekindle that old flame with Meg."

Roarke gave him the hard stare he usually reserved for interrogations. Chet held up his hands. "Okay, just kidding. Seriously, though, I can't thank you enough for your offer. This is the first time in months I've felt our kid has a fighting chance."

Thankful he could provide that chance, he clapped his stepbrother on the back. "Holly deserves it."

"Thanks, Roarke. Want to stick around for dinner?"

"I have a lot of work waiting for me."

He almost ran to his car, waved at Chet and then sped away before Holly or Nancy could come outside, gushing over his offer. A nugget of guilt winked at him deep inside. He should have been there all along for Holly. Family was supposed to stick together. But he had assumed, and made an ass of himself for assuming, that their paternal and stately grandparents would take care of their only great-granddaughter. Or Livi would.

Why Livi had cut Chet out of her will, he didn't know. Made no sense, except Livi was peculiar when it came to her defense of Roarke. *Maybe I was the one who tainted Chet for Livi.*

Yet Meg had said Chet and his family were on good terms with Livi. She had even babysat Holly at times after school when Nancy had to work late.

Why leave me in your will, Livi? Why me, and why the hell Megan?

His cell dinged a text message. Roarke put it on Bluetooth and a computerized voice droned out that Meg was at the house and had started inventory. Irritation filled him. *She should have waited for me. Something weird is going on in Livi's house.*

Roarke wished he could hire someone to simply list the house on the market and he could return home. But the murky details of Livi's death and the odd happenings at the house tied him to Cooper Falls until he figured out what was going on. If only Livi had left the house's contents to Chet, he wouldn't be in this predicament, forced to work alongside Megan.

He used to burn for Meg, feel as if he went up in damn flames each time he was around her. Couldn't wait to see her again, inhale the sweet smell of her hair, hold her soft hand and listen to her gurgling laugh. Meg had been his entire world when life looked so dark he thought he'd never leave Cooper Falls, never amount to anything, as everyone kept insisting.

Wasn't going to happen again. Not now. Meg was in the past and everything in his life pointed toward a promising future with the agency in DC. He'd no more wish to live back in Cooper Falls and all its small-town life and intrigue than he'd wish to cut off his right hand.

He drove to the market to get dog food. When he finally turned into the driveway of the big rambling mansion, Roarke parked and cut off the engine. For a moment he simply gazed at the house and let the memories float past, the good memories and the bad. The amazing stories Livi once told.

His gaze drifted up to the attic dormer windows. Sunlight glinted off the dirty glass. Roarke blinked.

What the…

He looked away and then looked again. Nothing there. Now.

Ghosts were not real.

But he'd swear on his mother's grave he saw someone dressed like a 1920s flapper standing in the attic window, staring down at him. Not a mannequin, either. But a breathing person.

Shaking his head, he went into the house with his purchases. Rigor ran to greet him, tail wagging. After feeding Rigor in the kitchen, he carried out a bowl of water onto the back porch and then let him out the kitchen door to run around outside on the property.

Meg had said something about a shotgun. Livi had hated guns. Logic said the most likely place to store one would be the hallway closet near the living room.

That closet had always been a mystery to him. Livi never allowed him to peer inside, claiming it was for adults. After she caught him inside, Lavinia had put a lock on the door.

Today there was no lock, only the antique glass knob as he pulled the door open.

Roarke opened the door and jumped back, expecting a plethora of sporting equipment, boxes, clothing and other items to topple outward.

Nothing.

A normal closet. Nothing except coats packed tight on hangers and a jumble of hatboxes on the floor. Normal.

Except for the gleam of white on the floor…bone-white. Roarke stared at it, his blood racing.

He'd heard of the saying every family had a skeleton in its closet.

But this was the real deal.

Chapter 7

His past returned to haunt him. Roarke wanted to curse, but held his tongue.

"Funny how you come back and dead bodies show up, Roarke Calhoun."

Sheriff Toby Doyle bent down and studied the skull found in Livi's front hall closet. Roarke's stomach clenched as he struggled to rein in his temper. The skeleton head grinned up at him, a haunting reminder of how final death was.

Now he was beginning to regret the decision to call the police. He'd forgotten what an ass Doyle could be.

"I haven't been home in years. You think I did this?" Roarke snapped.

Doyle glanced up. "Didn't say that. You sure are quick to jump to conclusions."

Sheriff Doyle stood, removed his hat and ran a thumb around the brim. Roarke narrowed his eyes as one of Doyle's deputies stood near the opened closet.

"My aunt is—" he took a deep breath, struggling with fresh grief and anguish "—was not a killer. Neither am I."

Megan put a hand on his arm. He wanted to shake it off, rage at Doyle's casual attitude, but as she had in the past, Megan calmed him and allowed him to focus. He breathed in the warmth of her floral perfume, the scent of woman, and forced his temper to subside.

The sheriff shook his head. "It's a real skull."

"I know," he shot back. He should know. He'd seen enough skeletal remains working for the FBI.

"Hmm." Doyle crouched down. "It's like that other skeleton."

He felt blood drain from his face. "What other skeleton?"

Doyle glanced up, his mouth tight. "You wouldn't know. You weren't here."

"I think I can clear up the mystery," Meg said. "This skull is real. Livi bought it when she was studying forensic anthropology. You know how she was always trying to learn new things."

He glanced at the old coats and hats. "What else did she keep in here?"

"This." Megan pointed to the upper shelf. "She didn't want anyone getting hurt."

He reached up and pulled down a long object wrapped in oilcloth. After laying it on the floor, he unwrapped it.

Shotgun.

"Double-barrel 12 gauge. This is an antique, could have been in the family for years. Is this the shotgun you mentioned her using, Meg? I doubt this would even fire."

"No, but this one will."

Megan tried reaching up for the shelf, but her fingertips barely grazed the surface. Roarke joined her, his body brushing against hers, and she startled. For a minute he basked in the warmth of their bodies touching, memories surging.

Megan glanced upward.

"Allow me."

Damn, they'd barely touched and he felt it down to his bones as if he were that same horny teen who'd seen her the first time, all long legs and laughter, as she ran to the lake.

Roarke took another deep breath and removed the second object.

Not wrapped in oilcloth. This shotgun was new and would definitely fire. He checked the weapon. Empty, thank goodness, but he found a case of shells on the shelf.

"Remington 870. Dammit, what the hell was Livi doing with this?"

Time to really explore this closet. Roarke found a step stool and climbed it. He brought out a box containing two handguns, a 9mm Luger and a revolver.

The house of mirrors spun crazily. Roarke glanced at the sheriff.

"She had permits," Doyle said calmly, as if Roarke had found a bouquet of flowers in the closet instead of weapons. "Livi insisted. Home defense. I went with her to pick them out."

The fact that his gentle, zany aunt had harbored what amounted to a personal armory bothered him on a visceral level. "Three guns? Why would she need to defend herself? Who was threatening her?"

How many other secrets had Livi kept from him?

"Never learned to fire them," Doyle said, ignoring his questions and taking the guns and placing them back on the shelf. "Just thought waving them around would scare off an intruder."

"Waving them around? Who threatened her?" he repeated.

Doyle didn't answer and averted his gaze.

Roarke took a deep breath. "I find a skull in Livi's closet

and a stack of weapons. What happened that neither of you are telling me?"

He wondered what else had been going on. The nail in the floor, the sawed-off stairs and now a skull left in the hall closet?

Did Livi die of natural causes or something much more ominous?

Roarke folded his arms. "Someone had better tell me what the hell is going on around here."

Doyle and Meg exchanged glances. Meg sighed. "Livi didn't want to worry you, Roarke…"

"Go on."

"About three months ago, human remains were found on the property in the woods." Meg clasped and unclasped her hands. "They were old bones."

He felt as if someone had punched him in the stomach. "A body was buried here?"

Doyle studied him as if Roarke had done that particular burial. "Forensics showed the body had been dead for decades, maybe since the 1930s."

"Cause of death?"

"Undetermined."

Frustrated, he took a deep breath. "Did you ID the vic?" Bones buried for that long meant Livi had nothing to do with it. She'd been born in 1938.

"No. Missing person records, as you well know, were nonexistent back then. The coroner determined the body was a male, maybe his late twenties to early thirties. We investigated, but no one could remember anyone going missing that far back. Not even rumors. Livi buried the bones in the county cemetery and that was it."

"That was it? You find human remains on my aunt's property and shrug them off?"

Doyle locked gazes with him, as if he wanted to win a

staring contest. "We investigated and couldn't find the victim. Livi said she would hire a private detective to trace any family members through DNA and as far as I know, the man's investigation met with a dead end."

Doyle grinned. "Pun intended."

He didn't appreciate the man's sense of humor. Roarke raked a hand through his hair. "I had no idea Livi was going through this."

"How would you know, Calhoun? You haven't been home to see her since you left."

Doyle's words cut to the quick. He wanted to slug the smirking expression off the man's face. Meg squeezed his arm and smiled at the sheriff. "Thank you for all your help. We'll take it from here, Sheriff."

When did Meg acquire that take-charge attitude? He liked it, because it gave him breathing room to process what had happened. Hard to do with Doyle hovering around, staring at him as if Roarke were sixteen all over again and caught smashing the windows of his grandparents' Bentley.

Doyle touched the brim of his hat. "Aim to serve, Miss Megan. Have a good day and let us know if you have any other problems."

Ignoring Roarke, the sheriff and two deputies left the house. He didn't care. Like many townspeople, Doyle had a less than charitable view of Roarke, no matter how much he'd redeemed himself as an adult. Hell, he could be a saint and Doyle would still see him as the same reckless boy.

The same kid who'd stolen his aunt's car.

The same kid who'd fallen in love with Megan—the most striking, intriguing girl in Lakefront High—and dared to date her, despite her esteemed father's protests.

That didn't matter now. He had more questions than answers. A simple case of putting the mansion on the market to sell it and fund Holly's kidney transplant had turned even more complicated.

"Doyle never did like me," Roarke mused. "Still doesn't."

Meg sighed. "He never forgave you for all your teenage transgressions."

"Like most of the town. Or was it that my mother and I lived on the wrong side of the railroad tracks?"

"That was a long time ago, Roarke," she said softly. "You've changed and so have they. Everyone should remember that."

Right. Ignoring that, he shut the closet door and leaned against it. "Time to level with me, Meggie. Tell me about the body found on the property."

"I will. Better yet, I'll show you where it was found. Rather, where I found it."

Another surprise. Damn, he hated surprises. "I don't suppose Livi kept gloves and plastic ziplock bags around."

Meg shot him a puzzled look. "There's gardening gloves in the deck box out back that the handyman used for trimming the hedges, and yes, she had a box of sandwich bags. Why do you need them?"

"Evidence."

"For what?" She shook her head. "Doyle already went through everything after the body was found."

Right. He'd bet his next paycheck that investigation had been hasty. "Doing a little investigating of my own."

Rigor ran to greet them as they went out the kitchen door onto the back porch. The dog loped ahead of them as they stepped onto the pathway leading to the lake and the beach. Trees covered most of the property, except for a broad swatch of green yard marching down to the sand and the lakefront.

The grounds looked in better condition than the house.

The grass had been mowed and the stone walkway splitting off into a garden near the trees was fairly clean. Even from this distance he could tell the garden looked tended, unlike the house itself.

Roarke jammed his hands into the pockets of his jeans. "Let me guess. You also helped Livi with the gardening?"

She sighed. "I love to garden and it was a way to help Livi and get my green thumb going again. She helped me. I think she enjoyed being out of that house. It seemed to suffocate her at times."

Instead of heading for the garden, Meg made a left turn, heading for the barn and the gravel road cutting through the forest. Oscar, Livi's father, had cut the roadway through the property years ago. Each autumn he'd drive the tractor through the woods to cut trees for firewood to last through the winter.

Rigor ran ahead of them, pausing now and then to investigate a particular smell. They walked through the forest, the birds chattering in the trees, the distant splash of water lapping against the sandy beach.

"Meg, how did Livi die and who found her?"

Meg bit her lip. "Heart attack. The sheriff found her on the property, by the rose garden."

He frowned. "She was alone?"

"It was a Saturday, one of the few busy days at the bookstore. I promised to stop by after the store closed. Unfortunately, I got delayed by a last-minute donation of rare books, so I was there later than I wanted to be. I tried her cell phone and got no answer. So I called the sheriff and asked him to do a welfare check on Livi."

He felt gut-punched that Livi had died that way, without anyone to help.

"I'm so sorry I couldn't be there for her."

"It wasn't your fault. I'm more at fault for not coming

to visit and insisting she move into assisted living where nurses would be nearby." Roarke frowned. "So the death was ruled natural causes? Did the sheriff even investigate to see what caused the heart attack?"

"No autopsy. Livi insisted in her will. If anything happened to her, she wanted a quick burial, no fuss. She was well-liked." She shook her head. "I can't think of a soul who'd wish to hurt her."

"Someone wanted to."

Roarke craned his neck upward to regard the sharp blue sky, enjoying the crisp feel of autumn approaching. "This property alone is worth at least two-million dollars."

Meg sniffed. "Some things have more value than dollars and cents, Roarke Calhoun. I would think you would understand that."

The rebuke, coming on the heels of Sheriff Doyle's caustic attitude, stung more than he'd ever admit. "Wouldn't want to ruin my image, princess. I'm all about cold hard cash."

She glanced at him. "You'd have to convince me of that. I know how much you loved and adored your aunt, and her legacy."

Grief welled up. He pushed it aside. "How far are we going to walk?"

Silently she pointed ahead to a dilapidated woodshed used to store firewood and equipment. Meg hesitated. Then she gestured to a small clearing beyond the shed.

"There. You can still see the crime scene tape marking the spot." She shuddered. "I'll stay here. I have no desire to get any closer." She whistled for Rigor, who ran toward her.

He approached the site, squatted down and examined the disturbed earth. A simple cross had been set aside, as if it marked the grave. Roarke slipped on the gloves. They were a little tight, but sufficed. With extreme care, he sifted through the dirt.

Sunlight dappled the pine and oak trees overhead, spilling in patches onto the ground. This area was cleared of leaves and decaying forest matter, making it easier for him to spot the object glittering in the sunlight. He pulled it free and examined it.

Doyle's men hadn't been thorough. Or maybe they were simply too rushed.

Rushed because the good sheriff told them to avoid a thorough investigation?

He pulled out a man's gold pocket watch with a fob and chain. Definitely an antique. Roarke tried to open the cover, but it was jammed shut. A professional jeweler could resolve this.

Roarke removed the plastic baggie he'd taken from the kitchen and snapped it open. He dropped the watch into the baggie and continued his search.

After several minutes, he found nothing. Dusting off his jeans, he returned to the woodshed. Megan was inside, going through stacks of old newspapers. Rigor sniffed around the shed, his tail wagging.

She waved a hand. "These were always used for kindling. Livi had them stored here after she read the daily paper. I thought maybe they would be useful in finding clues to the body. *The Cooper Falls Herald* always had a special edition each Halloween of mysteries that were never solved."

He admired her resolve. "Yeah, like the haunted train tracks on the old Barton Road and the ghost train. Any luck? I imagine someone reported missing for years would be newsworthy each year."

"No. I have a year's worth of back issues and every single issue is here, even that Halloween edition. But the section with the article about the mysteries is missing."

Worry needled him. What was Livi hiding? "The town library would have that edition digitized. Was Livi the only one who ever came out here?"

Megan frowned. "I don't think she'd been here recently. The yardman would chop and stack the wood and store the newspapers. But as you can see, the shed isn't locked."

Which meant anyone had access. But why remove that? Unless it had a clue about the identity of the body…and someone did not want anyone making that connection.

He'd hate to think Livi had known the real story and hidden the truth.

Outside, he took a deep breath of the fresh piney air. What had seemed like a cut-and-dried visit to sell a house and save a life grew more complicated by the minute. He squatted down and petted Rigor's head. The dog grinned up at him.

"I need to find that Halloween edition of the paper," he mused.

"Easy enough to do. We can check the library later, if you think it will provide a clue to that poor man's identity. It always bothered me that he was listed as a John Doe, his family never knowing what happened to him." Meg glanced at him. "I suppose you feel the same with some cases you work on."

The parallel was similar, but he was surprised she made the connection. "Sometimes."

She stared into the woods. "I went to the cemetery with Livi when the body was buried. Livi always talked about you and the importance of the work you do with the FBI. But I didn't want to hear about it because any mention of you was too painful and you were my past. And then she told me how critical your job is."

Another surprise. "What do you mean, Megan?"

"You help find missing children and reunite them with their families. Even if…you can't save them, you use all your skills and resources at your disposal to find them and bring them home." She bit her lip, her eyes filling with moisture. "Even if home ends up being a lonely graveyard. At least they are found."

He steeled himself against reaching out to hold her hand and provide comfort. Once he would easily have done so, but years stretched between them, and too much hurt. Distance was safer. Impartiality as well. "Sometimes the end result is painful, but the families do have closure and can bury their child and move on."

Could he sound any more like a robot? But it was easier than admitting the truth about how much it broke him inside when he didn't bring home happy endings to frantic parents.

"I don't know how you manage that kind of hard emotional toll, Roarke." Gone was all trace of tears, replaced with a steady resolve in her eyes. "Whatever else I may have thought of you since we broke up, I admire the work you've done, both with the military and the FBI. You help to save lives. That's amazing."

Man, he so did not want this to happen—Meg standing there, confessing her respect for him. Or for his profession, at least. For a wild moment he wondered if the old feelings could be rekindled. Roarke lifted his hand to reach out and touch hers.

Then Megan turned around and gave a little laugh.

"I guess you didn't expect to return home and then suddenly have to investigate another body. Not that you have to, but you have a skill set Doyle and his men haven't perfected. It would be nice to put a name on John Doe's headstone."

The moment vanished. Skill set. She talked about him as if he were providing a professional service. Not as a man she admired.

Yeah, the past remained in the past. He dropped his hand. "We'd best return. I need to find a jeweler. Is Clements Fine Jewels still in town?"

"Yes. Simon Clements still runs the store. Why?"

Roarke held up the baggie with the gold pocket watch. "It may have belonged to the vic. Pocket watch that needs to be professionally cleaned. Could be a clue to his ID…"

Meg studied the bag. "You think the watch can tell you all that, as old as it is?"

"Maybe. I had to dig a little to find it, which doesn't reflect well on the good sheriff and his deputies as far as their investigative techniques go. How did you find the body?"

In his profession he was used to interrogating suspects and watching for signs of lying. Considered himself pretty good at it as well. Roarke studied Meg's face as she pushed a hand through her hair, sighed and then stared off into the distance as if gathering her thoughts.

"I like coming out here. Or I used to, until now. Livi let me roam all over the property and walking through the woods was good for my soul. I'd gather my thoughts."

"What would you think about?" he asked softly.

Meg sighed again. "The book I was writing with Livi."

Roarke blinked. "You were writing a book?"

"A history book. I do have my master's in history." She waved a hand at the shed. "This manor has such a rich and fascinating history. Did you know your great-grandfather used to be a rumrunner? Livi told me about the runs he made during Prohibition, smuggling rum from Canada. I was out in the woods behind the shed and saw this cross. It looked handmade and I wondered what it marked. I asked

Livi and she told me her father told her he put it there after he buried her pet rabbit."

She shivered and hugged herself. "The next time I walked in the woods by the shed, I had Rigor with me. It had been raining and the cross was a little crooked. I went to straighten it and Rigor started digging and… I saw a glimpse of a skull. Not rabbit bones. I guess you're used to it with your job, but I wanted to throw up. I ran all the way back to the mansion with Rigor."

Roarke touched her arm, intending comfort. "You never get used to it."

She gestured at the crime scene tape. "It was a shock."

"What did Livi say? Was she surprised?" His great-aunt's reaction was important. It would indicate if Livi knew about the body, or at the very least had heard rumors about it.

Meg flexed her hands. "She was shocked and insisted on calling the sheriff herself. Spent quite a while talking with him when he showed up at the house." She looked away, bit her lip. "They shut themselves away in the drawing room, and Livi sent me to make coffee for the deputies, and sandwiches."

Coffee and sandwiches to keep Meg occupied while Livi had a private convo with the sheriff after a body was found? Roarke wanted to groan. This was so not good.

Understanding dawned in her pretty blue eyes. His ex had never been stupid. "Livi only made herself look suspicious, and the sheriff as well, when they did that. I tried to coax it out of her what they discussed, but she was tight-lipped. Soon after, the deputies unearthed the body and brought him to the county coroner. Death was ruled accidental, probably a vagrant camping out in the woods. There were many of those during the Great Depression."

Roarke pocketed the baggie with the watch, thinking

about the timing of the body's discovery and the ominous threats made against his aunt. It was too coincidental, and in his line of work, he learned there were no such things as coincidences.

"Meg, what happened after? Were there newspaper articles? Any publicity at all about the body?"

Dread filled him as she shook her head. "No. It seemed to be hushed up. I think that's what Livi and the sheriff discussed. They didn't want anyone knowing about it. I can't blame her because you know what would happen—the curiosity seekers trespassing on her property."

But hushing it up made his beloved aunt look even more suspicious. "Who knew about the discovery besides you, and the sheriff and my aunt?"

A little laugh escaped her. "That's the ironic part, Roarke. This is a small town and people talk, no matter how you try to keep a secret. One of the deputies told his wife who went to the beauty parlor and from there..."

"Everyone knew."

The peaceful, pretty day suddenly turned cold and gray as winter. Roarke gazed around, wondering what other secrets were hidden by his family. When Livi mentioned her family's history, he'd never paid much attention, feeling he truly didn't belong to either his father's side of the family or the town.

Now he wished he had listened.

"I need to get this watch to the jeweler and then get something to eat." He jammed his hands into his pockets, his skin crawling. *And I need to get the hell out of here, figure out what's going on.*

"Park Place Diner still has the fried turkey sandwich you used to like. We can drop off the watch first and then eat."

"Sounds terrific." Right now he'd settle for fried road-kill. Didn't matter, as long as it was prepared far from this place.

Because something was terribly wrong here, and he needed answers.

Chapter 8

Park Place Diner hadn't changed much since Roarke had left town. Megan wondered if he'd noticed. Same booths with the faux-leather seats, photos of celebrities from the 1950s adorning the faded rose wallpaper. Same menu with sandwiches named after Monopoly board places.

She didn't like going here with Roarke and causing the town gossips to wag their tongues, but after telling Roarke about the human remains she'd found, Meg needed to get away from the manor. The woods near the shed felt thick and haunted.

Her own past, and Roarke's, seemed mild by comparison. Plenty of emotional pain, but they hadn't physically hurt anyone.

Much less killed someone. She'd suspected the body on the grounds had been murdered, and Livi and the sheriff conspired to hastily bury the victim in hopes of stifling an investigation.

But now that Roarke was home, Roarke the FBI agent with dogged determination to deliver justice, she knew he wouldn't be content to keep the past buried.

Roarke leaned back and looked out the window at the passing traffic on Main Street, the pedestrians streaming past. Most of these people Meg knew. She'd lived here all her life and they knew her as the professor's dutiful daughter, the bookworm who ran the bookshop.

Newly married Mrs. Jenkins walked her two golden retriever dogs, Tango and Cash, struggling to keep up with the adventurous pups. Bald, bespectacled Town Commissioner Larry Rankin hurried past, glancing at his watch as if he were late for an appointment.

They knew her. Many had been a comfort after Dad died. But did they really know her, the quiet daughter of the professor and bookseller they admired? Did they know her inner longings and regrets? Did they know Roarke, or did they think of him only as Bad Boy Calhoun who joined the Navy, made everyone proud with his service as a Navy SEAL and now was an FBI agent dedicated to saving children?

Did Roarke even care to give *them* another chance?

A few people saw him, stared or pointed. Heads bent together, obviously whispering outside and in the diner as well, as one would look on in abject fascination at a hometown celebrity. She felt his discomfort, smiled to try to ease the tension.

"They're curious, that's all. They've heard a lot about you. Hometown hero Navy SEAL, FBI agent who searches for missing children. You're a local hero."

He snorted. "Some hero. This town will always think of me as Bad Boy Calhoun arrested for trespassing on Mayor Temple's prized rose garden."

She couldn't help a slight smile, glad they no longer talked about the dead body. "And for picking a few pink roses for me for Valentine's Day."

Something flickered across his expression. "Doyle only

released me after I agreed to pay for the damage. Livi paid the charges. And made me spend two weekends cleaning out her garage to pay her back. It was easy work, especially because you were there to help me."

The corners of his mouth twitched. "We did more in that garage than clean up spare auto parts."

A flush ignited her cheeks. She ducked her head to hide it. So many memories. She should remember as well the hurt he'd caused when charming Roarke Calhoun left and never returned.

She'd never understood why Roarke never gave Cooper Falls a second chance. It was almost as if he'd deliberately sabotaged himself and any chance for the townspeople to like him.

He leaned back, stretched out one long arm across the booth's back. The move made muscle and sinew flex beneath skin.

Megan's breath hitched at the memory of a similar time they'd shared a booth like this after school. When he'd stared at her, sin in his eyes, and she felt her entire body glowing in response. Sweet anticipation of the night to come.

Those days were gone, she reminded herself. Stick to the business at hand.

Hand... Her gaze drifted to those long elegant fingers, the faint dusting of hair on the back. A pianist's hands. He used to make her sing, the crescendo shattering them both in the back seat of his ancient Mustang...

Fingers snapped in front of her. "Megan? You still on planet Earth?"

Her mouth quirked as she dropped her gaze to the ground. "Left for a short break, but I'm back now."

Those green eyes softened. "You, too, huh? All the memories we made here in this diner."

And elsewhere, the spark in his gaze indicated.

"That was in the past. Let's drop it. I'm not the same girl you knew once," she said, struggling with her emotions.

He leaned back. "I wonder. Is she still hiding behind that sensible dress and shoes? The Meg who Rollerbladed between the marching band during the July Fourth parade down Main Street and laughed when the cops tried to stop her? The Meg who insisted on learning to play guitar so she could sneak into the Wild Child concert backstage by pretending she was with the band? The Meg who dyed her hair pink to match her pink jeans and socks?"

Some diners glanced their way. She squirmed in her seat, recognizing some customers. "Drop it, Roarke. You can't go back in time. I don't look good in pink hair. That was a stupid teenage whim."

"I think you looked amazing," he said softly. "You could shave all the hair off your head and you'd still remain the prettiest girl in Lakefront High."

Too long since anyone had paid her such an endearing compliment. Most guys she dated were too busy talking about themselves. Roarke turned on the charm full blast, a heater in a snowstorm. Maybe coming here was a bad idea.

Anywhere in town was a bad idea. They'd explored so much together before stamping their own memories on public spaces that were now bittersweet for her, thanks to their lovemaking. Same reason she couldn't bear to look at his aunt's classic car.

She had to stop this. Now. She scowled. "Listen to me, Roarke Calhoun. I don't dye my hair anymore. I have a wardrobe for business and I don't Rollerblade or play guitar."

Roarke leaned forward. "What happened, Meg? What happened to you? What happened to that wild spirit hiding behind that bookish exterior?"

Her mouth trembled. "I grew up, Roarke. Life, responsibilities, they change you. I have a bookstore to run."

"I know." He kept studying her. "I grew up as well. I had a hell of a lot of growing up to do. The Navy does that to you, makes you into a man. But you…you had that spark of life, that passion and drive for more than old books."

"Stop it," she said, her temper rising. "Stop criticizing me. You have no right."

Roarke's mouth compressed. "Yeah. Sorry. I don't."

"Besides, I don't see you wearing your old leather jacket and riding your motorcycle around town."

"No, you won't, either. I'm not eager to have Sheriff Doyle find another excuse to arrest me simply for breathing."

Ouch. Meg winced, remembering that incident. "Sorry. I forgot about that time."

The corners of his mouth tipped upward. "Doyle never let me forget it."

They both had changed. Her gaze dropped to her hands, the nails clipped short. Respectable. Sensible. When was the last time she got a manicure? Or painted her toenails anything other than ordinary pink? Once she adored lime green nails for St. Patrick's Day, and black and orange for Halloween.

"As long as you brought up the past, let me ask you something, Roarke? Why did you really leave Cooper Falls and never return?" Megan folded and unfolded her linen napkin.

Funny thing, napkins. The diner's owner always used paper ones in the past. Over the years, he'd gotten fancy.

He said nothing for a moment, only studied the sidewalk just outside their window.

Clay pots of purple and fuchsia petunias decorated the sidewalks. The tree-lined street with its antique streetlamps retained the original charm of the town he knew as a boy. Cooper Falls always did try to keep up appearances.

Even if he hadn't cared one whit about appearances. That was part of Roarke's charm. He was fiercely independent and a nonconformist in a town filled with conformity.

"I had no future. Where would I go? Work at Bill's garage? Get a job at the high school, pushing a broom? No good employer would take a chance on me, with my checkered past. There was nothing here for me, Megan."

"You're too quick to judge. Plenty of people would have given you a chance. You just never gave them the chance to try."

His mouth worked. "Name one person who would have given me a job, Megan. Just one."

When she delivered a list of ten names, all reputable employers in town, he looked less bristling. "All of them because of Livi. I know. But I had to make a name for myself, Megan, find my own path, without my aunt running interference for me. The Navy helped me to become the man Livi said she knew I could become."

"You went into the Navy after high school. I understood. But you never returned."

His gaze glittered with anger. "I kept in touch. The first and only time I ever heard from you was in that restaurant in DC five years ago."

Her heart skipped a beat and she could only stare at him. "I wrote to you, and you never wrote back."

He swore softly, shaking his head. "Don't lie to me. Aw, hell, it doesn't matter. I swore I wouldn't get into this with you… It's in the past."

"No, it isn't," she cried out. "I'm not lying, dammit!"

People turned and glanced at them. Flustered by the attention, she took a deep breath.

Roarke drummed his fingers on the booth's back. "Why were you in DC five years ago, Meg?"

Her father's friend, who taught at Georgetown, had invited them to visit when he secured a coveted grant to write an extensive nonfiction book on the history of piracy and government in the Caribbean, specifically Jamaica's Port Royal, a pirate stronghold.

And Dan Rogers offered Meg a job as his research assistant. The money hadn't been substantial, but she knew she could supplement the income. Didn't matter if she worked as a waitress. She would find a way.

Dan promised he would help her find a second job. Dad had to be coaxed into letting her go, but she'd already worked out what to say.

The three of them went to that fancy steak house in DC to celebrate the grant and discuss Meg's potential employment and there was Roarke Calhoun, two tables away, laughing with a pretty blonde over wine and lobster.

When they returned to Cooper Falls, her father had told her he'd changed his mind about her moving to DC and needed her help at the bookstore. Meg had given up the dream of moving.

Strike one—her own fear of the unknown. Strike two—Roarke Calhoun. Here in Cooper Falls, only the shadow of him remained. Old ghosts that had faded with each passing year. In DC she might turn a corner and there he'd be, the only man she ever truly loved, who never truly loved her back.

Strike three had been cancer that began riddling her father's body. He'd discovered it after the DC trip, but kept it quiet for months, until he could no longer hide it.

"Meg? You lost?" Roarke waved a hand before her face.

Meg shrugged. "My father and I were visiting a friend."

"You didn't even say hello. Just stared at me, and then

the three of you walked off to another table," he said, his voice icy.

How could I say hello when all you had wanted to do was tell me goodbye?

"You're right. It's in the past."

Tension crackled in the air, broken by a waitress coming over to take their orders. The server brightened as she recognized Roarke. "I'll be spit on a stick. Roarke Calhoun! Heard you were back. How long you staying this time?"

Megan watched his reaction. Sally had been working at Park Place since they were both kids. Honest and direct, she was one of the few people in town Roarke had liked.

"Hey, Sally." Roarke's smile seemed genuine. At least Sally could coax him to smile, she thought with bitterness.

He rattled off his order, then Megan gave hers. Sally didn't rush off to hand it over to the cook, but remained at their table, eyeing Roarke the way she had in the past when he'd swapped out the sugar container with salt.

"You're amazing. We've all kept up with your adventures and after you left the Navy SEALs, the people you saved. You're a real hero, Roarke."

Sally seemed to be totally enraptured with him. Roarke cleared his throat.

"Ah, thanks." He seemed embarrassed by the praise. Typical Roarke. He might appear arrogant on the surface, but in reality, he was humble.

Life had made him that way. With all the hard knocks he'd experienced, Roarke learned humility.

"Everyone's now in awe of you," Meg murmured.

He shook his head, his gaze tracking movement at the cash register. She turned around to see Sheriff Doyle staring at them as he paid for the take-out container sitting on the counter before him.

"Not everyone," Roarke drawled.

"You never answered my question. How long you staying?" Sally repeated.

"As long as it takes to sell Livi's house."

"Sorry about Livi. Everyone loved her. But you could have hired a real estate agent." Sally's pen thumped against her notepad. "Why are you really back here, Roarke?"

Roarke gave Sally a level look. "Why? Plan to hide the sugar and salt containers?"

Sally's mouth twitched. "No, just thought I'd fix you up a few special meals to take to Chet's house if you planned to stay there a spell."

Now this was news to Megan. She watched him closely.

"Why would I stay with my stepbrother? Not like we're close."

"Can't fool me, Calhoun. Couldn't fool me into thinking you were so tough when you were sixteen, and can't fool me into thinking you don't care about that little girl—and that's the real reason you're in town."

Sally waved her pad toward the kitchen at the diner's longtime cook. "Hey, Michelle! Get over here! Bad Boy Calhoun is back in town. Minus that noisy motorcycle of his."

Amusement and pity filled Megan. Roarke looked as if he wanted to slide beneath the table. A petite blonde, her hair pulled back in a short ponytail, emerged from the kitchen, drying her hands on a paper towel.

"I'll be damned. Calhoun, it's about time you returned to see Megan again and make an honest woman of her," Michelle said in a thick Boston accent as she winked at Megan.

Now it was her turn to slink beneath the table. "Roarke didn't…" she began.

A slow smile tipped her ex's mouth upward. "No, Michelle. I came back to make a dishonest woman out of Megan."

The cook laughed, while Sally grinned. Megan felt a hot flush race up her face as a few other diners chuckled.

"Roarke Calhoun, honest? That'll be the day," someone in the next booth said.

"Heard he was working in DC. Not surprised he went there, with all the like-minded crooks and thieves and politicians. Just his kind." This from old man Osther, who never liked Roarke, or anyone, for that matter.

Roarke's smirk dropped.

Her own embarrassment fled. "Ignore him," Megan whispered. "He's a cranky old man."

"Why are you back in town? Should have stayed away," Osther continued.

Fury glittered in his green eyes. "I'm here because of my great-aunt's death," Roarke said in a strong loud voice. "Anyone got a problem with that?"

Diners whose attention had focused on Roarke fell silent. Most glanced away, or suddenly became interested in their meals again.

Roarke's mouth tightened. He turned and glared at those who had stopped eating.

"That's right. Show's over, folks. There's no encore or repeat performance, so go back to eating," he snapped.

"Whoa, okay, big guy. I'll get started on your order," Michelle said, patting his shoulder.

As the cook and Sally hurried away, Megan shook her head. "I told you to ignore him. His opinion shouldn't matter to you."

"I know what people in this town think of me." But he seemed distracted, drumming his fingers on the table as if that wasn't the true reason he'd snapped at them.

Once she'd been able to read him like a menu. No longer. The chasm between them seemed too wide to breach.

His hatred of his childhood home too strong to overcome.

"Don't judge them, Roarke. Most people aren't as nasty as Osther."

"Who said I'm judging?" Roarke leaned back.

"Give them a chance, Roarke. You've been gone a long time and most people in this town know you're not the same wild boy Calhoun you were."

He didn't meet her gaze. "Maybe they're wrong. Maybe I still am."

"I doubt Holly would think so. Everyone loves your niece, Roarke. She's a sweetheart."

"Stepniece," he corrected.

Megan ignored that. "You're not here simply to sell the house. You plan to help Chet and Nancy with Holly."

"Don't make me into some kind of superhero, princess. You'll be sorely disappointed."

Meg sipped the iced tea Sally brought them both. "No worries, superhero. I'm not raising the bar for you."

His mouth twitched in apparent amusement. "That bar was set pretty low, huh?"

Not a good idea to answer that.

Their orders arrived at the same time a little girl came into the diner lugging a battered teddy bear. Lost in thought, Megan smiled.

"I had a big teddy like that. Theo. My father insisted I get rid of him when I turned sixteen. He told me, *You're older now. You need a boyfriend, not a teddy bear.*"

Roarke grinned. "I remember. We started dating shortly after that."

"And after our first date, my dad brought home another giant stuffed teddy. He told me, *Changed my mind. You need a stuffed animal, not a boyfriend.*"

"Ah, the esteemed professor, who eyed me as if I were the devil himself dating his only beloved daughter."

Her smile dropped. "Dad never gave you a chance. No

matter how nice you were to him, how much you tried to engage him in conversation, he never seemed to like you. I wish he could have seen the man you've become."

"Would it have changed his opinion of me?" Roarke drank some iced tea. "Doubt it."

"Maybe not back then, but he kept an eye on all your accomplishments, Roarke. Livi made sure to tell him. She was proud of you. And the townspeople, they were as well."

He wiped off his mouth. "Princess, don't get stars in your eyes about me. I'm still the same complete and utter jerk your dad said I was."

Megan focused on her salad. Why did he have to ruin everything she said? "Fine. I'll take your word for it."

They ate in uncomfortable silence for a minute. The delicious salad no longer held any appeal for her.

"Look, can't we just be civil to each other?" she began.

Then she spotted two familiar faces. This was so not the place to be seen arguing with her ex. Megan inclined her head. "Bob and Vivian Parker on the horizon at two o'clock."

A grin touched his mouth. "Our old code to signal nosy adults approaching. You still remember."

"Of course." Meg lowered her voice as the couple approached. "And they're still considered the best way to spread news in town, so watch what you say. They like knowing everything about everyone."

"No warning necessary, princess."

"Stop calling me that," she whispered and then shut her mouth as the pair reached their booth.

"Well, I'll be a monkey's uncle! Roarke Calhoun, returned home." Bob practically bellowed the words.

Nice man. Bob was younger than Vivian, and Livi used to joke her friend was a cougar since Vivian was seventy-five to Bob's seventy-two. Bob had grown slightly deaf through the years, but he still acted as if he were only in his forties. The Parkers said hello to Megan, Vivian reaching down to hug her.

Roarke shook Bob's hand and then Vivian's. "Good to see you both. You still working part-time at the library, Mr. Parker?"

Bob beamed. "Couldn't drag me away from the place."

Vivian gazed fondly at her husband. "I've tried to get Bob to retire, but he refuses. My work with the historical society and the antique store keeps us both busy."

Gray-haired and well-dressed, the Parkers were a genial couple adored by the townspeople. Meg had a special fondness for Vivian, who had been one of her father's frequent customers. On days when her father was too busy with his studies or the store, she'd fled to the antiques shop, spending happy hours listening to Vivian tell stories about Cooper Falls and its history.

Megan had seldom seen Vivian not wearing a dress and sensible heels, except when she and Bob ventured on one of their long walks around town to *keep our bones fit* as Bob put it.

When the Parkers started gushing about his work with the FBI, he modestly shrugged off their compliments and asked Vivian about her work with the historical society.

"Say, Mrs. Parker…"

"Please, Roarke. I'm Vivian."

"Thanks for your compliments about my job. And yes, it does take good detective work to find a missing child. Or anyone who is missing. You know a lot about this town's history. Do you remember any reports of missing persons over the years in Cooper Falls?"

Vivian frowned. "Not really. There was Nora Jean back in 1974, who ran away from home and she was later found living in San Francisco with a hippie cult. I can check if you wish."

"That would be terrific." Roarke sipped his drink.

Her eyes grew bright. "Are you investigating the disappearance of a child in Cooper Falls? Who?"

"Not exactly. Thought I'd check out cold cases as long as I'm in town." He shrugged. "Hobby of mine."

Bob sniffed. "I'm hungry. Let's eat."

Vivian's eyes grew bright with unbridled curiosity. "Are you two seeing each other again?"

"Viv!" her husband scolded.

"Well, they were quite an item a few years ago and they are sitting together, look at them…"

"I'm hungry," Bob insisted.

Viv sighed. "We'd better get to our table before Bob gnaws on the saltshaker, and his doctor advised him to cut back on salt. Good to see you again, Roarke, Megan."

Roarke glanced around, then dug into his wallet and left money on the table. "Let's get out of here. I need to talk to you and not where people can overhear us."

"I can pay my own way. I have a credit card." She started to reach for the check.

"Not today. I don't want to wait on a credit card. Livi gave me something and you need to be there when I open it."

He let Megan drive, requesting she pick a place that was quiet and private. Roarke was never one to insist that he drive all the time since he was the man. He'd been raised by two strong independent women and respected women too much. Besides, Megan knew the town, and he trusted her to find a safe area.

Livi had trusted her as well, though Roarke kept wondering what part his ex had played in his aunt's life after he'd left town.

She drove down Main Street, passing all the shops with their terra-cotta flowerpots, the summer marigolds and wildflowers still blooming. Soon the flowers would die with the approaching cold season.

Megan turned left on a road bordering the lake. He recognized the road, and the park a short distance away.

She drove into the park, parked in the nearly empty lot and cut the engine. Few visitors were here in autumn, and most of the sailboats and leisure craft were docked at the marina instead of peppering the tranquil lake waters.

"Let's go walk like we used to," she suggested. "There's a park bench that has a great view of the water and it's quiet and private."

A paved walkway bordered the shoreline. Dead ash and oak leaves littered the pathway. A few people were on the beach, enjoying the last warm weather before autumn set in.

Megan had always been cautious and thoughtful. The only time he'd see her become spontaneous was when they'd first made love in the back of the '69 Shelby.

He saw the worn wood bench sandwiched between the trees and had to smile. "Our bench," he mused.

Surprise flickered in her blue eyes. "I can't believe you remembered."

Hard to forget. They'd first met here. He'd been looking for a place to sail the toy boat his grandparents had given him as compensation for them throwing Chet a huge birthday party, and not inviting him. The grands had given the excuse that it would be awkward, with Roarke's father at the party, the father who never remembered Roarke's birthday, but young Roarke had only felt the shame and hurt.

Roarke had never owned a toy that needed batteries. The boat delighted him.

The girl with the freckled face reading on the bench had asked what he was doing, showed him how to power the remote and didn't mock him for not understanding how to work it. From there, they became friends.

"I guess this is private enough," he mused.

They sat, his stomach tight. Whatever Livi had to say, it couldn't be good. Roarke unfolded the letter and began to read aloud.

"My darling Roarke,
I had hoped to never write this to you, but you must know the truth.

This past summer, I became aware that someone had knowledge of our family's historical treasure and wished to steal it. It had remained hidden for years on the estate, but I realized the treasure had been compromised when someone gained knowledge of its existence.

So I moved it and hid it in the attic. But someone came snooping around the property one night and if not for Rigor scaring them off, they could have threatened to hurt me until I confessed the location. Someone knows, Roarke. It isn't safe.

I knew only you and Megan would figure out the new hiding place because you both know me well and Megan knows my hobbies. I hid the treasure in plain sight where you can plainly see it. I trust you will find it if something happens to me.

It is yours, my dear boy. You are the one I care about the most. Be careful. Whoever snuck onto my land that night will probably kill to get their hands on it.

When you do find the treasure, I trust that you will save that precious niece of yours and share some with

Megan, who is a priceless treasure herself. I trust you will be fair and equitable. I'm counting on you to do the right thing.
Your loving aunt,
Livi

P.S. I am certain you are wondering what a great deal of money is in my eyes, dear Roarke. The family trust, which my father set up to give myself and Abigail a quarterly allowance of $100,000, with instructions to go to charity when we die, is worth $3 million. However, the family treasure, which is yours, is worth around $10 million. Spend it wisely when you find it."

The letter fell to the ground. Meg stared at him. "What? *What?*"

"Ten-million dollars? Damn, no wonder Livi was scared someone was trying to kill her." Wanting to kick himself, he punched his thigh instead. "Why didn't she say something to me?"

Meg picked up the letter. "Don't blame her, Roarke. She was stubborn, like you. She wanted to remain independent and was too proud to ask for help. She only let me assist her when I told her about the book I needed her help to write. She reasoned it was a fair exchange, and then when she found out I needed…"

"Needed what?"

Meg looked away, her pale skin flushing. "I was in a bit of a financial bind after the funeral and she was paying me to help her around the house."

"How much? Ten-million dollars' worth?"

Her eyes narrowed. "Roarke Calhoun, that's not fair.

I would no more steal your inheritance than I would run down Main Street naked."

He considered. "That would be an interesting sight. I'd like to see it. Maybe even pay ten-million dollars for the privilege."

No return smile at his mocking grin. What a crude thing to say. When had he lost his manners? Once he could tease her with remarks like that. Coax a pretty blush to those fair cheeks, and then steal a kiss and more…

Meg wasn't his girlfriend anymore. Or even a friend. No familiarity existed between them now. He'd seen that the day she'd come into the restaurant in DC five years ago and the look on her face could have made it snow in Miami.

Roarke raked a hand through his hair again. He caught her wrist gently as she started to rise. "I'm sorry, Meg. I'm a little rattled right now. I came home thinking to sell the house and help Holly, and now this has turned far more complicated than I ever imagined."

Her expression shuttered, but she sat again. He wasn't sure if she accepted his apology. Or if she believed him.

Did it matter? His jaw tensed. Did he want it to matter?

He'd failed too many times in his past. Failed to keep his mom from dying from cancer. Failed Livi when she needed him the most.

Failed his first big case for the FBI. Sonia, damn, that one hurt a lot. Sonia had been Holly's age…and he'd been so close to finding her kidnapper…and then…

Failed to hold on to Meg.

I won't fail with Holly. Somehow I'll find the money for that kidney transplant. Then I'll get the hell out of this damn town and go back to Washington.

Once he and Meg had been best friends. They knew each other's innermost thoughts. He couldn't even tell what she was thinking about now. Or what secrets she harbored.

Much as he hated to admit it, he needed her help. His own great-aunt had kept much information from him and apparently Meg knew her better than he did. She might be the only source he had to find the missing money. She knew Livi's daily habits and quirks.

The thought irritated him as much as filled him with guilt. *I should have been here for Livi.*

Roarke took the letter from her, folded it and stuffed it back into the pocket of his jeans. "Did you help Livi sort through her possessions? Put them away? Do you have any clue what treasure she's talking about?"

"No."

"What about when you were working on the book? Could the treasure be related to something historical? Something easily hidden in the house. Jewelry makes sense. A rare necklace?"

"She loved to collect a lot of things. It was why she enlisted my help in trying to reduce the clutter in the house." Meg shrugged. "There are only so many ancient spears one can own."

Remembering everything in the house, he wanted to bury his head into his hands. So much stuff to go through.

"Can you think of anything she mentioned, or anything you came across, that would be worth a fortune?"

Meg sighed. "She had so much in that house, and so many valuables. And junk. Remember the snake venom she kept in a jar she got from a mystic who used to charm cobras?"

Roarke had to grin. "She still has that snake venom?"

"Unless she used it on your grandmother. She once told Abigail dried snake venom was a terrific aphrodisiac and maybe your grandfather could use a gallon or twelve in his old age."

Laughter burst out of him in an unexpected wave. He

could imagine the shock on his stately, proud grandmother's face as Livi waved the bottle of venom before her, claiming it was better than the blue pill. Meg laughed as well.

Then she wiped her eyes. "I miss her."

"I miss her, too." His chest tightened. He couldn't fail Livi now in her last request. And he certainly couldn't fail Holly. The pragmatic side of him nudged action.

Roarke glanced around the park, at the sailboats on the lake enjoying the last warmth. Anyone could have murdered Livi. Anyone who knew she had the equivalent of ten-million dollars on the estate.

Now Meg could be in danger as well. Every protective instinct flared. They weren't together anymore but he wasn't going to let anything bad happen to her.

"We need to change the locks on the house right now," he decided. "I'll stop by the hardware store on the way back."

Meg put a hand on his arm. "Roarke, about what Livi wrote in the letter—it's your inheritance. Your money. I want no part of it. You need to know this, even if you don't believe me."

The tightness in his chest eased. Despite the friction between them, Meg hadn't changed. She could have claimed a stake in the treasure, since the will clearly stated the contents of the mansion were hers to sell as she pleased.

He brushed a lock of hair away from her face. "We'll deal with that when we find what Livi hid. Part of it's yours as well. What am I going to do with ten-million dollars after Holly's operation and everything she needs is paid for?"

At first she leaned toward his touch, like a flower opening to the sun. Then she abruptly pulled away. "It's too late for me."

He wondered what she meant by that. Too late to ignite old passions? Or too late for the money to do any good?

She looked at him, but he couldn't read her expression. "What are we going to do, Roarke? Search the manor?"

"Yes. But I need to check it out first, in case there are more traps waiting for us."

As they made their way back to her car, he wondered what kind of financial troubles she faced, and if they could ever patch up the hurt between them. He was no longer Bad Boy Calhoun.

For a moment he wished he were. Bad Boy Calhoun, who roared off into the sunset and never looked back, never cared—never seemed to care, anyway.

If only that were true. Then Meg could never have broken his heart all those years ago.

Chapter 9

After his wild youth and drinking whiskey out of a bottle, then after his enlistment, Roarke had quit drinking for a long time. Now he occasionally drank socially, usually beers with his buddies. But even in the Navy, he had never downed more than a couple of beers while others chugged the hard stuff.

But today he needed a good stiff drink. Maybe ten.

After Meg dropped him off before heading back to her bookstore, he drove downtown, bought new security cameras and installed them at Livi's.

He was reeling. The news that Livi had hidden a ten-million-dollar treasure in the house rattled him deeply. He had wanted to sell the house and return to his home. Now he felt even more entangled.

He checked on Rigor, who was happily snoozing away in his doghouse. After setting out fresh water for the dog, he changed into jeans, a baseball shirt and sneakers. Roarke headed for his rental sedan and Clancey's Irish Tavern and Grill.

The bar, on the outskirts of town near the old mill, still stood. Maybe it was a little different, the neon sign brighter and purple instead of green, but to him it looked like a palace. Instead of motorcycles and rusty cars in the parking lot, there were sedans and a minivan.

How many times had he come here as a teen, ordering a soft drink, glaring at everyone? But Pat Clancey had been the kind of guy everyone knew—and trusted. Roarke had poured out all his troubles to him.

He walked into the bar, blinking from the strong sunshine outside. Smells of frying hamburgers and steaks filled the air. Good smells of food and a faint undertone of beer reminded him of the old days.

But unlike the Park Place Diner, the decor had changed. Gone was the scarred wood bar where Roarke once carved his initials with his switchblade. The wobbly stools that hosted many a town drunk had been replaced with chrome ones, and the ancient tabletops and booths were new. Even the faded photos of Ireland from Clancey's travels had been swapped out with gleaming chrome and neon lights and sparkling balls hanging from the ceiling. Five couples and a family sat in the booths, but no one was at the bar.

His old drinking establishment had vanished.

Feeling a sting of nostalgic longing, Roarke sat gingerly on one of the elite chrome stools, wondering if it would break beneath his weight. A man came out from the swinging double doors, saw him and approached. No, not a man, more like a teenager with a baby face.

"May I help you, sir?" the kid squeaked.

Sir? No one called him sir. He raised a brow. "You old enough to serve liquor?"

The kid nodded. "I'm twenty-one."

"Whiskey, neat," he told him.

When the kid served it, he downed it in one gulp, relishing the exquisite burn. Roarke pointed to his glass. "Another."

The kid's brows raised, but he dutifully poured another. This time Roarke sipped, his mind in a whirl.

He called to the kid. "Where's Clancey?"

The bartender frowned. "Who's Clancey?"

He pointed to the sign. The kid brightened. "Oh, Grandpa. He's out fishing. Retired. Gave this place to Pops."

Pops? Suddenly the facial features became stronger as Roarke racked his memory. "Is Pops Bryan O'Brien?"

"Yeah. My uncle. No one calls him that, but yeah. You know him? He's in the kitchen." The kid made a half-hearted attempt at swiping a cloth across the shiny chrome bar top.

A slow smile touched Roarke's mouth. "Tell your uncle that Viper wants to see him."

"Viper?" The kid looked puzzled.

"Nickname he gave me. Said I was as lethal to the ladies as a viper." Roarke winked.

The kid left through the swinging doors. Minutes later, a tall lanky redhead wearing jeans, a white T-shirt and a stained apron emerged. He saw Roarke and his face lit up.

"Irish!" Roarke shouted.

"Viper! I can't believe it."

Pops rounded the bar with a shout and made a whooping noise that caused the stoic couples seated nearby to pause in their eating.

"How the hell are you?" Roarke clapped him on the back. "Good to see you."

"You say that like you mean it."

"I do. You're one person in this damn town I still like." Roarke pointed to the empty seat next to him. "Take a load off for a few."

"Just a few. I have steaks on the grill." Bryan sat, grin- ning like a fool at Roarke. "Never thought I'd see you in this town again. Thought for a minute you were a ghost."

Seeing Bryan, he almost felt like one. "My great-aunt died."

His friend's expression dropped. "I heard. I'm so sorry, Roarke. I know how much she meant to you."

No condemnation or inquiries of why he hadn't been here for Livi. It felt good. "You still in the Navy or did you get out permanently?"

Friends in high school who frequently got into trouble together, they had gone to basic training together. Bryan had been shipped out and Roarke lost track of him.

"Naw. Did my time, that's all. The military gave me a ticket out of here, but Helen lured me back." He grinned. "You remember Helen, Clancey's daughter?"

Everyone remembered Helen. Helen was a classic beauty, off-limits to everyone. Roarke hadn't cared be- cause his heart belonged with Megan.

"You finally settled down," he realized. "She actually married you, you loser?"

Bryan smiled and flipped out his cell phone. "We just had a little boy. Our second."

Roarke made admiring sounds at the baby photo, which looked like a wrinkled old man. All baby photos looked like wrinkled old men to him, except this time seeing one caused an ache he couldn't pinpoint.

He sipped more whisky. "Hope you didn't name him Bryan."

A grin at the familiar joke. Bryan's father had named him in a rush, for they had expected a girl when he was born. No one realized how Bryan O'Brien would sound in school.

"Nope. Charles, after my grandfather. Safe enough

name. We're calling him Charlie already since he'll probably get called that in school."

"And now you're Pops."

Bryan beamed. "Customers started calling me that after son number one."

Feeling a wistful tug of regret about his lost opportunities, Roarke raised his glass. "Cheers, Pops. And now you're the proud owner of a bar."

His friend waved a hand. "Clancey gave us this place. Said I'd better take damn good care of it."

"Hey, the seventies called and forgot their disco ball." He nodded at the decor.

Bryan laughed. "Helen's idea. Said if we were running the place, we need to spruce it up to attract new customers instead of the seedy lot we used to have. The disco ball was Clancey's. Only thing he insisted on. Said it reminded him of his youth."

Laughter died. "You and me, man, we had some times here. Good times, but not so good times. How are you? Really, Viper?"

As much as he didn't want to discuss his current problems, he also didn't want to stroll down memory lane. Roarke changed the subject. "Your wife sounds like a businesswoman."

Beaming proudly, his friend nodded. "She is, my Helen. We're now running in the black, thanks to her putting a marketing spin on the tavern. We make the best stacked sandwiches in town. The menu's expanded and we cater."

With idle interest he listened to Bryan prattle, his mind flicking back to his own money issues. Ten-million dollars! He'd be rich. Even after paying for Holly's surgery and ensuring she would be set for life for all her needs, he'd have enough money to do whatever he wished.

Travel. Buy a huge house in DC. Help several worthy charities.

And yet he had no desire to be rich. In his work he'd seen how money didn't mean squat when your child went missing, and worse.

He loved his work. It fed him purpose, set him on the right road.

It was only being here, back home, that he felt lost.

Bryan finished talking and glanced toward the kitchen. "Gotta go, man. We have a new cook and she's good, but still needs a little supervision. You staying in town long?"

"Soon as I can sell Livi's house."

"With all that junk?" Bryan exclaimed.

He shook his head. "It's not all junk according to Megan. She inherited the contents."

"Huh."

"What, *huh*?" he demanded.

Instead his friend changed the subject. "Megan. She's the town darling, you know. Everyone loves her. She rallied everyone to hold the fundraiser for your stepniece."

Bryan shook his head. "I don't know how she did it, what with her bookstore failing and all."

Roarke sat up straighter. "Failing?"

A shrug. "Rumor has it she'll be bankrupt in a couple of months. But that's just a rumor."

Rumors often held more than a grain of truth.

"I thought the bookstore was running in the black. Albert Robinson had plenty of money."

"He might have, but cancer ate up a lot of it. That coupled with the rent increases slapped on her, well, it's a wonder she can survive. She's tough, but there's only so much a person can take."

Proud Megan hadn't uttered a word to him, not even after reading there was a ten-million-dollar treasure to be found. He inwardly cursed. Why couldn't he have seen it? Her eagerness to find anything valuable in the manor, and her clear disappointment that many of Livi's valuables were gone.

"She should be here soon." His friend consulted his watch. "Deke said he wanted a private booth for the two of them."

Jealousy bit, hard and nasty. "Megan has better taste."

"Maybe." His friend's gaze twinkled. "She used to, anyway, but then you left."

Bryan slid off the stool, shook his hand. "Good to see you… Uh-oh. Here comes trouble."

Turning, Roarke squinted at the front door. He stiffened. Bryan slapped him on the back. "No fighting here, Viper. I just got the place fixed up."

By the time his friend vanished into the kitchen, trouble had joined him at the bar, looking down his long nose at Roarke the way he had in high school.

"I heard you were back. Pity. I thought you were gone for good. Or dead," Deke Kinkaid said.

Blond hair, blue eyes, all ego. Dressed in a charcoal gray suit with a starched blue shirt and a red tie, he looked ready to wheel and deal. His smile wide as Lake Michigan, only less sincere.

More whiskey was needed to deal with this. Roarke drained his drink. Hell, an entire bottle wouldn't suffice.

"More's the pity to see you. I had never-seeing-your-ugly-face-again on my bucket list," Roarke drawled.

An incredulous frown dented Kinkaid's expression, as if no one ever spoke back to him. About time someone did. Maybe if someone had long ago, Kinkaid wouldn't have grown up to be the bastard he was now.

"You always were crude and rude, Calhoun. This establishment has changed, thank goodness, and decent people eat here now, not thugs, so you should leave." A smug smile touched Kinkaid's mouth. "I have a date and she's refined and not accustomed to trailer trash like you. Megan Robinson is a lady."

Good thing he'd learned long ago in the field to control his facial expressions. Fury pummeled through him. Megan, dating this loser? He couldn't believe it.

He could take Kinkaid's elitist insults; hell, he'd endured much worse. But the thought of Megan with him...

Forcing a dry chuckle, Roarke traced a line on his glass. "Right. In your dreams."

"Certainly not in yours. She is not part of your knuckle-dragging world, Calhoun. Megan is the daughter of an intellectual and she enjoys the same pastimes as I. We saw each other at the university theater over the summer. Excellent play. *King Lear.* Not that Shakespeare is something you would comprehend."

Roarke raised his eyebrows. "'Hell is empty and all the devils are here.'"

At that quote from *The Tempest*, Kinkaid seemed at a loss for words. Finally he straightened his sleeve and sniffed. "Megan is special. She and I have a special...rather intimate...relationship." Kinkaid smirked, as if hinting the physical details of that particular relationship.

Roarke ordered another whiskey, sipping it slowly as the kid poured it quickly, glancing from him to Kinkaid. Kinkaid was still talking, but he couldn't hear the words for the buzzing in his ears. He felt as if he'd walked onto an accident scene, only he was the vic lying on the pavement, staring at the sky.

He should leave. He had no claim on Megan, she could date whoever the hell she wished. That ship sailed years ago. But the same peculiar stubbornness that had made him write to Megan over and over until that final email that told him to get lost, made him stick his butt in the chair. He wanted to see Megan walk through that door.

See if her date with Kinkaid was the real thing and if her face lit up like a torch in a dark cave, the way it did once when she saw him. She had been his light, his love, his purpose.

Until she wasn't.

By the time the tavern door opened, he had almost finished his third whiskey. The room spun around a little and for a moment he saw two lovely women silhouetted by the brightness outside, shining like a halo around her. Squinting, he tracked with his gaze the flowing lines of her polka-dotted dress and the red sweater she wore. So curvy and cute. Red heels complemented the outfit. Megan looked good in everything she wore.

But he'd loved her best when she wore his shirt like an oversized dress as she puttered around the cottage's kitchen the morning after they'd made love their third time together...

Pain squeezed his insides. He rubbed his chest.

Her expression didn't light up as she advanced farther into the room and saw Kinkaid. Rather, even though he no longer saw two Megans, he could tell she wasn't happy.

Maybe because she hadn't expected seeing Roarke as well.

"Roarke, what are you doing here?" she murmured, her hand on his arm. Such soft hands, elegant and patrician. A lady, with supple peach-smooth skin. A lady who'd shuddered and cried out in his arms when he'd showed her the heights of passion.

He raised his glass. Shook it. She sighed.

"What about you?" he asked.

"She's with me," Kinkaid shot out before Meg could answer.

Piercing longing shot through him. Maybe he was truly drunk and this was a nightmare, her in this bar, pairing off with his nemesis. "You seeing this loser?" he demanded.

His words slurred, but he didn't care. Megan remained his focus. Nothing else mattered. He felt a funny tickle in his chest, irritating, but there, reminding him he still breathed and his heart still beat, even though he felt dead inside.

Twin Megans compressed two lush carnation-pink mouths. "Roarke, this isn't your business. Let it go. I'll call you a ride."

"Megan," Kinkaid called out. He tapped his watch. "My time is limited."

She turned, two spots of color in her high patrician cheeks. "Then perhaps we should postpone our discussion until tomorrow. I wouldn't want to waste your precious time."

Such anger, barely controlled. Roarke felt a surge of delight.

"You're ditching time with me for this lowlife?" Kinkaid snorted. "I was wrong about you, Megan. I thought you had better taste. You're as much trailer trash as he is."

The words made her flinch slightly, but stirred a fury inside him. Shaking off her hand, Roarke slid off the barstool. The ground spun a little, but he forced himself to concentrate. "You can insult me all you want, you sack of crap, but not her. Apologize to the lady."

Deke snorted. "Don't order me around, Calhoun. Do you know who I am?"

"Last time I checked, you're still the same jerk you were in high school," he drawled.

"Roarke, please." Megan tugged at his arm.

"Yeah?" Kinkaid drank from his glass of Scotch. "And

you're a loser. Too bad you didn't get arrested and thrown in jail permanently for torching my family's lake house."

"I never touched your damn house and you know it."

Kinkaid finished his Scotch and smiled. "I know it. Maybe I know who did it. Maybe someone was there for a quickie with a cute girl and the candles they had tipped over. Maybe it was an accident, but maybe that same someone had the same kind of leather jacket as you and that someone saw an opportunity to send a criminal-in-training away for good and do this town a favor."

Roarke's chest tightened and he slammed down his glass on the counter. His hands curled into fists. "I knew it. You set me up."

"Prove it," Kinkaid taunted.

"I'll prove it outside. Let's settle this once and for all."

The soft hand on his arm again. A softer plea. "Roarke, please, let's leave. I've got my car. I'll drive you home."

For a sheer moment the offer tempted him. Home, with Megan. Sounded so tempting, so right. He reached into his wallet, threw bills on the counter and turned to leave.

He glanced at Megan's paling face, feeling more sober by the minute. Acute awareness shot through him. *Listen to her.*

Harder to obey when he and Megan walked outside and Kinkaid followed, shouting his name. As Roarke reached for the passenger door handle, he felt a hard jab in his back.

"Don't walk away from me when I'm talking to you, dumbass." Kinkaid poked him again. "People in this town listen to me."

"Deke, leave him alone," Megan ordered.

"Shut up, bitch," Kinkaid snapped.

Roarke slowly turned. "What did you say to her?"

Jeering, Kinkaid pushed at him. "You heard me. What

she is. What your mother was as well… A dirt scraping, low-class…"

Roarke punched him in the face.

Ignoring Megan's gasp, he ducked as Kinkaid recoiled and came back swinging. Bastard managed to hit him in the stomach. Roarke grunted, then hit Kinkaid again, vaguely aware of Megan's cries.

"Roarke, please, stop it, you're going to kill him!"

Pulling in deep lungfuls of air, he glanced down at the man moaning in the dirt. "Hardly. I barely touched him."

He didn't care about spending the night in jail, but he didn't want Megan in trouble.

She opened her door. "Your bare touch could land him in the hospital. Get in."

He didn't need an engraved invitation. Roarke climbed inside and slammed the door.

She sped out of the parking lot, her expression tight. "What were you thinking? You're hardly evenly matched to that jerk and you know he hates you. Now he'll do everything he can to make things difficult for you."

He snorted. "He doesn't have that kind of influence."

"I wish you'd remember other people who live here who have to deal with him. Your stepbrother, who's employed by a subsidiary of Deke's company. Your stepniece, who gets dialysis at the medical center funded by his family. Me…" her voice trailed off.

"You? What is it, Meg? What hold does Kinkaid have on you?" Worry replaced the anger his nemesis had stirred in him.

"Nothing."

"I can help…"

"I don't need your help," she shot back. "Dammit Roarke, I didn't need you to play knight in shining armor. I've managed well enough without you for years, so quit it."

He ran a hand through his hair. "Well, thank you very much, Roarke, for standing up for me," he muttered.

Tossed forward, the seat belt held him in place as she stomped on the brakes and the Jeep jerked to a halt. "Stop that. Please, just stop it. Stop trying to be my champion. You drew unnecessary attention to me. You don't live here. You don't know the power Deke Kinkaid holds."

Roarke heard the desperation beneath the words. Deke wasn't dating Megan. He'd wanted to see her for another reason.

"What power does he hold over you, Megan?"

She depressed the gas pedal and they moved forward again. "None of your business."

Money, he guessed.

He tried to press her for answers, but her pretty mouth clamped shut and she remained silent until pulling into the gravel drive of Greystone Manor. Megan stopped and faced him.

"I'd ice that hand if I were you. And stay away from Deke Kinkaid. You have no idea how dangerous he is."

Considering her words, he wanted to drive back to the tavern and punch Kinkaid all over again. Dangerous? He'd faced real danger in Afghanistan from armed insurgents and in his job when he once cornered an armed kidnapper holding an innocent kid hostage.

It had been a long time since he'd confronted a different kind of danger—the kind that came from people society held in high esteem, who could frame you for a crime you didn't commit.

He climbed out, looked at her. "I know what he is, Megan. He's destructive, likes to bully others to boost his considerable ego. I'd watch your back. Kinkaid is good at ruining lives. Don't let him ruin yours."

A small sniff and headshake. "He'll never get that distinction, Roarke. Because you already did."

With a screech of tires, spitting gravel, the Jeep took off, leaving him to stare after her in utter disbelief and disgust.

Not at her.

But himself, for being so blind to her own desperation.

Chapter 10

Once her knight in shining armor, whose armor had gotten tarnished in the years, Roarke Calhoun was an arrogant jerk. Meg kept telling herself that as she drove to the bookstore, her cheeks burning.

All she'd wanted to do was make him aware that the town never saw his past. Losers like Deke Kinkaid were not representative of Cooper Falls. But Roarke was determined to see things only as they were. Now Roarke had an even worse impression of his hometown, thanks to the fistfight with Deke. Even if she secretly reveled in watching Deke get the beating he deserved, she knew it was bad for Roarke.

And her. Meg had no idea what the consequences would be. Deke had an ocean of pride.

She trudged upstairs to her apartment, feeling a familiar comfort as she closed and locked the door. At least here, in the quiet of her home, she could escape and forget the world's woes. And Roarke.

No way could she forget the grim reminder hovering overhead that she could lose everything.

That night she tossed and turned in her bed. Ten-million dollars! For that amount, not only could Holly get her transplant, but the manor could be fixed up, maybe turned around...

She laughed as she plumped up her pillow. Who was she fooling? It was Roarke's money and he'd made it clear he wanted to leave Cooper Falls as soon as he could finish with his obligations.

Leave her and leave the town forever.

Sleep was fleeting, so she rose early, made coffee and sipped it as she gazed out onto the street.

Sales were so slow she could have closed and it wouldn't make a dime of difference. But it provided a good reason for her to get away from Roarke and to gather her lost composure.

Who was she fooling? She could drive to California and it wouldn't be far enough to escape the devastating feelings she still held for Roarke.

After showering and dressing in a yellow-and-white floral dress and heels, she went downstairs onto Main Street. A cool breeze ruffled her hair as she walked. The bookstore was at the south end of Main Street, a prime location, but with a six-month lease. Deke had raised the rent so high on the last lease she wasn't certain how she could manage. Throughout it all, she'd remained cool and calm, totally professional.

Not so much with Roarke. One stupid remark and her emotions spiraled out of control. The rakish glint in his eyes as he said he'd like to see her run down Main Street naked had sparked all the old desire and reminders of when his teasing remarks had led to hot and heavy necking sessions.

And more.

His blustering tone when he'd told her he didn't need her help, or anyone else's.

Main Street hosted a variety of shops, and the town's Chamber of Commerce had recently beautified downtown with cedarwood planters and oak saplings to line the streets. Store owners had painted their shops to add to the color. Yet now Meg noticed the shops on their block weren't bustling with customers. It was past Labor Day, marking the end of tourist season, so the boutiques and the restaurants weren't as crowded. Still, with all the college students nearby, Main shouldn't be this dead in the middle of the week.

No amount of pretty flowers, fresh paint or trees would lure in more customers. She stopped before Vivi's Antiques.

With her vivacious warmth, Vivi provided a spark of life on traditional Main Street. And she made the most delicious oatmeal cookies, which she always kept in a glass jar on the counter, free to customers.

The silver bell on the door jingled as she entered the shop. Megan helped herself to a cookie and gazed around.

"Hi, hon." Vivi climbed down from a ladder and dusted off her hands. "What brings you here?"

"Viv, you need to stop climbing ladders. What if you fell?"

A shrug. "I can take care of myself."

"How's your business doing?"

The older woman shook her head. "My rent is killing the business. Deke raised it last month and going into winter, it doesn't look promising."

"My rent went up almost forty percent as well on the bookstore. I don't know how I'll manage through the fall and winter," Megan confessed.

Vivi's rheumy blue gaze sharpened. "Deke raised the rent on the other businesses on this block as well. I heard a rumor he wants to raze the buildings and construct new stores with condos above the stores. Less space, more income from rent."

"He'd never get the zoning approval." Megan wished she felt more confident than she sounded.

"Of course he would." Vivian blew out a breath. "Town needs the increased revenue from taxes if they're going to build that new fire station over on Tenth."

Another Kinkaid project. Was there any place in town that family didn't have their hands in?

Vivi glanced away. "I'd love to retire. If Bob and I had the money, we would."

The oatmeal cookie tasted delicious, but her appetite suddenly vanished. Megan swallowed past the lump in her throat. "We could fight him. Get a group together, a petition…"

"What's the use? I'm too old to fight. I just want to retire and enjoy what's left of my life, but we don't have the money." Vivian's mouth compressed. "Some people have it all, while others are left with scraps."

She felt the need to reassure the elderly woman. "You have a devoted spouse and everyone loves you, Vivi. That's something Deke will never have."

The woman flashed a brief smile. "I suppose."

Meg gazed around the shop, instinctively knowing Vivi wouldn't take any more antiques on commission.

"I'm trying to find a dealer who would take Livi's belongings and give me a fair market price for them. Got any ideas? I know a couple of rare book collectors, but if you have more, I'd appreciate it."

Vivi went behind the counter. "I'm afraid you won't get much. That old house has a lot of junk in it."

"So many memories, too," she murmured.

"Livi did know how to enjoy herself." Vivi scribbled down a few names and numbers and handed her the paper.

Thanking her again, Megan saw herself out.

She walked back to her father's bookstore, but instead

of feeling familiar relief and comfort at the gold lettering on the store window, Megan felt empty. Lingering on the sidewalk, she stared into the store, hearing the ghosts of the past and the bustle of a busy business.

Once college students frequented this dusty magical place. They bought textbooks and history books and reading material for pleasure. Books And More had been a popular place, with her father holding lively discussions with students about the past and literature. She'd started a coffee and tea bar as an added attraction.

But now the coffee bar was empty and few customers bought anything. Not with digital textbooks.

It seemed that when her father fell sick and died, the spirit and life of the bookstore died with him.

Throat tight, she went inside and headed for the back. Paul Underwood, a local college student she'd hired to tend the store, was working at the computer.

She couldn't afford to pay him much, so instead bartered with him and gave him a private place to study, use the internet for free and write his thesis. Paul was graduating at the end of the year. When he left, she'd have to find a replacement.

Not that she could afford to hire anyone else.

It didn't take long to go over the previous day's sales with Paul. Two books, totaling thirty dollars. Meg didn't know whether to laugh or cry. She thanked Paul, who had a class to attend, watched him walk away and unlock his bike and take off toward the college.

Meg sat at the desk, staring at the spreadsheet showing the month's sales, the cursor blinking on and off like an accusation.

You are letting your father's dream die.

Yet she wondered if it was simply a sign of the times or something else. Certainly it wasn't a coincidence that all four stores on this block were suffering, when the other shops on Main seemed to be running in the black. Her instinct warned something was off about the poor sales, and the rent increase.

Her cell phone pinged a message. Megan broke into a smile reading it. Dawn, her bestie from high school, wanted a late lunch date. Amazingly Dawn had a free day.

She texted back the name of a more upscale restaurant. She had tutored the owner's son and Ralph had told her he wanted her to have lunch on the house to return the favor.

The Lakeside Grille was off Main Street on a quiet side street. It offered a prime view of sparkling blue lake waters. Diners could sit outside on the shaded patio, watching the last of the summer tourist holdouts paddleboat near the sandy shore. Today she chose the quieter inside dining room. The maître d' beamed at her and escorted her to a window table with a view of the terrace and the lake, assuring her lunch was on the house and for her guest as well.

Dawn arrived soon after. They hugged and Megan stepped back to study her friend. Gone were the nearly waist-length blond locks that were Dawn's signature.

"You cut your hair!" she told her.

Touching the pixie-style locks, Dawn sighed. "This is what happens when you have kids who think your hair is their personal gym rope for climbing up Mommy."

"It looks great," she assured her as they sat.

A waiter dressed in elegant black came over. They ordered—unsweetened iced tea for both, and Dawn chose a salad with salmon, while Megan settled on steak with her salad.

Dawn tossed her head, though she had no more long hair to fling back. She ran a hand through her short locks. "This is so hard to get used to. I used to have hair. And time for our weekly lunches."

"Now you have kids and short hair and a darling husband." Megan smiled at her. "I'd say that's a good trade."

Dawn's mouth twisted upward. "True. So when are you finally settling down? Or at least dating someone?"

"I am settled down. I'm married to my business."

"Oh, that."

Not caring for the flash of sympathy on her friend's face, she changed subjects, asking about the children and Dawn's pride—her vegetable garden.

The waiter brought over their iced teas and a silver bread basket. Dawn selected a multigrain bun.

"I heard Roarke's in town. How is he? Still as sexy as ever?"

The question almost made her choke. "I wouldn't know."

"Right." Her friend's mouth pursed. She knew when Megan was bluffing.

"I caught a glimpse of him driving through town. He's even better-looking now than in high school. Such a hunk." Dawn sighed. "I used to get jealous once in a while, but after I met Hal, I only had eyes for him. Besides, Roarke was too wild for me. Perfect for you. You two belong together. Always did. So, have you done anything together other than try to clean up that old termite trap of Livi's? Go out to dinner, maybe find a little snuggle time?"

At her friend's sly wink, Megan shook her head. "We went for a walk by the lake."

That seemed safe enough.

Waving a hand, Dawn smirked. "Darling Meg, you need to take advantage of that fine man. These days it's Netflix and chill. Walking by the lake is as exciting as renting roller skates."

"I like roller skating," she protested. "And how would you know about Netflix and chill? You're married with kids."

"How do you think number three came about?" Dawn laughed and then her attention riveted to the doorway.

Meg chewed more salad as Dawn sipped her water.

"I can think of more interesting activities to do with Roarke Calhoun, and none involves skates. Or walks. Speak of the handsome devil…" Dawn flicked a finger in the direction of the door.

Roarke had walked into the restaurant, his big frame seeming to take up all the space in the cool, elegant surroundings. Gone were the jeans and the blue chambray work shirt. He wore the same charcoal gray suit, white shirt and red tie he'd sported at the attorney's reading of Livi's will.

A delicate shiver snaked down her spine. "Skating is safer."

"Who wants safe when you can have all that?" Dawn gave a dreamy sigh as she stared at Roarke like a starving woman.

Amused, Megan forked a tomato and swished it in the dressing. "You're supposed to be a happily married woman."

"I am happy and I am married. But I can look. No harm in looking."

Barely had her friend said that when Roarke glanced in their direction. His cool green gaze locked with hers and he nodded. Breath caught in her throat. Seeing him like this at a distance reminded her of all the times they'd pretended not to be together, for the sake of gossip. And all those times it proved fruitless because she knew she'd looked at him with her heart shining in her eyes.

Roarke headed for a table near the window. Tracking him with her eyes, she was surprised to see him sit with Amanda Rawlings, the president of the Chamber of Commerce. Amanda owned the town's most successful real estate agency. She always wore red or mulberry designer dresses with heels that added a good four inches to her petite frame. One would think the woman, with all her energy, was in her thirties instead of her fifties.

What business did he have with the town matriarch? She asked Dawn. Dawn kept up more with gossip than she did.

Her friend shrugged. "It probably has something to do with the last fundraiser for Chet and Nancy's daughter. You know how much clout Amanda has in town. Maybe they want to do another one."

Roarke wasn't the society fundraiser type. She turned her attention to her food as the waiter set down a silver gravy boat filled with vinaigrette. With these prices, she needed to eat every single leaf of arugula.

"Dreamboat." Dawn sighed. "You two belong together. Always did."

Time to change the subject again. She talked about Holly and tutoring students. Dawn was active on the PTA and had sent a few students her way. She appreciated the extra income, though it wasn't enough to pay the bills.

Out of the corner of her eye, she saw Roarke leave the table. That lunch date hadn't taken long.

He stopped by her table, nodded at Dawn.

"I'm headed back to the house to start looking through everything, Megan. Do you have to get back to the bookstore?"

She thought of her dismal sales. "No. I can meet you there and I can help you."

"I bought new locks and installed a security system. No one is coming in or out without me knowing." Roarke scrolled through his cell phone and then held up a screen showing a system of cameras.

"I wish Livi had done that long ago."

"When you're ready, meet me at the cottage." With another nod at Dawn, he left.

Dawn sighed. "Still so dreamy. What are you checking out?"

Oh, nothing. Booby traps, making sure we don't get killed by one before we find a ten-million-dollar treasure. "Stuff. Lots to do to clean up Livi's house."

Then she saw Amanda head in their direction.

"Heads-up. Amanda coming in for a landing," she whispered to Dawn.

The president of the Cooper Falls Chamber of Commerce glided over. Much as she wanted to have a quiet private lunch with her bestie, politeness forced Megan to ask Amanda to join them.

"I'll join you only for a minute. I have to return to the office." Amanda beckoned to the waiter. "Earl Grey tea, please."

The waiter scurried to fill her need. Amanda frequented this restaurant and town gossips said she had dated the owner, so the waitstaff feared displeasing her.

"Now, Megan, I have something I wish to discuss with you." Amanda nodded at the waiter as he brought a tray with a china pot, steam wafting out of the spout, a delicate floral cup and a box filled with specialty teas.

She selected her tea, added the bag to the pot and turned to Megan with the same kind of purpose Megan had seen her display at town council meetings when she wanted land rezoned.

"I have heard an unpleasant rumor that you are in financial straits and may lose the bookstore."

Dawn's fork clattered to the soft linen tablecloth. Megan's heart skipped a beat. "Oh? Who is saying this?"

Amanda waved a hand. "It does not matter. I do not say this to distress you, but give you advice and an opportunity. Why do you wish to stay at that bookstore, Megan? You have so much potential, more than the bookstore needs." The woman tapped an elegant nail on the table. "You could come work for me."

"Real estate?" Megan's nose wrinkled. "I'm not the sales type."

"You could learn. Become my helper and then get your real estate license. It's more of a future than tending to antique books. Besides, as president of the historical society, I could set you up with a side project of documenting historical properties. Vivian is our new vice president and will help. I understand you were writing a book on the Carlson family and Greystone Manor."

She murmured something about putting her book on hold. After Livi had died, Megan felt the project should die with her. Livi had brought it to life with her vibrant and cheerful personality.

"I've wrangled a few large donors into supporting the society and my new project. Our coffers have increased, and I'm now on the hunt for acquiring a home to preserve and turn into a museum showpiece." Amanda sipped her tea.

She hoped Amanda wasn't eyeing the house. More time was needed to search the premises in hopes of finding the ten-million-dollar treasure. Silly of her to even think Amanda would use her clout to buy Greystone Manor. The society didn't have the money, no matter how many wealthy patrons they boasted.

Dawn wiped her mouth. "I heard one of your new donors is Victor Kinkaid and his son."

Her already waning appetite headed south. She pushed aside her salad bowl. "Deke Kinkaid? Why would he be interested in preserving old homes?"

"Tax reasons," Amanda said, pushing aside her teacup. "Deke and his father are invested in this town."

Dawn made an unladylike sound. "He's as much of a jerk now as he was in high school. Maybe even more so now."

"Language, Dawn." Amanda shrugged. "He may act as if he owns the entire town, but he does not."

"He owns our building with the bookstore and apartment." She sighed. "And keeps reminding me of it."

"He doesn't own Livi's house. Now there's a real treasure."

The hairs on Megan's neck stood at end. "It is a lovely house, but needs work."

Amanda toyed with her teaspoon. "That old house is filled with secrets."

"You have no idea," she murmured.

"Lavinia was such a collector. Does she still have those uncirculated Morgan silver dollars lying around? I recall one was from 1883. Bright and shiny, it looked as if it had been minted yesterday. There's less than seven million of them that are uncirculated. Hers were not only uncirculated, but nearly perfect."

Meg tried to control her rising excitement. "I'm not a numismatist, but I do know antiques and I know everything has a price on it."

The woman raised a perfectly arched brow. "I do believe she paid about four-thousand dollars for twenty-five of those coins."

Her excitement plummeted. So much for her theory on finding the treasure.

Amanda glanced at her gold watch. "I'm afraid I must be running along."

Before Megan could ask her about her meeting with Roarke, the woman swept away like a tornado, leaving a trail of Chanel in her wake. Dawn shook her head.

"She always was larger than life. Be careful, Meg. You'd

best sell everything in that house before Amanda gets her hands on the valuables. What Amanda wants, Amanda gets. And usually at rock-bottom prices. She didn't make her millions being kind."

She wondered about that. What did Amanda want with Roarke, and why did she have a bad feeling about it?

Chapter 11

After lunch, she returned to the manor, waiting for Roarke on the cottage porch as she watched Rigor chase squirrels. The afternoon sun dappled the pine and oak trees on the property, shining off the mirror-like lake.

Roarke emerged from the back of the manor house. She admired his easy swagger as he headed toward the cottage. She frowned. When had he started limping?

When he reached the porch, she pointed at his legs. "What happened? I thought you hurt your hand, not your legs, when you hit Deke."

Roarke glanced at his hand. "My hand's a little sore. What do you mean?"

"You're limping."

A crooked smile touched his mouth. "Happened a long while ago, princess. Back in Afghanistan. Blew my knee and had to get it replaced at Walter Reed Hospital in DC. Every once in a while, when I'm real tired, I limp."

Her heart twisted. "Oh, Roarke. I'm sorry."

Shrugging, he climbed the porch steps and joined her

on a rocking chair. For a moment she said nothing. Then she reached out and touched his arm. "What happened?"

His green gaze widened. "What do you mean?"

"A knee doesn't merely get blown out. Were you injured?"

"I don't like talking about it to anyone."

"I'm not anyone, Roarke. Tell me about your time in the Navy."

He didn't speak right away. Then he drew in a deep breath. "It was great for an adrenaline junkie like me until the day we were on patrol and we saw an insurgent holding a grenade."

As she gasped, his expression flattened. "He couldn't have been more than ten. Just a kid."

Megan couldn't imagine the horror and shock.

"We were with a Marine unit and I was with a guy named Sam. Sam was green, eager for action. I saw the grenade, should have taken the shot, taken the kid out. I hesitated. Sam got to the kid… I ran toward him, yelling for him to get back and…" Roarke flung out his hands. "Ka-pow. When I gained consciousness, I was lying in a hospital bed. I was in the hospital a long time. But I was alive. Sam was dead."

"Roarke, I never knew…"

A self-effacing shrug indicated the hurt went far deeper than he had admitted. "No one did. Not even Livi. No use complaining. What else was I going to do? I was still alive. Sam was eighteen years old, the best years of his life still ahead of him. Killed by a scared kid filled with hate, bearing a grenade."

He rubbed his chin. "I spent a long time, more than I want to admit, in therapy. Both kinds, Meg. When I could finally walk again, I wanted to return. But I couldn't. I kept seeing the desperate fear in that kid's eyes, how he kept shaking and couldn't think of what it took to push him into doing that, that level of hopelessness. Kept thinking about how I hesitated and cost Sam his life. Then I met Kyle. He came to the hospital to help vets and we clicked. The Navy saved my life, but Kyle gave me purpose."

His fingers strummed an absent beat on the table. "Kyle told me he needed a team player and SEALs are all about the team. I could save kids, find missing children, instead of seeing blood and death and war. I was damn good at hunting things down. Kyle wanted me on his team. He offered me a way out. I finished college and then entered the FBI."

Meg rubbed at the tears welling in her eyes. "Kyle sounds like a good man."

"He's a damn good boss, and friend. Enough about me."

She had to know. "Why were you meeting with Amanda at the restaurant?"

Roarke's expression turned guarded. "It's private business."

Much as she wanted to pry it out of him, she didn't. "Let's start the inventory and looking for the treasure."

"If it exists." He stood and started down the steps. "I'll believe it when or if we find it."

At the manor's back door, he reached for the knob, and hesitated.

"I can't believe I'm doing this," he muttered.

Maybe it was the flood of memories pushing at him because this house had meant so much to him. She didn't know.

Because she knew better than to pry, Meg waved her tablet. "I can do this by myself. As long as you're in the house with me, I don't foresee a problem."

"No. I'll help. It'll go faster. We need to get this place cleaned up. The sooner the better."

Odd thing to say, but she followed him into the house

through the kitchen and down the hallway. She paused there, studying the photos and portraits of his family. So much rich history here. Meg touched the portrait of Oscar Carlson II and felt familiar fascination, along with keen regret.

Would all this fade into dust if someone bought the house and tore it down to build a new, modern home?

"Let's get started."

His curt tone tore away the melancholy. Meg consulted her tablet.

"I'll make the list and if you can take the photos with my cell phone, it'll go faster. If you don't mind, I want to leave Livi's room alone for now," she told him.

Her heart wasn't in this. Going through all of Livi's things felt like a knife sticking her in the chest.

Roarke followed her into the library. Meg steeled her spine. How many times had she and Roarke met here, studied for classes while Livi quietly read her historical novels? She cleared her throat.

"One antique needlepoint chair, Queen Anne legs. One side table, inlaid marble."

Her voice cracked. "I can't do this right now, not this room. I still see her there, sitting in the corner and reading in that chair. It's her, Roarke. So much of her."

Memories of their past and Livi were so thick they wrapped around her like a blanket.

Roarke rubbed her shoulder, his touch comforting and familiar. "I miss her terribly as well."

"If I'm to sell some of these things as soon as possible, I need to push on."

He gave her a quizzical look. "Do you need money that badly?"

Instead of answering, she consulted her iPad again. "That's private."

Using his own words worked. Roarke shut up. Meg began taking stock of the valuables in Livi's library. It didn't take long to see something was terribly wrong.

The Chinese porcelain vase was missing from the room, but Livi could have moved it. Why then did she remove the oil painting and replace it with a cheap imitation watercolor? Meg searched her memory. Gone, too, was the silver coin collection she'd kept in a vintage candy dish. Most troubling was the missing collection of women's suffrage memorabilia from 1916, proudly displayed behind a specially made glass case. Livi's aunt had been a keen advocate of gaining the right to vote for women and passed her collection on to her niece. Livi had sworn to never sell it, but to keep the mementos as a reminder of how her family fought hard for the basic right to vote. She loved telling stories about her aunt Emma being dragged off to jail after a volatile march.

Roarke's aunt loved this room and storing her precious possessions here, mainly for others to enjoy. She believed art and treasures shouldn't be hidden away like secrets.

Why were they missing?

She told Roarke, who frowned. "I don't know. Maybe she sold them before she died?"

Two hours later, the discoveries they'd made left her depressed and worried. Most of the antiques and expensive items were gone. They searched the house, the attic, but they had vanished. The vases, paintings and coin collections. All gone.

They weren't any closer to finding any kind of treasure, either.

Roarke consulted his cell phone. "Lab got back to me on that email sent to you about the tapestries. The IP address was traced back to an internet café here in town."

Meg lowered her tablet. "Can we tell who sent it? Can someone check it out?"

"I already did. The user paid cash and there's no security cameras there, nor does the clerk in charge that day remember anyone." He pocketed his phone.

Of course. Whoever had sent that email had covered their tracks well. "Does it prove anything?"

"Not really. But it is suspicious. It could be the same person who sawed off the bottom steps." Roarke paced in the library. "I really don't think we'll find much here, Meg. Livi must have sold off the valuables. Sorry about that."

"She specifically wanted you and me to figure out where she would hide something of tremendous value, Roarke. She trusted that you and I knew her best, knew her likes, dislikes, how she spent her days."

Meg plopped into the chair Livi once loved, and ran her hands over the worn wooden armrests. "She spent a great deal of time here, in this room. It was her favorite. I've combed over everything in here. I was hoping this room would give us some clues. But we haven't found anything!"

"It was on us to try. Doesn't mean that it would work out, or go right."

He almost sounded as if he talked about their past relationship. She gazed around the room. "Why would she lie about a ten-million-dollar treasure? There's no point to it."

He sighed. "It's Livi. She adored mysteries. And pulling pranks."

"When she was alive, yes. When you were living here, of course. But in the past few years, she grew more serious. She had no good reason to lie to you, Roarke. Not about something as important as hidden money."

He looked troubled. "Unless her mind was going…"

"No!" She said it with more force than intended. "Livi wasn't senile. Far from it."

His mouth curled into a smile. "You always did defend her," he mused. "Fierce Megan. Never did thank you for taking care of my aunt the way you did."

She shrugged. "She needed me for a change, after Livi had always been there for me. I was happy to return the favor."

He touched her nose. "You've got dust there."

The pad of his fingertip came away black. Roarke stared into her eyes. She could drown in his green gaze, always had in the past… He only had to snap his fingers and she'd melt into him, into his warm drugging kisses, and never want to leave his arms. Meg licked her lips, drawn to him, the fine curvature of his lips, the slight bristles on his lean cheeks, the intensity searing her…

Roarke pulled away, killing the moment.

Turning away, she hid her feelings. Good times with Roarke, oh, she missed them, and these days she tried not to get nostalgic because she missed many things. Not only her father and Livi, but Roarke.

Everything about him. The way he made her laugh and bolstered her confidence. His engaging grin. The sex, oh, yes, she really missed that. Even the smell of him.

They returned to inventorying. The dining room furniture wasn't original and neither was the sideboard. She opened a drawer.

Mismatched silver. If it was even silver. It might even be silver plate.

Roarke picked up a spoon. "Livi told me Abigail got all the good silverware when their mother died, along with the heirloom place settings. Livi didn't care. She was traveling too much to worry about setting tables for formal dinner parties."

"The hallway." She sighed, realizing her hopes were dimming of selling anything of value.

They entered the hallway and began to make notes, Roarke photographing each item she wrote down. Most of it wasn't worth much to her experienced eyes. Whimsical and fun, like the spear she'd threatened Roarke with, or the flamingo umbrella and the stained glass windowpane hanging on the wall.

But worth little. Not enough to pay the back rent on the bookstore. Certainly not enough to aid Holly in her transplant operation.

Megan glanced upward at the elk-horn chandelier. It easily weighed one hundred pounds. The lead crystal chandelier Livi had bought in France and shipped over to hang in the dining room was gone. Perhaps she'd sold it long ago. She'd never noticed.

But this chandelier was an interesting piece that someone might want to collect. Vivian's antique shop could easily sell it. Perhaps Vivian could take it and give her five-hundred dollars, and that would satisfy Deke for the moment.

Then she remembered Vivian complaining her sales were down this summer as well and the rent had gone up, so it was doubtful her friend had five-hundred dollars to spend on a chandelier that might be tough to sell.

Roarke craned his neck upward. "That's going to be tough to dismantle."

"I might be able to find an estate company interested in this."

"Hire them to clean everything out."

She glared at him. "Their percentages aren't high enough. I can make more money selling some of these items on my own."

Roarke's expression tightened. "How much are you in debt, Meg?"

Now was a good time to tell him the truth. Yet pride

prevented her from spilling everything. "A little. Not your problem."

Such tough words in the past might have pushed him away. Not now. He kept looking at her with that burning intensity he sported when he'd wanted to make love in the past. As if she were everything to him, his very life, and he'd die without her.

It was a reminder of the closeness they'd shared, and all she'd lost as well. It was more than she could take.

"What?" she snapped.

His expression became guarded. "I want to help, Megan. Just as you helped my great-aunt. Tell me, how much do you need? I have some savings. Let me help you."

"I don't need help. I need—" she waved her iPad "—to get this done."

Roarke sighed and rubbed the back of his neck. "Understood. I can float you a loan and you can pay me back when you sell the contents of the manor."

Yet another reminder of their past. He'd always been there for her. Until the day he was not.

Megan gave a little nod. "Thank you. But I'm fine."

His intense gaze studied her. "There's another option, Meg. You can sign over the contents to me in a notarized letter and I'll give you cash. It would expedite a potential sale and put funds into your bank account right now."

Generous offer. Tempting, even. "And what would you do with all these…treasures?"

All the items were fascinating to her, and had been more than Livi's life. They were part of a cherished history few people chose to honor these days.

His broad shoulders lifted. "I might sell everything to the buyer, let them dispense of everything as they choose. It would be faster."

Fast, but not thorough. Meg's heart squeezed tight. He

would dispense of everything and give it to a stranger simply for money. Even if the money funded Holly's transplant, it still felt wrong.

Meg gave a little laugh. "Or you could kill me and get off the hook that way. Livi's will stated that if I die, the contents go to you, anyway."

He didn't crack a smile. "That's not funny, princess." Roarke touched her cheek and dropped his hand. "Death is nothing to laugh about. I would never want anything to happen to you. I've lost too many I've cared about."

As if realizing the importance of his words, he dropped his hand and turned around, his shoulders stiffening. Meg had trouble believing what she'd heard.

He still harbored feelings for her. After all these years and all this hurt...

Admitting she felt the same was not a good idea. Megan wished she did not. It ripped open the old wounds, let them bleed fresh. If only she could flick her feelings for him on and off like a light switch.

Never mind her emotions. She had a mansion to inventory.

Biting her lip, she flipped the chandelier's switch.

"Okay, this was working the other day when I came inside. What is going on?"

The lights remained off. Annoyed, she flicked it again. Overhead, the chandelier gently swayed as if caught in an earthquake.

A rumble sounded. This wasn't good...

"What the hell?" Roarke yanked her back roughly, just before the chandelier crashed to the floor.

It would have fallen on her head, at the very least causing a head injury. Those antlers... She shivered.

Megan wrapped her arms around herself as she stared at the broken antlers, the shattered glass light bulbs across the floor. "Wow. You almost didn't have to worry about waiting on me selling the contents of the manor."

Roarke kept her cradled against his broad chest, and she felt the rumble of his chuckle reverberate against her ear. "You okay, Meg?"

He'd used the same gentle, tender tone right after the first time they'd had sex and all her feelings had been jumbled, her body sore and aching, but well satisfied. Megan flushed at the memory.

"I'm fine. Physically. What's going on here, Roarke?"

His brows drew together. "That chandelier worked fine the day I arrived. And the day you arrived, you turned it on as well. After that, you used the hallway lamp."

"I preferred the lamp on the table because it's less glaring."

"Let's check the security cameras."

They went into the study off the hallway where he'd set up a monitor. After going through the footage, they didn't see anything suspicious.

Her stomach roiled as they returned to the hallway. "Someone's been in the house and tampered with it after we were here and before you installed the cameras."

He nodded, his jaw tight. "We have more questions than answers right now. But we're going to leave here until I have the chance to check out every inch of this place. It isn't safe."

Roarke shifted into command mode. She knew this mood, the way his thick dark eyebrows scrunched together. She'd referred to it as the Brick Wall.

When his mind was made up, there was no sweet-talking him into anything else.

Megan flexed her hands as if ready to take him on in a bout in the boxing ring. "I'm a big girl and I can take care of myself."

"Not if another chandelier falls on you. Not that I'll let that happen." His grim tone made her shiver, glad they were on the same side, reminding her this was a man who'd fought the enemy, killed for his country and put his life on the line.

Now he was willing to do the same for her, much as he had in the past. Emotion tightened her throat. The trauma of nearly getting speared by a funky chandelier warred with her confused feelings over this man who once vowed his undying love to her. No, not a man. A lovestruck teenager, much as she had been.

Roarke was no teen. He was a man, with a man's muscled physique and emotional maturity. In so many ways he'd changed. In this he had not.

She'd wanted to distance herself. His reaction made it harder. She couldn't think.

"I need some fresh air and I want to check on Rigor," she murmured, pulling out of his arms.

Livi's guard dog was happily snoozing on the grass beneath the sun-dappled shade of a sheltering oak tree. He gave a woof upon seeing them, and bounded toward them. Megan bent down and rubbed behind his ears. Dogs were so easy. Their needs were basic, their motives understandable. People, not so much.

Sitting on the grass beside her, Roarke stretched out his long legs. "Someone clearly had it in for Livi. It's a miracle she survived sleeping in the manor without anything happening to her."

Her lower lip wobbled as she remembered Livi's deep laugh and her spark for life, a spark extinguished far too soon. Instinctively she sought comfort and rested against him, listening to the steady thrum of his heart.

"Comfortable?" he asked.

Megan glanced down and realized she'd pillowed her

head against the rigid muscles of his abdomen. It was a familiar position in the past when they'd lie on the grass together, either gazing at white clouds scuttling across the sky or at the stars.

"Oh. Sorry." Flushing, she started to pull away.

"It's okay." He patted his chest. "Unless you'd rather lean against the dog."

She gazed at the dog. "Naw. At least you had a shower."

He raised his eyebrows, wiggled them.

"You did shower today, right, Roarke?"

Suddenly he laughed and pulled her down with him so she lay against his chest. "You always did coax me out of a bad mood."

Unable to resist she curled against his warm solid body. So many regrets. She missed this closeness. She missed him. When they'd first dated, Megan was certain she'd found her soul mate. They shared the same likes and the chemistry was instantaneous. They also had bonded in their loneliness.

None of their friends knew what it was like to be raised by a parent too busy to bother with them...

"What happened to us, Roarke?" She had to ask. "Why did you leave and never look back?"

His mouth opened and closed. Staring skyward, he inhaled deeply, her head rising and falling with his breath. "I needed to shake the dust of this town off my feet."

"I get it. I understand. But me..." She bit her lip. "I would have followed you anywhere."

Openness and honesty.

"I... You what?" His chuckle this time contained no humor. "Right."

"You ghosted *me*, Roarke. Not only Cooper Falls."

Looking stunned, he sat up suddenly. She propped up her head on a fist. "There's no need to make excuses now.

You walked out the door and never looked back. I get it, even though I wish you'd have given Cooper Falls a chance. There are many good people here. But I thought I mattered more to you."

She couldn't say *love*. Not that word. It hurt too much to say it. What they'd shared was teenage passion. Nothing more.

Now who's being dishonest? She ignored the niggling prick of her conscience.

For a few minutes he said nothing, the silence draping between them broken by Rigor's soft snores and the lake water splashing in the distance against the rocks.

"I ghosted you?" he finally asked.

"Of course you did."

He raked a hand through his wavy hair, messing it. "I didn't ghost you, Megan. You're the one who sent the Dear John letter."

"I, dear…what?"

He made an impatient dismissal gesture with one hand. "Broke up with me, in an email. Not even a phone call. A damn email."

She sat up and scowled. "Never. I never broke up with you. We were without internet for a while and then Dad changed service providers, so I couldn't email you until after you got out of basic training."

Judging from his look, he thought she was lying. "I'm telling you the truth."

"An email," he continued. "One line. I memorized it. Roarke, you have a new life now and it's best I never see you again. Megan."

"I didn't write that!" She drew in a breath. "I wrote you letters, real letters that were mailed. I tried to call a couple of times, but your phone was disconnected."

"Cell phones aren't allowed in basic. They remove your

cell and put it in a bag with your civies, your civilian clothing, and ship it to your family. In my case, I had mine stored
in a locker near the base. Even if you tried calling me, the
Navy only allows one to two calls a month after basic training from their call centers."

"I wrote you after you got out of basic. Livi gave me
the address. All those letters, packages, I baked cookies.
Cakes. Sent them to you, the chocolate chip cookies you
loved."

"Never got any of it. I got packages and letters from
Livi. That was it."

"Then what happened to everything?" Her voice rose
on a shrill note. Meg made a sweeping gesture. "Did they
vanish into thin air?"

"You tell me," he said tightly. "There's no evidence you
sent a single postcard. All I know is that except for that
email, I didn't hear from you until that day in DC five
years ago when you walked into the restaurant with that
man and your father. Even after the emails I sent you and
the letters. I heard nada."

"But I sent them! I packaged everything up and left
them with my father to mail because he always drove past
the university post office each day where we have a PO
box... Oh."

Suddenly she remembered the trouble she'd had with
her laptop and how slow the internet had been, and the
software she'd discovered installed on it. Her father had
told her the laptop had been hacked and had a tech wipe
out the hard drive. There were no cloud servers storing her
email, he'd told her.

"My computer... I had trouble with it not long after you
left. My father took it to be fixed."

"Your father." He rubbed his chin. "He hated me."

"He didn't hate you. You scared him. He was afraid of

losing me. Maybe he didn't mail everything, after all." She hooked her arms around her knees, grief spiraling through her. The dual losses of Roarke and her father made her chest squeeze tight. Worse was the realization her own father had lied to her about mailing her correspondence to Roarke.

Roarke drew in a breath. "But did you really try hard enough, Meg?"

It was her turn to be stunned. "I tried! He must have intercepted everything."

"You could have mailed the letters yourself."

The tightness increased. "I thought…after basic training when I didn't hear from you, that it didn't matter. You must have moved on, made new friends, maybe met someone new. Maybe it was better that we drifted apart."

All those assumptions. He gave her a penetrating look. "Better? After I promised you I loved you and would do anything to be with you?"

She couldn't argue with his point.

"I didn't need you to boot me out of your life. I needed you to fight for me. I needed you to fight for the reasons we got together in the first place. Remind me of why you were my first choice, my only choice."

If she felt bad before, his words made her feel worse. "I wanted to fight for you. I kept in touch. But to be honest, after a while I realized there were too many obstacles and it seemed impossible. I was seventeen, Roarke. I had to finish school."

She felt guilty and added, "It's a two-way street. You could have fought for me as well, Roarke. You let an email break us up, after all we'd said to each other?"

He stared into the distance again. "Doesn't matter. It's in the past. We need to focus on the here and now. I have some business to attend to and you have your bookstore. Good night Megan."

Roarke stood, striding off toward the manor house. It was like that day all over again when he cut his ties and walked out the door and hadn't looked back.

Leaving her behind once more.

Chapter 12

The next day Megan spent the morning with receipts. Even with all the frugal measures she'd taken, the figures showed the bleak news.

Not good. Not even a flurry of customers would save her. And this morning she'd had only two sales, barely enough to pay for groceries.

The silver bell over the door jingled. Meg walked from the office into the storefront. Her optimistic mood slipped several notches.

Deke Kinkaid stood in the store. Despite the shiner he sported on his right eye, courtesy of Roarke and something she noted with no small measure of glee, he looked polished and urbane in his tan summer suit and light blue shirt.

So charming. Debonair. And as dangerous to her as the Great Lakes during a violent storm.

Deke and his father's company owned the building housing the bookstore and her apartment above it. Her stomach roiled. He wasn't here to purchase ancient poetry books or textbooks. Only one thing would draw him to her father's store.

Money.

Or worse, considering that Deke had hit on her in the past for dates and each time she had turned him down. Not that she remembered what a date was like, since her social life had taken a crash dive with the diagnosis of her father's cancer.

Meg closed the door to the office and leaned against it. "Looking for a good read?"

His disdainful expression as he scanned the stacks of old books said everything. "Smells musty in here."

"Oh? I love that old book smell. I always thought they should bottle it." Her nose wrinkled. *It smells much better than the expensive cologne you bathe in, chum.*

Dusting off his hands, he gave her a wide smile as sincere as someone trying to sell her an extended warranty. "I stopped by to see you, Meg. How are you?"

Cut to the chase. "You saw me yesterday at the bar. What's going on, Deke? Why are you really here?"

He studied a well-manicured nail. Brief envy flickered through her as she realized it had been weeks, no, months, since she'd had a mani-pedi. No time, or money, for such luxuries.

"I'm afraid I have bad news for you, Meg. The lease on the apartment is expiring Monday. You have seven days to move out."

Good thing she had the door to support her back because she felt like collapsing. Meg inwardly cursed. The fight with Roarke and her reaction had probably wounded his considerable pride. She now had to pay the price.

"What? I've given you a little money to pay off the back rent on the store and I know...the bookstore will start to make money..."

"I'm talking about the apartment upstairs you shared with your father. Not the bookstore. Your father never signed a new lease. He said he was going to, but never did. I had to increase the rent and he paid up for six months, but the lease is now up. Alas, I found a tenant willing to pay twice the amount for the apartment." He heaved a dramatic sigh. "Unfortunately, I have no choice but to ask you to leave. I promised him I'd renovate and I have to start immediately."

Her mind whirled. She wanted to groan but didn't wish him to know how she felt. *Dad, you promised me the lease was taken care of before you died. You had negotiated it for another year! Not six months!*

Not his fault. The cancer had eaten away at his good sense until he became too weak to manage.

Meg steeled her spine and gave Deke a level look.

"It will take that long to pack and get the furniture into storage."

Deke came closer, his body language too suggestive. "If you need more time, I can get you another month. We could talk about it over dinner."

She stiffened. "No, thank you. I have plans."

Dinner with Deke meant only one thing, and she wasn't sleeping with him to stave off eviction.

"Where will you go? I worry about you." He stroked a finger along her arm.

"I'll be fine."

"I have an extra bedroom in my house." A slow smile curled his lips. "Or you could keep me warm in mine. It is getting cold out."

Meg shuddered. "I'd rather sleep on the street. In the freezing cold. Please leave. I have to close shop."

His eyes narrowed. "You'll regret not taking me up on my offer."

"Not as much as I'd regret taking it. Do you really think I'd sleep with you to avoid eviction?" She leaned forward now, her fury barely contained. "There are laws against that. It's called sexual harassment. Your father might not look kindly upon his good name being tarnished with a lawsuit."

Scowling, he shook his head. "Have your things moved out by next Monday."

She decided to risk it. "I need seven business days."

"Monday you'd better be gone from the apartment. Don't make me call the sheriff on you, Meg. I'd hate to do that."

He slammed the door as he left, nearly knocking the pretty silver bell off its chain. Meg fisted her hands, remembering that bell. Her mother had presented it as a gift to her father, the day he opened the store as a way for them to supplement his professor salary. She'd been pregnant with Meg and wanted to work, but work close to home. Leasing the bookstore space and the apartment above it had been a perfect solution.

Where am I going to live now, Dad? Got any answers?

Much as she hated doing it, she called Roarke. He answered on the first ring, his tone guarded. "Hi, Megan."

She cleared her throat, feeling awkward. "Hi. Does your hand still hurt?"

"Not as sore as Deke Kinkaid's eye, I'd say."

She laughed breathlessly. "I must admit a guilty pleasure watching him get what he's doled out to me."

Mistake. She shouldn't have said that.

Silence on the other line. Then he spoke in low dangerous voice. "That bastard… Did he hit you? Is he threatening you, Meg?"

She hesitated. That protective note in his voice warned Roarke wouldn't hesitate to go after her landlord and punch him again, maybe this time into next week. "He's never touched me. I have no relationship with him, Roarke, other than through business and I'll deal with that. Anyway, that's not why I called. I need a favor."

"What kind?"

A ten-million-dollar one. Megan bit her lip. "I need to move into the caretaker's cottage for a little while."

"Sure. That's fine. What's wrong with your place?"

"It's being renovated." A white lie, for she knew Deke planned to renovate. *Just not while I'm his tenant.* "So can I have it?"

"Bring your stuff over and you can have it tonight. First I need to check it out to make sure it's safe. I think the gas needs to be turned on and the electric. You need anything? Groceries? Fresh linens, of course."

Tears filled her eyes at his thoughtfulness. After Deke's callous treatment, Roarke's consideration made her crumble. She couldn't. *I have to get through this. I will.*

"Livi had the gas turned on a couple of months ago and the power, so I should be fine."

"Okay. When can I expect you?"

Glad for a diversion, she glanced around the office. "Give me half an hour to close up shop and I'll meet you at the manor."

Tomorrow she'd stop by to clear out her things from the apartment. For now she needed to get out of here and erase that horrid taste in her mouth left by Deke Kinkaid.

Roarke waited for her by the front door as she pulled up to the manor. Deeply curious as to why she really needed the cottage, he kept his mouth shut. He'd done enough talking about their breakup and that had gotten him into trouble.

Megan carried a suitcase. She thanked him as they went

around the back, taking the stone path to the small cottage at the property's back end.

Once he'd imagined a life with Meg living in a cozy cottage like this. Roarke climbed up the porch steps and looked around. The wide porch overlooked the lake and a pathway marched down to the sandy beach where he'd once played happily, daring to dash into the cold waters of Lake Worth.

Those days were gone. It was just a pretty sky blue cottage now, not a vacation refuge for him and his mother.

He opened the screen door. He keyed in the code, glad he'd changed the locks, and opened the glass door.

The original cottage was built in the 1920s as a summer cottage for guests, and Livi's family had hired a caretaker to remain on the estate during the harsh winter months to ensure the horses and other animals were cared for. Last year Livi had written to Roarke, telling him she'd renovated the cottage to bring it up to modern standards.

The side door opened to a small kitchen with white appliances, glass cabinets and a microwave. Livi had spent a considerable amount upgrading it and renovating it last year, which made him wonder if she had planned to live here. White tile covered the kitchen area, a practical choice. The cottage retained its original hardwood flooring, lath-and-plaster ceiling and paneled walls. Everything was painted white and pale blue, a cheery contrast to the mansion. White curtains with navy blue tiebacks bedecked the many windows. Livi had informed him she had updated the plumbing as well. He grinned, remembering the cold water he'd endured as a boy, and the trickle of water that barely allowed him to shower.

As he walked from the kitchen to the tiny living room area with its brick fireplace and white wicker credenza hiding a very modern flat-screen television, Roarke was pleased she'd retained the original charm of the cottage.

Above the white leather sofa hung a whimsical oil painting of boxes. He glanced at the signature, but couldn't make out the artist's name.

Roarke inspected the rest of the cottage, checking for traps. Nothing. Livi had stacked fresh linens and towels in the hall closet. He opened a drawer and smelled lavender memories of when he and Megan used to sneak inside the cottage to make love…

The click of heels on the hardwood floor jarred away his memories. Blinking, he watched Megan enter the room and her expression softened. "I love this place. She spent a lot of money on renovations."

Roarke glanced at his cell phone. "Okay, you should be all set. I have to go. Simon the jeweler called and said the watch is ready."

"Want some company?"

"No, I have a few errands to run after."

Surely the real estate agent would understand. She'd told him to drop by anytime.

"Will you be back soon?" Megan took out her cell phone. "I wanted to inventory the house. I'll start while you're gone."

"No," he said flatly. "Under any circumstances, do not go into that house without me."

She saluted him. "Yes, sir."

He softened his tone. "It's safer with me there. I won't be long. Get settled, and when I return, we'll search again."

She nibbled on her bottom lip. "Maybe we can brainstorm on what we know about Livi and where she would hide something worth ten-million dollars."

Much as he hated to disillusion her, he had serious doubts Livi actually possessed anything worth that much money. "Meg, about that letter, Livi could have grossly overestimated the object's value."

Her hopeful look faded.

He had to let her down gently. "If there were such a thing as a hidden treasure with my family, don't you think I would have heard about it over the years? All the stories she told about my family's past? I never heard her mention anything about it, or even hint at it."

Her crestfallen look tightened his chest. "I guess. She did love to tell stories. It's worth it to try to look. No harm in looking, Roarke. We owe it to her, and to Holly. That money will save her."

Relying on a treasure hunt to save Holly was not an option. Not when he might get a solid offer on the house and property. "I won't stake my stepniece's life on a treasure that might be more myth than fact. Holly needs more than stories to save her."

Meg threw up her hands. "I'm still going to believe that we can find this. I won't give up."

"You did years ago when I went into the Navy."

The wounded look in her eyes said everything. He walked out of the cottage, guilt riding his shoulders and a sinking feeling she was chasing a dream.

Much as she had years ago, when they were young and in love.

You should have fought for her.

The self-accusation rang through his head as he drove the rental car. Yeah, he should have. Could have picked up the phone years ago and insisted on speaking to her instead of letting her old man dictate her life. Find a way around him. Hell, even return to Cooper Falls in person to see if she really meant that email.

Instead he'd moved on, or thought he had. But five years ago, seeing her in that restaurant in DC, the years had melted away and he'd wanted her with the same dogged determination he'd felt in high school.

Except five years ago he'd been a new FBI recruit and needed to focus on his career. Not on Megan Robinson.

Roarke Bluetoothed his cell phone and listened to messages. In one Kyle, his new boss and former partner, assured him he could take all the time he needed in Michigan.

When he picked up the watch and paid for it, he itched to see if it provided any clues. Roarke waited until he returned to his car and then opened the box.

Simon had cleaned the watch as best as he could, but it had been badly damaged by the years in the dirt. He squinted. Initials were on the inside, but he couldn't decipher them. He set the watch in the glove compartment.

Roarke thought about the manor and who the hell could have accessed it while Livi still lived there. He'd heard Livi talk of secret tunnels and bootlegging, and wished he'd paid more attention to his great-aunt's ramblings of the past.

There had to be a way of getting to the house other than the driveway or the lake. He felt it in his bones. Livi had told them in her letter there was a ten-million-dollar treasure, but he had serious doubts. Livi loved spinning tales and if there were such a treasure, his great-grandfather would have disposed of it long ago. The old man loved adventure and travel as much as Livi did.

What he did know was that the family heirlooms Livi did own were now missing. Roarke doubted Livi would sell all of them, especially the coin collection. She knew how much he'd loved playing with it as a child, and specifically left it to him in her will.

If he could find a secret tunnel, Roarke felt confident he'd find how thieves had accessed the house without anyone's knowledge.

Public libraries were great sources of information.

Two hours later, he returned to the cottage, the watch in his pocket. Megan was in the kitchen, sitting at the table with her laptop. She shut it as he entered the room. "Did you get the watch?"

Roarke showed her. "Can you make out these initials?"

She frowned. "The first letter could be an *i*. It's hard to tell."

He dropped it on the table. "I was hoping it would provide a clue to the body's identity."

"We could keep searching for those missing Halloween editions of the paper. I can call Bob at the library, ask him to look again."

"I talked to the assistant librarian. She said those papers were never microfiched." He sighed. "The local newspaper might have back editions, but they went out of business earlier this year."

Megan exhaled. "Too bad. Do you want to help me now with inventory?"

"I have something to do, heading out again."

"Where are you going now?"

"Going to check out the old train depot and the pedestrian tunnel."

"I should go with you."

On guard, he jingled the keys in his hand. "Why?"

"Why are you going there?" she countered.

Usually he did the interrogating. Roarke considered. "I need to check something out."

"Such as…"

"You ask a lot of questions," he shot back, unsure as to why she irritated him right now. Perhaps it was seeing her standing there, in the same cottage where they used to make love.

Or maybe it was plain instinct, wondering why she was curious to know why he was headed there.

She stood and approached him. "I've documented that depot and the tunnel and I know a lot about it. I'll go with you."

"No."

Meg actually took a step back as if his words had slapped her. Inside he regretted his sharp tone, but knew it was for the best.

"It's too dangerous," he told her.

A slight laugh. She shook her head. "It wasn't dangerous when I mapped out the pedestrian tunnel a year ago for the historical society, and wrote a paper detailing the events leading to it. Let me go with you."

If his suspicions proved right, it was dangerous and he didn't want her to accompany him. "I'd rather go alone. I researched it at the library and I'll leave you here to get settled."

Without another word he headed to the manor, taking care to cautiously navigate through the house. In his bedroom he changed into a long-sleeved flannel shirt, old jeans and steel-toed boots. No knowing what or whom he might encounter down there. He packed water and a few granola bars and a powerful flashlight in a backpack.

As an extra precaution he strapped on his pistol, leaving the flannel shirt untucked and hiding it.

Minutes later he was driving toward the old depot. Bob hadn't been available during his visit, but the assistant librarian had been most helpful in detailing where the old section of the town had developed. Roarke hadn't told him what he was interested in, because it was no one's business.

No one's but his. The less who knew the better. He didn't trust the townspeople, nice as they seemed.

From the main road leading out of town, he crossed over the railroad tracks and drove on the road paralleling the train tracks not far from Greystone Manor.

Roarke rolled down his window and hung his arm on the ledge, studying the train tracks. The rail line used to run passengers. Now it ferried only freight, hauling chemicals, limestone and coal. There was a railroad depot in the area where he'd found Rigor tied up. Cooper Falls had developed around that depot more than one hundred years ago.

He'd remembered Livi's idle talk of secret tunnels and bootlegging whiskey, and the ways her father had thwarted the law by having his own private access to the train depot...

As he drew closer, and the road became more buckled, showing clear signs of abandonment, he glanced in his rearview mirror. Dismay shot through him.

A bright red Jeep tailed him.

Swearing softly, he thought about stopping and yelling at her, but knowing her stubborn streak, knew it wouldn't work. The road became more difficult to drive, and he had to navigate around several large potholes.

Years ago the road had accommodated traffic, but must have fallen into disrepair as the town's center moved farther south. Now what was left of the pavement was uneven and broken. Finally the old depot came into view. Roarke parked nearby. Grass and weeds shot up against the sagging building, adding to the abandoned feeling.

The remains of the old train depot, a wooden skeleton of a building, stood out starkly against the grassy field and the woods beyond. The ghostly whistle of an approaching train echoed across the plains. He climbed out, grabbed his backpack and waited for Meg.

She pulled up beside him and jumped out. Exasperation warred with admiration. She also had dressed in old jeans, and a long-sleeved T-shirt that fit smoothly over her curves and the delicious roundness of her bottom. She carried a backpack. She was always ready for adventure in the past.

Now it were as though the old Meg from their teenage years had whisked away the older cautious Megan.

Scowling at her as she approached, he shook his head.

"I told you I don't want company," he snapped.

Meg gave a little shrug. "Maybe I don't want to go with you. Maybe I'm exploring on my own. But if you wish to team with me, someone who knows this place better than you ever could, then you're welcome to join me."

With some resigned amusement, he saw she'd brought her own flashlight. "I see I can't stop you."

"No, you can't."

"Then stick with me and stay behind me." Roarke studied the fields surrounding the depot.

"Why, in case of rats?"

Her tone was light and unconcerned. He lifted the corner of his shirt, displaying his sidearm. "In case of two-legged ones."

Blood drained from her face. She got the message. Meg nodded. "All right. But let me fill you in on the history of this area. It may help."

Weeds tangled at their knees as they headed for the old pedestrian tunnel. The undergrowth had been cleared around the tunnel, with a paved area that stopped a few feet away, as if construction had begun here and halted. Pitted iron railings framed the entrance, with stone steps leading down into pitch-blackness. Roarke stopped short a few hundred feet away, listening to the wind sweep across the grass.

Megan began reciting as if lecturing one of her father's classes.

"Cooper Falls was founded in 1862 as a lumber town and had a large train depot for passengers and unloading and loading freight. It fell into disrepair and was abandoned in the 1950s when the lumber industry fell on hard times."

Intent on scoping out the area, he listened, scanning the

depot for signs of life, and then the ground for signs someone else had been here recently. There! Broken field grass
and faint footprints. Probably the same bastard who had
tied Rigor to the train tracks.

"Cooper Falls industry center was not Main Street,"
Meg continued. "The town actually developed as a lumber town to the north and spread from there. Town fathers
built shops, a school and homes. The train tracks divided
the town. The depot was on one side, where most of the low-
income homes were, and the school across from it a mile
or so down the road. The crossing was closer to the school,
which was dangerous because kids cut across the tracks all
the time instead of walking to the railroad crossing.

"In 1885 there was a terrible accident. A child was killed
crossing the train tracks, trying to get to school. So the town
council put a special tax on businesses and homeowners to
dig an underground pedestrian tunnel for the kids to safely
get to school from the depot side."

Squatting down, he examined the footprints. Looked
like a man's boot, but he couldn't be certain. "Livi said
the tunnel was abandoned after World War II when the
town built a new train station for passengers and the lumber business died out."

Meg squatted down next to him. "Yes. The entire town
shifted northward—commerce, the school, everything.
Roarke, what are you looking for?"

Standing, he pointed to the bricked entrance of the tunnel near the train tracks. "I'll know when I find it."

His curt tone didn't seem to bother her. With a wide arc
of her arm, she continued, "The tunnel was maintained,
courtesy of an anonymous wealthy donor. The historical
society put a marker up to memorialize Sid Sykes, the ten-
year-old who was killed in 1885."

Then she fell silent. Too silent. Megan glanced downward and when she looked up, her expression grew troubled. "You found Rigor tied to the train tracks. It was around here, wasn't it?"

He nodded.

"Consider this. Livi's dad ran illegal alcohol, so how did he do it?" She pushed a hand through her thick hair. "He'd have had to ship it out, probably by trains in disguised containers. This tunnel...you think it has an access way to the manor's property."

Roarke drew in a breath. "Yeah. You figured it out. Someone used it to get to the manor the back way." He pointed to the tunnel. "Someone's getting into Livi's house and sabotaging it without being seen. They could be in the tunnel right now."

She started for the entrance. "I'm not scared. Let's do this."

Knowing her fear of dark enclosed places, he had to admire her bravado. "Stay behind me at all times."

They advanced down the steps and peered into the yawning darkness.

Megan shivered. "I believe the lights still work."

He found the switch on the brick wall halfway down the steps. Yellow light flooded the tunnel. She breathed an audible sigh of relief as they reached the bottom.

Walls of brick alternated with sections of aged wood. Meg kept talking, but her voice had a distinct quaver to it now. "There was a storage area down here for railroad equipment. It was a way for them to pay for construction of the pedestrian tunnel, with the railroad donating money as long as they could use the storage room."

Although he'd done extensive research in the library, her knowledge of this structure was probably more accurate. He had a suspicion about that particular room. "Got an idea where that storage room is?"

She pointed it out.

The wooden center accessing the storage area was square in the middle of the pedestrian tunnel. It swung open after Roarke yanked hard. He jiggled the light switch on the wall and when it failed to work, flipped on his flashlight. The room showed brick walls, and a short passageway littered with railroad spikes, lamps and equipment. It wasn't a room, but extended farther into the darkness. Another tunnel. Satisfaction filled him.

Roarke shone his light into the darkness. "You should go back now. It may not be safe."

She started forward, but he caught her arm. "Let me go in first," he growled. "Were you always this stubborn?"

Her smile could melt butter. Good thing he wasn't butter. "Not as much as you were," she shot back.

The walls seemed closer as they walked farther inside. Roarke was glad he wasn't claustrophobic, but remembering Megan's fear, he glanced backward. Her color was pale and she was breathing a little too heavily. Stopping, he turned around, flashed his light over her face.

"You okay?" he asked quietly.

She gulped down another breath. "I forgot how much I hate small spaces."

He could only imagine how much. Roarke studied the blackness they'd traversed. Too far in now for her to return. "Take my hand. It'll help center you."

Her palm in his seemed so small, perspiring and fragile. Yet he knew Megan, knew she might look frail but harbored a resolve and inner strength that would put some of his former teammates to shame. He gave her hand a reassuring squeeze before starting forward again.

This was the price she paid for her pride, and anger at Roarke.

Meg's stomach tightened as she breathed in the musty

air. She focused on the man holding her hand as they walked, the slight trickle of sweat making his flannel shirt cling to the chiseled muscles of his back.

Roarke would never willingly lead her into danger. She'd been the one insisting on accompanying him.

They navigated through the tunnel until it dead-ended. He swept the flashlight beam over the ceiling and walls.

"What are you looking for?" she asked.

"A hidden entrance." In the dim light she saw his gaze sharpen. "Do you know where it is?"

"I have an idea."

Ignoring the pounding in her head and the tightness in her stomach, Meg ran a hand over the brick wall. *Focus on the task at hand. You're fine. Nothing will happen to you.*

"Livi did say something about a secret tunnel near the pedestrian passageway… She debated putting it into the book. Said the historical council didn't know about it and those old geezers would turn blue if they found out."

For the first time since she'd caught up with him, Roarke flashed a brief grin. "I bet she got a kick out of knowing something they didn't. Especially since it was part of her family's skeleton in the closet."

Intent on finding the hidden door, she swept her light over the brick wall. "Look for the outline of a door."

Roarke prodded the wall. "Here."

He pushed and the wall suddenly swung open. Megan forgot her suffocating anxiety. "I'll be damned!"

"Only if you were drinking booze back then, princess." He grinned at her and then sniffed the air. "Smells musty, but the air is clear. Safe to venture inside."

The passageway led deeper and deeper. Overhead the brick ceiling began to shake as she heard a train thunder past. Dust sprinkled like raindrops on their heads. Fear kicked up, bright and sharp. A faint buzzing sounded in her ears. The entire tunnel could collapse on top of them and they'd be buried here for months, years, no one finding them, no one hearing her panicked cries for help…

Roarke shone his light on the ceiling. "Regular freight. We're not far from the tracks."

Then he noticed her. "Damn, Meg, you look ready to pass out."

Two warm hands gently gripped her shoulders, made her lean over. Blood rushed to her head. She swallowed hard. "I'm okay," she managed to say, and straightened.

He squeezed her shoulders lightly. "I'm right here. Nothing's going to happen to you."

She took a long pull of water from the bottle he fished out of her pack and forced herself to regain her composure. This was temporary, her fear silly and shallow. The real problems lay outside these walls, back at her bookstore and the lack of money in the bank. That was worth getting scared over.

Meg finished the entire bottle and then capped it and placed it into her backpack. "Let's push on."

She needed to move, get going, not stand here with thoughts winking in her mind like neon signs, her imagination going wild. Roarke took her hand, rubbed his thumb over her chilled knuckles.

"Remember when we explored Harlow's Hill outside of town, climbed over those rocks and you slipped and nearly fell?"

Her skin quivered as she recalled that terrifying moment, and how his reassuring grip had calmed her, along with his encouraging smile as he urged her to continue the climb.

"I could never forget. My thighs ached for days," she joked.

Roarke's expression turned serious. Her smile faded. "I never did thank you for catching me, and saving my life."

A self-deprecating shrug from him. "I didn't save your life, princess. Just saved you from a few bumps and bruises."

"But you were there, catching me. That meant a lot to me, Roarke," she told him, feeling something in her chest ease. "It felt good to know you watched over me. I've... missed that."

His caress, barely a brush against her skin, warmed her from the inside out. When was the last time a man, or anyone, had made her feel this alive, this safe?

"I told you something that day I meant, and never forgot. I'll always be there to catch you when you fall...if you need me. That never changed, Meg."

Megan wanted to lean into his touch, relish his warmth and strength, and forget all her cares and woes. She wanted to tell him how much she cherished him holding her, but all the old hurt urged against it. Rejection had never been something she tolerated well. With more than a little reluctance, she pulled her hand out of his.

"We're here now, and that's all that matters, Roarke. Not the past. Finding out who stole from Livi, and how they did it. I don't need your help or anyone else's."

His expression shuttered. "Yeah. Guess I should have remembered that as well. Knew I should have gone it alone without you."

Turning away, he shouldered his pack and kept walking, this time without taking her hand. She felt bereft. No matter. She'd gotten used to it years ago.

Except this time she was the one pushing him away.

To her relief a faint light shone ahead of them. The tunnel forked. An obvious cave-in to the left, the tunnel boarded up. Meg shuddered.

The fork to the right looked clear. Roarke kept walking as she followed. Fresh air and a slight breeze wafted through the passageway. Meg's nostrils twitched as she gripped her flashlight in her sweaty hand. She caught up to him.

"We must be close to the lake," he mused.

The beam of his flashlight bounced over a large wooden chest and a few wrapped items pushed against the left side of the passageway. The chest looked old, perhaps dating back to the 1930s. Excitement filled her.

Roarke touched the chest. "Here it is. Pirate's booty. Knew we'd find something."

Memories flooded back of the stories Livi told about hauntings on the estate, and the stories her father deliberately told to keep strangers away, and nosy townspeople.

"Think there's anything good in here? Aged rum? Got a glass handy?" she joked.

His lips twitched in a faint smile.

"I bet the old man used it to store the rum and would come down here and sneak a few sips before packing it up for shipping to the speakeasies. Maybe we'll find a martini glass, a few olives and a shaker as well."

Roarke opened the chest. "No rum. No martini glass. Not unless I'm hallucinating."

Meg gasped.

Inside were all the items missing from the manor's library. The vintage candy dish. Meg lifted the lid and there were all the coins, including the uncirculated Morgan silver dollars. Roarke quietly swore as he fingered a silver dollar.

"She knew how much these coins meant to me. They belonged to her father, who inherited them from his father. Livi would bring out the coins and tell me stories about her grandfather mining silver in Colorado and how harsh the conditions were. I would sit at her feet, enthralled, and then she'd let me count every single coin so I could feel the edges, feel the heavy weight of each one in my palm. When I touched them, it was like touching history, my history, connecting me to a family I'd never have known without Livi."

Megan's heart squeezed tight. Whoever stole these saw only the material value, not the priceless memories connected to them.

"I'm sorry they violated your memories."

Shadows played over his handsome face as he replaced the coin in the candy dish. "What else did they steal?"

After unwrapping an old blanket, she found the glass case displaying women's suffrage memorabilia from 1916.

She unwrapped another piece of cloth and uncovered a lovely blue Chinese porcelain vase. "I remember this. Livi kept it in the library. It's from the Qing dynasty, one of Livi's pieces she acquired years ago when she was going through her China period and was wild about Chinese art. She told me the vase is worth about twenty-thousand dollars."

Her throat went dry as she glanced at Roarke. He'd gone still, the way he'd done when sensing a worrisome problem. Roarke always had a sixth sense for trouble. Even when he was the one who ended up with it as his best friend.

"All the antiques from Livi's house, the valuable ones except for the furniture, they're here. Who stored them here?"

"I don't know. It could be a hiding place. Or something else."

"Or someone stealing from a sweet old lady behind her back. But why leave them here? Why not get them out of town and sell them right away?"

He stroked a thumb across his mouth, a gesture she knew meant he was deep in thought. Roarke shook his head. "Livi was many things. Sweet? No. Perhaps a little too trusting at times. If the items were stolen, why are they still here? Most thieves move the stolen items as soon as they can. You said Livi knew something about this tunnel?"

"She did tell me something about a tunnel her father

used near the railroad depot for smuggling rum. Livi never told me the exact location."

"How much did my great-aunt tell you, Megan?" He held up his light to his face and gestured to the items. "You knew about this tunnel."

The suspicion in his green eyes hurt like a sharp slap. "I was helping her write and record your family's memories, Livi's memories, for future generations, for the town's history, so all her wonderful stories wouldn't fade into obscurity. I didn't steal from her."

She felt a rising, suffocating anxiety. Meg swept her flashlight beam over the darkness ahead and started forward.

He caught her arm. "Wait."

"What?"

"I owe you an apology." Roarke stiffened. "I'm sorry. I didn't mean to sound accusing."

In the past when he did or said something stupid, she'd forgive him and fling her arms around his neck, kissing him and assuring him everything was all right. She wasn't that same naive starry-eyed teenager in love with wild Roarke Calhoun, ready to forgive and forget because she loved him so much. Even now she was hyperaware of him, the slight tang of his cologne mingling with the very male sweat, the brooding intensity that made him uniquely Roarke. Her chest ached because deep inside, she wanted him with the same crazed passion and longing she'd had as a teenager. How hard it was to sweep away the memories of the man she'd once loved and would give up everything to be with, the man who'd sworn his unending devotion to her.

"Apology accepted," she muttered. "Let's get out of here."

She followed him as he progressed through the tunnel. The passageway wound uphill until it dead-ended at steps.

Above the steps was a door. Roarke grunted and strained as he struggled to push it open. It finally opened upward.

He whistled. "Son of a biscuit, I can't believe it."

After climbing upward, he held out a hand. She ignored it and climbed upward, her gorge rising as she realized where they were. If she felt suffocated previously by the dark enclosed tunnel, this place totally creeped her out.

On either side of them were marble tombs. One was labeled Walter Carlson. Another was labeled Geraldine Carlson, Livi's mother.

They were inside the Carlson private mausoleum. The air smelled musty and of the dead flowers someone had forgotten about on the window shelf, overlooked by a stained glass angel with a gentle expression on her face.

"The family cemetery." Meg swallowed her distaste. "Inventive and original. But quite disrespectful."

He glanced down at the tiled floor that disguised the hidden doorway. "I'll be damned. The old man probably built this, knowing no one would dare enter into a private mausoleum, and put out the stories about the cemetery being haunted to excuse the late-night goings if anyone should see them running rum. Clever."

She shuddered. "May we get out of here? Or are we locked in and have to spend the night with Uncle Walter?"

Much to her relief, the door leading outside wasn't locked. She ran down the two steps and took a deep lungful of fresh air, grateful to smell the nearby lake water, trees and the honeysuckle Livi's family had planted in the cemetery years ago.

Meg shrugged off her backpack, hunted for water, and withdrew the empty. Stupid, stupid, she'd only brought one bottle. The light-headedness got to her and she sagged to the ground.

He thrust a bottle of water at her. "Drink."

Taking the bottle with a shaky hand, she drank, gradually feeling her equilibrium return. She handed back the half-finished bottle, glad to see her hands no longer trembling.

Instead of capping it, he chugged down the rest of the water. Meg licked her lips as she watched in pure fascination as his throat muscles worked. As he backhanded his mouth, he glanced at her.

"You okay now? You're flushed."

Her cheeks heated further. She managed a nod. How could she think about sex, about the slide of water down his throat, remembering his mouth on hers, while in a cemetery? In a cemetery after they'd fought in the most claustrophobic place she'd ever entered. Her lady parts didn't agree. They liked the look of Roarke, remembered how good it had been when they got naked together...

At the sheer absurdity of everything, Meg began to laugh. Roarke squatted down. "Princess, calm down. I know I was a bastard back there, and you must be feeling terrible, but it's going to be all right."

This was the old Roarke, caring and concerned. Her throat closed. Better to have the new Roarke, who eyed her with suspicion and treated her like a stranger.

The new Roarke was safer. No memories, less chance of her falling in love with him all over again.

"I'm not hysterical." She drew in a breath. "I'm okay. Thanks."

He patted her shoulder. "Good. Easy hike from here back to the manor. You game?"

This time she took the hand he offered as Roarke pulled her upright. She dusted off her bottom and looked around.

"I remember last time I was here. It was shortly after your mom..."

Words failed her. Meg stared at the tombstones, swallowing hard as she recognized a familiar one.

Frowning, he glanced around and the blood drained from his face. As he ran toward one grave, she followed, wincing as he swore loudly. She couldn't say anything. All she could do was stand there stupidly, immobilized by shock and disgust.

The Carlson private family cemetery housed graves dating back generations. Roarke's mom was buried here. Meg had accompanied him to the gravesite after the marble tombstone had been placed here. Roarke had designed it himself, a teddy bear with angel wings surrounded by a heart. Moira had loved making teddy bears for children at the hospital. She had hunted in thrift stores for used clothing for the fabric and buttons for the eyes. It fed her purpose and joy when times were rough and bleak.

Even though she wasn't a Carlson, Moira was buried here after her fight with cancer ended. Livi had insisted, and Roarke's grandparents hadn't fought her. Livi had purchased the tombstone, one of the largest in the cemetery, and paid for the engraving.

That same tombstone now lay in pieces atop his mother's grave, the dirt covering the coffin below recently disturbed and hastily filled in. Desecrated and ruined, it felt like a knife to her heart. She went to him, put a hand on his arm.

Shock dawned in his vivid green gaze, gradually turning incandescent with fury. He swore in a low voice, raked a hand through his hair again.

"Oh, Roarke, I'm so sorry... Why would someone do this?" she whispered.

He fisted his trembling hands, a clear struggle to control the rage she knew roared inside him. A vein throbbed in his temple as sweat trickled down like teardrops.

Not only Moira's grave, but several graves had been disturbed, the tombstones knocked over or worse, smashed to rubble. Tears came to Meg's eyes as Roarke knelt by his mother's grave and gently brushed leaves from the cracked ruins of her tombstone. Words engraved that had memorialized Moira Calhoun had been splintered by a cruel hand, not recognizable now.

Roarke took another deep breath, his voice cracking as he spoke.

"She wanted to be buried here for me. Mom couldn't stand my dad's family, except for Livi. My grandparents, her in-laws, she would never accept help from them. Not that they offered much. But cancer treatments cost money, lots of money, and she didn't have much in the way of health insurance. Mom didn't want me burdened with funeral expenses, so she talked to Livi about paying for her damn funeral expenses. She was so sick in that final stage. If only she had gone to the doctor... By the time she told me, it was too late. She was only thirty-eight, too damn young to die."

Meg couldn't speak. She joined him by the grave and wrapped her arms around him, her heart shattered at the deep-set grief in his voice. "I'm so sorry."

Muscles in his arms quivered as he fisted his hands. Roarke inhaled deeply, wiped his eyes.

"I'm sorry, Mom. I'll get you a new stone, much grander than the old one. And I'll find whoever did this. I promise."

Grief flooded her as his voice broke. Roarke had loved his mother more than anyone else in the world, and would have done anything to save her. But she knew from her own experience, sometimes love wasn't enough to save someone from a terrible disease.

He turned and wrapped his arms around her. "Meg, I know... I've been a bastard..."

She put a finger to his lips and hugged him tight. Roarke rested his head against hers. They held each other for a few minutes, two souls bonded by sorrow, who had watched their beloved parents slowly suffer and die.

Then he untangled himself from her gentle grip and helped her to stand. "Whoever did this wanted more than a few stolen items from Livi's house. They knew Livi was hiding something of tremendous value. They found the tunnel and used it, probably to smuggle out everything they found worth selling on the black market."

"That's why they smashed the tombstones. They were searching for the entrance in the cemetery."

His mouth worked as he gazed around. "No. This is too destructive. Whoever destroyed these tombstones did so in a rage. I've seen these kinds of crimes before."

Meg couldn't fathom that level of anger, especially against the dead. "Roarke, who could be so angry at Livi's family that they'd do this? Everyone in town loves Livi and they've always respected the Carlsons."

"Everyone? Someone definitely has a problem with my father's side of the family."

She had to point out the obvious. "Except for your relationship with Livi, and the destruction of your mother's grave, you would make an excellent suspect. You've always loathed your father and his relatives."

He blinked. "True. I wonder…"

A calculating look came over him. She could almost see the wheels spinning. Then he took her hand. "Let's get the hell out of here, before whoever did this decides to return."

Good idea. But his next words caused a chill to race down her spine.

"Whoever did this is going to pay. You can count on that."

Chapter 13

Since they'd left both of their vehicles at the train depot, Roarke drove them there in the Shelby so she could pick up her Jeep. If not for the troubling scene at the cemetery, she might indulge in memories of when they'd go joyriding in this car. Or even more memorable—when they'd first made love in the back seat.

Seemingly lost in thought, he said nothing on the ride over. When they arrived, he stopped, his white-knuckled grip on the steering wheel indicating the emotions he felt.

"I'll stay here until you get into your vehicle and pull out." He stared into the distance.

"Roarke…" For the first time since her arrival, she felt worried for him. "What are you going to do?"

For a moment he said nothing, only tightened his grip on the wheel.

"What are you going to do? Tell me or I won't leave. I can stay here all day, Roarke."

He blew out a breath. Roarke unbuckled his seat belt and then removed the pistol at his side. He checked it and turned it over in his hands, as if it anchored him. "I'm going back in and tracing every inch of that tunnel to search for an entrance that leads either to the manor or the cottage and then I'm setting a trap for whoever stole those items and wrecked my mother's grave."

"No. You won't. You're going to drive the Shelby back to the manor, and then I'll drive you back here to get your rental car."

His jaw tightened.

Hoping he'd listen to reason, knowing his fierce protective streak, she took a gamble. "Please. It's getting late and I don't want to be alone. Not after what we discovered."

Grunting, he slid the pistol back into the holster. "All right. For now."

By the time they returned for good, the sun had sunk lower into the sky. Roarke fed Rigor on the porch while Meg changed his water bowl.

She sat in one of the rockers while Roarke paced back and forth on the porch.

"I bet that's why someone tied Rigor to the train tracks," he mused. "Rigor knows who was stealing from the manor. He's a witness."

The dog perked up at the mention of his name. Meg reached down and patted his head. "In all honesty, could Livi have moved everything? She was getting eccentric and worried, and we had been talking about the tunnel and how her father used it to run rum. Maybe she thought it was a safe place."

"Then who desecrated the graves?"

"I don't know, but we should tell the sheriff."

His expression darkened. "Not that I trust him to care." He walked back and forth the length of the porch, his boot heels clicking against the worn planks.

Meg sighed. "You hate him because he's always antagonized you."

"You're such an expert on this town, do you trust him?"

"Not necessarily. But I do know pacing like a caged dog won't do you any good."

Rigor lifted his head again and whined.

"I think better when I walk around," he muttered.

"You could walk back to Washington and you're not going to solve anything right now. Neither of us are. So what do we do now?"

Finally he halted. "We keep this strictly between us. And you, avoid the manor unless I'm with you. Even with security cameras, it's not safe. I'm moving into the cottage until I figure out what the hell is going on. If there's a secret entrance that leads to the manor and the cottage, I'll sleep better knowing I'm armed and close by you."

"Isn't the cottage a little small for the two of us?" she blurted out.

His gaze remained steady. "There's two bedrooms, Meg."

A hot flush crept up her neck. When they were teenagers, they used one of the bedrooms for their clandestine lovemaking.

Her phone buzzed. She glanced down at the text from Deke Kinkaid, her heart racing.

Tick tock. You have three days left until I call the sheriff to evict you, the text read.

The clock wasn't merely ticking, the minutes were speeding by. Maybe she could find something of value to fend Deke off.

Livi had hinted about a hiding place in the main guest bedroom closet when Meg had asked about secrets the old house had hidden. There could be a clue to the treasure there.

"What are your plans now?" she asked Roarke.

He rubbed the back of his neck. "A shower, after I move my things into the cottage. You?"

She sniffed the air. "You smell fine."

He did. Even when sweating, Roarke Calhoun smelled like spices and his own unique scent that always drew her to him like a lodestone.

Amusement played over his face. "Yeah, you're not so bad yourself, Megan. Got any plans for dinner?"

Once she would have jumped at the chance to dine alone with him, but not with the eviction looming over her head. "I have to return to the bookstore. I plan to spend the night at my apartment. Tomorrow is Saturday and I have things I have to get done at the bookstore, so you're on your own, but there's a leftover casserole I made in the fridge if you get hungry."

His gaze softened. "Thanks. Same old Megan, always taking care of me."

"What are your plans for tomorrow?" she asked.

"Going into town to do a little more research at the library tomorrow morning. I found some old journals from around the time Oscar was smuggling alcohol. I should be a few hours. Then I want to tackle repairs on the front of the manor."

"Huh. Old journals at the library?"

He nodded.

"Did you find any of Geraldine's journals? Livi told me her mother kept diaries, but never could find them. The diaries were personal and might contain useful information."

"No. These journals are more about inventory of Oscar's business. But thanks for the info."

She watched him go into the cottage. Megan pushed back at her hair. Pride prevented her from telling Roarke about the eviction. She didn't want him to ask questions or try to make it easier. Or harder. She didn't need his pity.

First she had a call to make. After seeing the raw hurt in Roarke's eyes about the destruction in the cemetery, she needed to do something.

She headed for the Jeep and drove to her destination. After a short visit she headed to her apartment. For the next few hours, she packed all her personal things into boxes she found at the local grocery store. Meg felt a loss knowing she couldn't afford storage for the furniture and her father's belongings. The idea of seeing them on the street twisted her heart, but what choice did she have?

Deke Kinkaid had texted her he expected the apartment to be vacant and clean by Monday at 9:00 a.m. or she'd lose the security deposit.

The apartment over the bookstore that had been home for thirty years was more than a living space. It was crammed with memories and sang with the past as she drifted from room to room, staring helplessly at her father's cuff links still on the dresser, at the framed photos of her mother and father smiling at her from the antique table in the living room. If only she'd spent time going through her father's items after he'd died! Too late now. She had only the weekend to deal with everything.

How did one clean out an entire lifetime of memories with a parent? Her throat tightened as she began sifting through her father's personal belongings. His beloved book collection. The photos of him with favorite students. His shirts, always pressed and clean. Meg buried her face into a blue sweater he'd always worn on exam day because he said blue was a soothing color.

Tears gathered in her eyes, but she refused to let them fall. Grief was a luxury for those who didn't face eviction.

If she'd learned one thing from her father's death, it was survival.

A hollowness settled in her chest. Meg folded the sweater and set it aside. She hadn't the emotional energy yet to go through her dad's clothing and belongings, sort it all out and give it away.

She was too busy trying to save his bookstore.

Save the bookstore, save the apartment, but what about your needs? a little voice inside her whispered. *Is this the life you really want? Stuck in a dusty bookstore when there's adventure waiting beyond the boundaries of this small town?*

One thing at a time. She needed to store all her belongings and her father's as well… Then Meg looked around at the furniture, her father's favorite easy chair in the corner with the antique gooseneck lamp. She laughed. Not enough to store everything. She had to get rid of it.

Exhausted, she collapsed on the bed and fell into a dreamless sleep. When she woke, the sky outside was leaden with dawn, rose and gold streaking the horizon.

Dread filled her as she showered and dressed. Today she'd have to choose which of her father's belongings would be saved, and which would be tossed onto the street with the trash.

As she finished braiding her hair, the doorbell rang. Probably Deke demanding to know if she had cleaned everything out yet.

Instead Holly's mom stood in the hallway, a cardboard container in her hands.

"I heard what happened, what Deke did, and I came here to help you move." Nancy marched inside and placed the box on the living room floor.

Word traveled fast in small towns. Her pride no longer mattered. Not in the face of the seemingly insurmountable task of moving an entire apartment in two days.

Meg took a deep breath. "Thank you. But what about Holly?"

"My parents are watching her. Chet and I figure you could use the help, and you'd be too proud to ask, so we're here. Consider it payback for all those times you tutored Holly and read to her."

Suddenly an army of people marched up the stairs and down the hallway. Not only Chet, but more than two dozen people had joined him, including Dawn. Seeing her almost made Meg break down.

"I had to come," Dawn said, stepping forward with a large cooler in hand. "I brought pop, water and fruit juice. My brother's watching the kids. I wish I'd have been able to help sooner, Meg. But I'm here now."

Meg's throat closed with emotion. "Thank you, Dawn. Thank you, everyone."

This was the good part of small-town life, people rallying to come to your aid when they knew you needed help the most. The same thing had happened after Dad died. Casseroles, offers to help with the funeral arrangements and much more.

Roarke had remembered only the negative aspects. She wished he could see this now.

More than twenty people piled into the spacious apartment, bearing boxes and packing tape and bubble wrap. Vivian and Bob came as well. The biggest surprise was Amanda, wearing gray pleated trousers and a gray-and-white silk blouse instead of her usual tailored dresses.

She squeezed Meg's arm. "Your father's class was a lifesaver for me. The professor kept me going through college when I wanted to quit. How many times would I sit in his library, crying, and he would assure me I could do it? Your dear mother kept piling homemade cookies and hot tea on me, and both of them helped me to regain the confidence I needed. I'm so sorry this is happening to you. I wish I had a place for you to live, but I have an empty storage unit that will accommodate all your belongings until you can get settled elsewhere."

The thoughtfulness, and mention of her mother, touched Meg. "Thank you," she said, struggling to hold back her own emotions.

Mrs. Rawlings gazed around. "You know, my dear, my own father pressured me to continue the family business. That's the main reason I ended up in college, pursuing a business degree. My first love was literature, but I felt obligated to follow in the family footsteps. Sometimes it isn't until we're older that we gather enough courage to pursue our own dreams. Endings can be new beginnings."

Words failed her. She didn't know where to start. Where did one begin packing up a lifetime of hopes, dreams and memories? But ever-efficient Amanda Rawlings seemed to understand Meg's inertia, and came equipped with a pad of paper and pen to make lists.

In no time Amanda had the volunteers sorted into groups. Able-bodied men took the furniture out the door. A tractor trailer truck outside, courtesy of Amanda's company, stood ready to haul everything to the waiting storage unit.

Flitting between rooms, Meg directed everyone, leaving the packing of her room and her own personal items to Nancy and Dawn.

When it was time for a break, they all sat on the floor and grabbed sodas from the cooler. Meg took a long drink of hers. She rolled the can on her forehead, relishing the coolness.

Amanda, too formal to sit on the floor, perched on the edge of the lone chair left in the living room. "What are you going to do, Megan?"

Everyone looked at her. Flushing, she set down her drink.

"I'm in the process of inventorying everything in the manor, and I'll try to find a buyer after for the contents."

"That will take quite a while," Chet said, shaking his head. "When you need money now, it seems like everything moves in slow motion."

Nancy put her hand over her husband's.

"I heard the manor and the property went to Roarke," Amanda said, sipping her diet cola.

"Yes. He wants to sell as soon as I can clean out the house." She thought of Holly's bravery, faced with such a critical disease.

"Maybe Roarke can buy you out," Chet suggested. "Give you cash now for the value of everything in the manor."

She shook her head. "I can't do that. I feel so connected to the house and the contents, and there's so much I want to preserve. Roarke doesn't feel the same. He indicated if he bought out my share, he might sell everything lock, stock and old wine barrel."

Amanda's expression grew dreamy. "I always adored that house and all the antiques Livi owned. I remember the cherry rolltop desk Livi purchased at an auction. Unfortunately, I was out of town on business when it went for sale and my designated buyer did not realize my obsession with that desk. It would have complemented my office perfectly. Livi always enjoyed beating me in purchasing antiques. I told her it killed me that she outbid me."

Amanda's wistful admission made her wonder. How badly did her friend want Livi's possessions? Enough to steal?

Realizing the woman stared at her, she hastily laughed. "You'd have to kill me to get to it," she joked weakly. "But if you did, everything would go to Roarke, anyway, and he'd probably give it to you just to get out of town."

Dawn shook her head. "I don't know, Meg. The way I saw him looking at you, seems like he found a good reason to stay."

Wishing to break the awkward silence that followed, Megan drained her soda and got back to work.

It wasn't much later that almost everything was packed up in the moving truck and only a few items remained. In the living room, at the vintage glass cocktail cart Amanda, Vivian and Nancy wanted to pack, Meg shook her head at the liquor. "Most of this can go," she said. "Except this... I'm keeping this."

Meg picked up the bottle of Glenfiddich 1937. The aged Scotch whiskey was valued at more than seventy-thousand dollars, but to her father it had been priceless.

Vivian peered at the bottle. "What is it?"

After telling her, Meg explained. "Keith Barnes, one of his students, gave Dad this as a gift for all the times Dad helped him out through college. Keith was a struggling student and Dad gave him a huge discount on books, even loaning him money, assuring him Keith could repay it later when he got a job. Keith went on to become CEO of one of the country's largest telecommunications companies. Dad was so proud of him."

Amanda nodded. "Your father was highly regarded in this town as well, Meg. Anything we can do to help."

Struggling to rein in her emotions, Meg exhaled. "You and everyone else have already done so much."

"Except for that horrible Deke Kinkaid," Dawn said, marching by with a box filled with clothing. "He's a bastard."

"Dawn! Language!" Amanda scolded.

"Deke *is* a bastard. I could kill him for how he's ruining my weekend," Meg joked weakly. "Vivian, please bring me one of those plastic cups. Maybe I should indulge to drown my sorrows."

The cap on the Scotch bottle twisted easily. She inhaled the scent of oak and cedar. "Dad and I drank out of this bottle only once, after I graduated."

She poured a finger into one of the plastic cups. Amanda Rawlings blinked. "My dear Meg, you cannot be serious! Whiskey that fine into a plastic cup? Your father would be appalled."

Winking, she shrugged. "Beats drinking from the bottle. Here's to you, Dad."

Downing the drink in one gulp, she relished the burn sliding down her throat and coughed. "Wow. I forgot… I guess it's been a long time since I had a drink."

"You sip fine whiskey, you do not down it like a college frat student." Amanda fetched a glass from the cart, poured a small amount into it and sipped. "Amazing. I haven't sampled whiskey this smooth in a long time."

Meg sighed and touched the bottle. "This stays. I'll return tomorrow night, use it to drink a toast to the apartment and Dad and then take it when I leave the keys."

Finally everything but for three boxes had been packed and hauled away. The Scotch bottle sat next to the boxes. Emotionally she couldn't take another minute here.

"What about these?" Vivian pointed to the remaining boxes.

"I can't. It's too much. I'll take those tomorrow night as well."

Amanda opened the door to let Chet and Hal, Dawn's husband, carry out the last chairs in the study. What came through the door next, and into the living room, caused an unpleasant jolt.

"This place is larger than I remember." Hands on hips,

Deke Kinkaid gazed around the empty dusty room. "Needs a good cleaning. Hope you plan to do that or you'll forfeit your security deposit."

Feeling as if a cockroach had crawled onto her, Meg scowled. "Why are you here?"

"Heard you organized people to move your stuff out. Came to see the progress."

Sticking his nose into her business, he meant. "You've seen it. Now leave."

"I own the place. You can't throw me out."

Seeing him walk over the hardwood floors she'd polished, the floors her father had paced while thinking of an outline for his book project, made her stomach roil.

"The apartment is mine until Monday morning at 9:00 a.m." Meg got in his face, glaring at him. "I can leave things here until then."

"True." Deke looked around, picked up the bottle of Scotch and whistled. "This is some fine whiskey. Say, I'd give you a hundred dollars for it."

She lurched forward, grabbed the bottle out of his hands. "This was my father's and I'd see you choke on it before you took a single drop. Now get the hell out of my place."

Deke gave a nervous laugh as he looked around at the angry faces surrounding him. "Yours until Monday. Don't forget that."

The door closed behind him.

"Deke Kinkaid is a rotten bastard. I wish he were dead," she whispered, more to herself than anyone.

But Amanda, Nancy and Vivian and others had heard, and glanced at her, sympathy on their faces. She steeled her spine. One thing she'd learned was to rely on herself and get through each obstacle. It was her life and she had to live it.

"That took some guts. Good for you," Nancy announced.

Meg put a hand to her spinning head. The whiskey had gone to it. She'd surprised herself. Never before had she stood up to someone the way she just had to Deke.

Maybe it was about time.

"We'll be taking off now." Vivian shook her head. "I hope you're not sleeping here."

The thought provided much disquiet. "No." Too many memories.

"But, honey, where will you sleep? We have a pullout sofa," Nancy told her.

"Don't worry about me." Pride prevented her from telling too much. "I have a temporary place and Sunday I'll come back, toast the apartment and Dad one last time. But for now, I need to get out of here. It's too much."

Nancy squeezed her shoulder. "I understand, honey. If you need anything else, let me know."

As she thanked everyone and watched them leave, Meg felt the weariness weigh her down. As much as it hurt to pack up everything and move out years of memories, she couldn't have done it without her friends. This was small-town life, where everyone knew everyone else's business, but they pitched in when needed.

If only Roarke had understood that and given the town a chance.

Her throat closed with emotion as she thought about telling Roarke of her downfall. Pride had prevented it up until now, but she'd have to inform him she'd lost her home, the only home she could ever remember. Meg bit her lip. Anger was better than tears.

As she took one last look at the apartment, tears welling in her eyes, she didn't know where home was. For the first time in thirty years, she felt groundless.

It wasn't as jarring as she'd thought. Along with sorrow

came a small feeling of relief and freedom. She could go where she wished now, after she sold Livi's things and had money to save the bookstore and find a new apartment. Perhaps even a small house of her own. New opportunities meant new possibilities in Cooper Falls.

Really? You want to stay here all your life? When you've been given a chance to start over? You can go anywhere you want. Do whatever you want.

Meg lugged her suitcase down to her car. Where did you go when you had nothing grounding you, no clear direction? Much as she wanted to fight to save the bookstore and her father's legacy, deep inside she knew it was pointless. Unless she could sell something of real value in Livi's house, the bookstore would close.

The idea of closing a bookstore that had helped hundreds of students over the years, had been a place of deep thought and learning for the entire town, left her shaking. But she had to prioritize. Two bedrooms in the manor had yet to be searched for the treasure. Suddenly she remembered Livi talking about a hidden compartment in the master closet used to store valuables.

She and Roarke could check it out. Maybe there was a slim chance the treasure was there.

Starting up the Jeep, she felt a pang of sorrow mixed with hope. This is what Roarke faced all those years ago. Starting over, heading in a new direction.

For the first time since he'd left, she had an understanding of the freedom he'd felt when he climbed onto his motorcycle and roared off. Wiping the slate clean, throwing out everything in his life like tossing out the trash. Starting over.

Except for you. He wanted to keep you.

This isn't about you and Roarke. Stop thinking about that little crooked smile of his, how strong he is and how he wanted to keep you safe from harm. You have to resolve your own problems. He's already stated he is leaving and needs to wipe his feet of this town.

She had to cling to hope, stop thinking this whole situation would have a bad outcome.

Or that she and Roarke could ever fall in love again.

Chapter 14

Roarke was outside, fixing the porch steps of the manor when Megan returned later that afternoon.

He wiped sweat off his forehead. "Hey, there. Get a good night's sleep and everything done you needed to get done?"

"I slept. Accomplished a lot. Listen, we need to search the upstairs rooms."

She told him about the conversation she'd had with Livi. He sat on the repaired step, dangling the hammer from one hand.

"If we do this, I go first," he said flatly. "I'm not having a chandelier fall on your head or have you tumble down sawed-off steps."

"And what about you? You could easily get hurt as well."

"I'll be careful."

Her gaze narrowed. "Have you been inside the house without me?"

He glanced away. "Yeah. Searched for an entrance to that tunnel. No luck yet. There's a dozen places it could be, including the basement. So I did the next best thing—bought more cameras and installed them throughout the house and set up the monitor in the cottage. I can also check on my phone to see if someone's inside the manor."

Probably a good idea.

They went inside the house. Meg trailed up the steps behind Roarke as he jumped on each step as if it would collapse beneath his weight. Dragging his feet down the hallway, he paused every few feet to study walls and the ceiling.

When they reached the master bedroom, she pointed to the closet. He went inside first, examining everything. A few articles of vintage clothing hung from the clothing rack, but otherwise it was fairly empty. Considering how many items Livi owned, it struck her as unusual.

Not only was the closet empty, it remained uncarpeted, the wood floor dusty and ancient.

Using the penknife he handed her, Megan lifted up a board. Beneath was an empty space, perfect for hiding a treasure. Her heart skipped a beat as she spied a tin cigar box.

"Wait." He stayed her hand. "It might be another trap."

Roarke prodded the box with the tip of the penknife. Nothing happened. He nudged it over to the opening, and then lifted it.

Hands shaking, she opened it. There was a packet of one-hundred-dollar bills and a pile of yellowed papers. She counted the money. Three-thousand dollars. Surely this money would buy her time with the bookstore at least.

Honesty kicked in. It wasn't hers. She handed the bills to Roarke.

"This belongs to you. It is your house."

He raised his eyebrows. "The will states the contents belong to you, Meg."

How she wished! But she'd read over the will until her

eyes grew bleary. "The will stated the contents, such as the antiques, furniture and other physical objects, are mine to sell. It stated any cash on the premises Livi had intended for you. If you don't want it, I'm sure Holly's parents could use it."

"Good point. I'll give it to Chet. Since he's taken more time off, it's been hard on all of them financially."

Always so honorable. She felt a wave of relief. At least Chet would have money to pay bills. She picked up the packet of papers, tied with a faded blue ribbon. Meg untied the ribbon and began reading the letters, handing a few to Roarke.

His brow wrinkled. "What is this? Sounds like an erotic romance novel."

"They're love letters, silly." She waved the one in her hand. "Love letters written to Oscar Carlson but not from Lavinia and Abigail's mother."

"Listen to this one! It's dated August 1941." She read aloud. "Darling, tonight will be our night. I will meet you at our love nest. JB says he loves me, but I told him I do not want to see him ever again. I can't wait for you to undress me, lay my trembling body down on the four-poster bed and guide your wonderful little Oscar into my body. I want to feel you all over, have your hands touch my body until we are both panting and longing for each other…"

Roarke whistled. "Oscar? The town's upstanding citizen and founder? My great-grandfather?"

"Little Oscar. I wonder how little?" she mused.

She giggled as he laughed. "Let me see the letter."

He read the rest aloud, making her blush. Meg fanned herself. "Whoever wrote those letters certainly had a flaming affair with your paternal great-grandfather."

"Secret lover." Roarke squinted at the letter. "It's signed *your kitten*. Must be a nickname."

She folded the paper. "Or not so secret. In those days, sometimes wives turned a blind eye to a husband's affairs."

"In those days, there was also no birth control. I wonder if Kitten and Oscar had more than a love affair in common."

Her heart raced. "You mean an illegitimate child? But something like that would be hard to keep secret in a small town like Cooper Falls."

"I wonder who poor JB was. Kitten's boyfriend probably had no clue she was sleeping with the town's richest citizen." Meg replaced the board.

Roarke thumbed through the money. "Would you like to give this to Chet and Nancy? You found it. You had an idea of the hidden space."

"They need to know it was from you."

They found an envelope in a rolltop desk in the guest room and Roarke put the money inside. "As long as we're here. I need to check out her bedroom."

His jaw tightened as he looked away. "Hope you understand… I need to be alone to do this, go through her stuff."

Meg's heart constricted. She understood. She felt the same way walking into her father's bedroom, seeing his comb and brush on the dresser, his reading glasses. Memories were painful.

"I'll put this in the cottage and then come back. I want to go through her books in the library."

He nodded. "Library's safe. I checked it out twice."

After she'd hidden the money in an empty flour canister in the cottage kitchen, Meg went to the library and combed through all of Livi's books, knowing some would fetch a nice price with a rare book dealer she knew. She had set aside ten books when she heard a loud noise and curses from upstairs.

Megan ran to the steps. "What happened?"

"Wait! Stay where you are."

Hand on the banister, she did, watching him climb down the stairs, his expression grim.

"I was positive the house was safe. I checked through every inch, except Livi's room." He drew in a deep breath. "That room… Well, it was tough to walk in there and comb through it, so I left it for last. Thought you might like some of her jewelry and things for yourself."

This was the old Roarke, thoughtful and caring. She drew a deep breath. "Thank you. I would."

"That's when I found two more traps."

Her stomach roiled. "What? What about the security cameras?"

"I'll check the footage, but I suspect this was done before I installed the cameras. Someone was here, sabotaging things, Meg. In Livi's room and the guest bath. These were intentionally set to seriously injure if not kill. The trap in the bathroom was left for Livi."

He held up a length of wire. "The bathroom shower was rigged with a strip of wire connected to the light fixture. It was hard to detect, but soon as you turned on the lights and turned on the shower knob, you'd be electrocuted."

Her stomach roiled. Roarke tossed down the wire and took her elbow, guiding her outside. On the rickety steps, he gently urged her to sit.

"You look pale. Put your head between your knees," he advised.

She pressed two fingers to her temples. "I'll be all right. I'm a little overwhelmed, hot and tired. This was not what I had hoped."

"Me, either, especially when I found the second trap in Livi's bedroom. That one wasn't as lethal, but it did surprise me in a most unpleasant way."

Her gaze scanned him up and down as she realized the

gravity of his words. "Oh, no! What was it? Did you get hurt?"

"Mostly my pride. Usually I'm not as careless." He held up his left palm. It sported a blue bandanna with a dark wet stain.

"Remember the silver coin collection Livi let me play with as a kid?" Roarke sighed. "This trap was cleverly baited. I opened a drawer to her dresser, saw the silver dollar beneath her collection of lace handkerchiefs, reached for it and sliced my hand on a knife sticking up. Damn sharp, too."

Forgetting all her recent woes, she took his palm into her hands and turned it over. "Ouch. Did you disinfect this?"

"Nope. Grabbed my old bandanna and wrapped it to stop the bleeding. Decided to wait until I got to the cottage. Didn't want to find another booby trap in the cabinet."

She stood and tugged him with her. "Come on. Livi outfitted the cottage with everything necessary, including a first-aid kit."

Inside the cottage bathroom, she found disinfectant and bandages. The cut wasn't deep, but it still bled. She made Roarke sit on the tub lip and knelt before him, stroking a cotton ball damp with peroxide. He didn't even wince. His green gaze grew stormy.

"Someone who knew I would sort through Livi's personal belongings soon…because I was putting the house up for sale and it needed to be cleaned out. Someone who knew you or I would open those drawers. But that's nothing compared to the shower trap."

Dread filled her as she realized what he was saying. "Livi had remodeled that bathroom to make it easier to access. No tub, just a shower."

His expression tightened. "Whoever did this intended to kill Livi."

A shiver raced down her spine. She placed her palm on his arm, feeling tensile strength beneath the hard muscle and sinew. Reassuring. Roarke might be some things, but he was a good person to have in a crisis.

Her area of expertise was history and research. Not sabotage and crime.

"Now I'm damn certain there's a secret entranceway to the manor. Maybe one that old Oscar and Kitten used for their love affair. What I can't figure out is how someone found it, and began using it as well," he mused.

She finished wrapping his hand. "How's that?"

Roarke flexed it. "Great. You're a good nurse. Got any ideas about who could have found the secret entrance from the tunnel?"

Megan sat back on her heels, thought hard. "There was that party Livi had, and many of the townspeople were here. She started talking about the history of the house… Maybe someone found it that night?"

He went still, his green gaze thoughtful. "Where were most of the guests?"

"The library and the drawing room."

"We'll check those after we look through the security footage."

Back at the cottage, they found no evidence of anyone entering or leaving. Roarke thumbed off the remote to the monitor. "Whoever set those traps did it before the cameras. Let's check out the library and the drawing room."

She remembered something she'd read in one of the love letters. "No. I want to read over the letters Kitten wrote to old Oscar. Correspondence like that can indicate a location, since they had a clandestine affair."

He gave her an approving look. "Good thinking."

The praise warmed her.

After retrieving the letters, they sat in the library. Roarke selected one and she took another as Rigor kept them company. The dog was a good watchdog and would alert them if someone came into the house.

Roarke sat up in the dainty needlepoint chair. "Listen to this! My darling Oscar, I tried to meet you at our love nest, but JB may suspect something. He still wants me. I had to remain working. You should fire him as your chauffeur. He has started to become a nuisance. Your wife also has been keeping an eye on me and I cannot escape her attention. After she goes to bed, I will use the library door and meet you in the cemetery at midnight. I pray this letter finds its way to you. There's something I must tell you…"

Megan read aloud the dates of all the letters. "The one you just read is the latest. There's no more after that. I guess their affair ended."

"I bet Kitten was a maid in his household."

"Oscar probably ended it if his wife suspected. He wouldn't risk a scandal. He had already faced town scrutiny when his illegal bootlegging brought him trouble," she mused. "I did a little research and found out he stopped running rum after the sheriff let him off with a warning and a promise not to alert the federal authorities if Oscar stopped."

Roarke tapped the letter on the side of his boot. "The sheriff was probably worried about the Purple Gang from Detroit getting involved. Cooper City was ripe for infiltration from the mob, so old Oscar did the right thing. Kitten mentioned a library door."

She set the letters down on the little table next to her chair. "The manor was built in the late 1800s, but records show Oscar renovated in the 1920s. That's when he probably constructed the tunnel and the secret entrance to the manor. The library was added on during the renovation process. It used to be a pantry, since it's adjacent to the kitchen…"

Roarke was already on his feet, examining the bookshelves. It seemed too cliché, too easy. She helped him pull books off the shelves and stack them on the floor.

"Look for a wider than normal opening," she advised. "These shelves are original from the renovation."

After examining every inch of the shelves, they found nothing. Roarke frowned. "Got any ideas?"

She glanced around the room. "Maybe we need to look down, not up."

He pointed to the heavy carpet covering the original oak hardwood floor. "Help me with this."

When they rolled it back, she saw the outline of a door in the middle of the room.

He grinned at her. "Got it."

He traced the outline of a hatch. There was a small latch at the end.

The hatch lifted easily. Hinges were well-oiled. Roarke glanced into the darkness and then at her. "Stay here."

When he returned, he carried a powerful flashlight and his pistol. He descended first after handing Megan the light.

They followed the passageway, Roarke leading with his pistol drawn. Finally it dead-ended at a door. He pushed at the door and it slowly swung open.

They found themselves in the tunnel that led into the cemetery. Roarke examined the door. "Brick facade to a wooden door, hinges on the inside of it to hide it from sight. Old Oscar was clever."

When they returned to the library, Megan breathed a sigh of relief as Roarke closed the hatchway.

"What are you going to do?"

"Nail it shut," he told her.

Some time later, the entrance was boarded up. Roarke

wiped his brow with his shirt. "That will give them a hell of a surprise."

Megan sat on one of the library chairs. "If someone was using this hidden entrance to the tunnel to smuggle out items, how did they lift the rug to get into the manor from the tunnel?"

His gaze sharpened. "They may have had help. Or there's another hidden entrance."

"Poor Livi, all this time someone sneaking into the house without her knowing." She shivered.

"I should have come back here." He looked haunted.

"You were busy with your career, Roarke. She knew that and she was so proud of you. Talked about you all the time."

Wry amusement filled his green gaze. "Bet that wasn't your favorite topic."

"Oh, it wasn't so bad. It made her happy, and I did enjoy listening to her stories about you and your work... Everyone in town was proud of you as well and the man you became."

Best to keep it impartial and not admit the full truth about how Livi's bragging about Roarke saddened her and made her long to see him again. In the years they had been apart, she had tried to forget him, but it was impossible.

How did you forget the one man who made you feel alive, fired you with a passion you would always remember, filled your life with daring and adventure, and listened, really listened, to your hopes and dreams?

You didn't.

His expression dropped. "Everyone in town? Hard to believe. I'm Bad Boy Calhoun, remember? Hard to erase that rep. I don't have that kind of respect."

This was one thing she could change his mind about. She took his hand. "There's something you need to see,

Roarke. Something to change your perception about this town and how they don't care about you."

He frowned. "What?"

"Come with me. We can take the golf cart. The batteries should be charged."

Although darkness had fallen, the headlights on the cart worked well. Megan drove through the woods, detouring at the road leading to the family cemetery. His breath hitched as she parked the cart before the iron gate.

"Why are we here?" he asked.

Megan tugged at his hand. "Come with me."

They walked into the cemetery. He stood, staring at the family plot, then rubbed his eyes as if in disbelief.

Every single smashed stone had been carted away, the graves restored. Nothing remained of the vile destruction they had seen. He strode over to his mother's grave. Roarke didn't speak. In the moonlight wetness glistened on his cheeks.

Megan felt her throat close up. She knew how much he'd loved and cherished his mother.

"You did this for me?" he asked quietly.

"I didn't have the money. But your grandmother does. I told her what happened, asked for her help and she made some calls. Several people volunteered to clean up. Today, on their day off." Megan pointed to the road leading away from the cemetery. "Hardest thing was to have it done without you knowing."

"That's why you wanted to know my plans." He squatted down, touched the simple headstone saying Moira Calhoun.

"I'm sorry they didn't have time to engrave much. Your grandparents paid extra to have a marker put in place until you decide what kind of headstone you want for your mom."

He stood, dusted off his hands. "Thank you. This is…"

Roarke was not an emotional person, but she knew this was an emotional moment for him. She put a finger to his lips. "No thanks are needed. I know you would have done the same for me, if our positions were reversed."

He nodded, looked at the gravestone again. There was the cement that forged their bond years ago. They were always there for each other in the past.

He exhaled. "You always had my back, princess. More than anyone else, even Livi. Always."

"This is what friends do for each other, Roarke."

He glanced at her. "Are we friends?"

Her heart skipped a beat. "I'd like to think so."

They drove back to the cottage. Inside, Roarke sat on the sofa, burying his head into his hands. Megan sat beside him.

"If you need privacy, I'll go outside, check on Rigor."

His expression was somber as he lifted his head. "Tell me what you went through when your dad died. I hope you had someone to lean on as I leaned on you when it happened to my mom."

The question stunned her. Megan licked her lips, struggling with her own emotions. She sat next to him as he took her hand.

"Did you, princess? Was anyone there for you?"

She managed to find the words. "No. It was…private. Just me and the nurse."

Grief had a funny way of surfacing when she least expected it. She didn't want to cry in front of him, she hadn't cried in front of anyone, not even when the hospice nurse pronounced the time of death. Roarke touched her face and his fingers came away wet.

"I'm sorry you had to go through that alone." His voice was soft.

She went into his opened arms, needing this, needing

him. For a few moments she let herself cry, releasing all the emotions she'd bottled inside her. So much pain and anger.

Finally she lifted her head. He handed her the box of tissues on the end table. Megan wiped her eyes and nose.

"Thanks. I'm so afraid I'm going to have nightmares tonight. I have no energy left to fight them. Sometimes I'm afraid to fall asleep."

Roarke gave her a thoughtful look. "Sometimes you need to vanquish the bad memories with rituals, bring them closure."

He vanished into the kitchen. She heard a cork pop.

When he returned, he had two filled champagne glasses.

"Livi always kept a bottle of sparkling wine in the fridge for special celebrations. We should toast your father and my mom."

So thoughtful of him, bringing much-needed closure for them both. Roarke handed her a glass and lifted his. "To Professor Albert Robinson, who loved teaching and adored his smart beautiful daughter, and Moira Calhoun, who would do anything for her wayward son."

She stayed his hand. "To Moira Calhoun, who was loved and cherished by a good man, a son who cared deeply for her."

They clinked glasses and drank. For a few moments they sat in companionable silence.

He looked at his glass, seemingly lost in thought. "Your dad wasn't a bad man, Megan. He was trying to protect you. Now that I'm older, I realize that. Let's face it, I wasn't a stellar example of the kind of guy a dad wants his daughter to marry."

Megan set down her glass. "He would be proud of the man you became. Don't sell yourself short, Calhoun. Ever."

Roarke put down his glass and caressed her hand, his thumb stroking over her skin, making her shiver with longing. Awareness of him shot through her, filled every cell. Her mind didn't wish to rekindle the passion they'd once shared, but it was hard to convince her body otherwise. Sex between them had been explosive, and everything inside her remembered the bliss they'd shared.

She lifted her head. Roarke stared at her mouth the way he had in the past.

The intensity of his gaze resembled a man who wanted her in his bed and would stop at nothing to have her. With other men, she shied away from such determination. Never with Roarke.

Finally he lowered his head and brushed his lips against hers. Megan closed her eyes, leaning forward. He deepened the kiss, pulling her hard against him. She lost herself and all the terrible memories in the promise of his hard warm mouth. She gripped the stiff muscles of his shoulders, knowing the years had lashed him with scars on the outside and inside.

It didn't matter. What mattered was here and now, with him. It felt so perfect, as if the years had melted away and they were young, foolish and desperately in love; their bodies molded against each other so they could barely tell where one began and the other ended.

Passion flared, the passion she'd felt when the world felt suffocating and Roarke had freed her from the restrictive cage placed around her by parental expectations. She was laughing inside, joyous, feelings she hadn't experienced in months.

Roarke groaned beneath her mouth and then he pulled away, his lips parted, his body rigid. He drew in a breath, raked a hand through his short dark hair.

"Damn, Megan. I forgot how good it could be with you…"

She gave a little laugh. "I did as well."

He drew in a deep breath. "I have no right to ask this of you, but I need you tonight, Megan. I hope you need me, too," he said quietly.

In answer she kissed him again. Roarke framed her face with his hands and kissed her back, his tongue sweeping into her mouth, his lips moving over hers with warm determination. He pulled away, leaned his forehead against hers.

"You're trembling," he murmured.

"I'm scared." Finally she admitted her worst fear. "I've thought of this for so long. What if this is a dream and I wake up?"

"Then we'll fall into the dream together." He took her hand and led her upstairs.

They didn't stop until reaching the bedroom. They kissed again, tearing their clothing off, and fell onto the bed naked.

Roarke's palms slid up the small of her back, stroking the curve of her spine. "I miss this, miss you," he muttered.

Then he fisted a hand in her hair, bent her head back and kissed her with such passion, she lost all her sense. Megan could only think of Roarke, the taste of him in her mouth, the feel of tensile muscles beneath taut skin, the wiry chest hair rubbing against her sensitive nipples.

She opened her legs and wrapped them around his hips, urging him closer as they kept kissing. Roarke slipped a hand between her legs and caressed her, drawing a finger through her swollen folds. He teased her and stroked, every touch drawing her higher and higher. Then he feathered his warm mouth across her neck, kissing and nipping as the tension climbed.

Screaming, she shattered, her nails digging into the hard muscles of his back.

Pride and masculine possession shone in his gaze as

he sat back, watching her. Roarke's gaze smoldered. He reached into the nightstand and withdrew a foil packet.

Panting, she sat up and helped him roll on the condom.

His limbs were long and sturdy and roped with muscle. Wide shoulders gave way to the classic V of narrow waist and hips. Her breath caught at the web of ugly scars knotting his leg.

Roarke diverted her attention away by kissing her cheeks, murmuring how he adored her freckles.

Then he was nudging her thighs open, settling between them. Roarke stared at her, his heavy body atop hers, his hard chest pressed against her soft breasts, his muscled flanks entwined with her slender legs, his heated gaze fused to hers.

His cock slid against her soaked folds. The slow teasing move made her grit her teeth. An impish grin as he drew out the anticipation, making her hot and eager. She pushed her hips upward, doing a little teasing of her own.

Roarke pushed into her, driving upward, sealing them together. Megan gasped, gripping his shoulders. It felt so good, so right.

Pleasure rippled through her as he began to move. Slowly out and then back inside her, building the heat between them. All the while his gaze was warm and soft on her, the look on his face making her believe this was more than casual sex.

It was reigniting the flame they both thought had died, had wanted to die.

It consumed them, sending them spiraling together into erotic bliss as his hips drove harder and faster. She pushed upward, meeting his frantic moves. She squeezed hard around him, feeling the incredible pressure build until she cried out and climaxed again, gasping for air, feeling as if she were flying.

Roarke closed his eyes and threw his head back, the corded muscles on his neck straining as he gave one last thrust and shouted her name.

Wrapping her arms around him, she held him close as he collapsed atop her, his muscled weight pressing her against the soft mattress. Roarke's ragged breathing bellowed into her ear as he pillowed his head next to hers.

Trembling, she curled up against him, hearing the rapid beating of his heart. They seemed perfectly in sync, the two of them recapturing what she'd thought was lost years ago.

Megan placed her hand upon his chest, reassured by the sound of life, the gentle breeze drifting through the open windows cooling the sweat on their bodies. She pillowed her head on his broad shoulder as he kissed her again.

Her eyes closed on the exhale of one breath and the inhale of another.

Roarke couldn't sleep. He kept thinking about the wild, explosive sex they'd had. He'd needed it. He had needed to shred the last barrier of clothing between them and slide into her warmth. Banish the icy nightmares of the past with her soft female flesh sheathing him. Making love with Megan had vanquished his demons when he was a teenager. Now fresh demons rode his shoulder as she snuggled into his arms.

With other women, it was only sex. Never with Megan, burrowed inside him and curled up like a kitten, snatching his heart.

Roarke slipped into a dream memory...

She couldn't be dying. Not his vital, strong mother who had slogged her way through lifting thirty-pound trays at her waitressing job, battled her in-laws for custody and loved with every fiber of her being.

Not Moira Calhoun. She was only thirty-eight. But cancer ignored age. Her bones poked through flesh, her cheeks were sunken.

"Mom," Roarke whispered, his fingers curling around hers. "Mom, don't go, please."

Vivid green eyes, mirrors of his own, opened. "Roarke, you'll be fine. Promise me to follow your heart. Promise me."

"I promise." He squeezed her hand tighter, as if that could prevent her from slipping through his grasp into the next world. "Mom, you're not going to die. You're going to be fine."

A small smile curled her cracked dry lips, the kind of smile she always had when telling him to be strong and take pride. "I love you, Roarke Calhoun."

Then the light faded from her vivid gaze.

Several moments passed, many heartbeats, his heart shattering but still beating. How could it beat when his world had collapsed?

Tears brimming in his eyes, he couldn't release her hand. The doctor came into the room to give the official news. Only when he smelled Meg, her sweet fragrance, and felt her arms slide around him, did he release his mother's hand.

He turned to her, this woman-child who refused to leave his side. Roarke fell into her embrace as strangers marched into the room and the harsh, grating sound of a zipper closed over his mother's face.

Megan took his hand and led him out of the cold dark room filled with death and grief. Now they were in the bedroom in the caretaker's cottage. Roarke acted on instinct, easing his grief in her young naked body, releasing his emotions as they tangled together on the cotton sheets. They were making love with a ferocity he'd never experienced, but she took everything he had to give, kept taking, her eyes trusting and shining with love.

When he finally slid off her sweating naked body, Megan turned to him, her expression changing. Panting, he stared at her.

"Touch me again, Roarke." She leaned forward and grabbed his arm. "You know you want to. Stay here with me."

"Megan...what's the matter with you?"

Her face changed, turned into sharp features, erasing the pretty freckles he adored kissing, her eyes dark and sunken... She looked like a phantom.

He struggled, trying to free himself from her tight grip on his arm.

"I'll keep you here with me. You'll never leave. Never be free. You'll die here like your mother did."

She laughed...

Roarke woke with a start. Moonlight streamed into the bedroom, pooling on the white carpeting and spilling onto the pretty white furniture. It glinted on the mirror, giving everything a ghostly effect.

He glanced down at Megan sleeping beside him. No wonder he'd dreamed about her and their past. It was a dream. Nothing more.

But it was a long time before his troubled mind allowed him to fall asleep again.

Chapter 15

Roarke's side of the bed was empty when she woke the next morning. Megan yawned, stretched, feeling a luxurious pull of muscles well used.

She showered, singing as the enticing smell of bacon and eggs floated in the air. Breakfast, courtesy of her man. She laughed a little. Her man.

The laughter faded as she realized he wasn't her man. She'd awakened in the middle of the night to find him staring at the ceiling. He assured her he was fine, but Roarke had seemed a little different afterward.

As she dressed in jeans, a plain lavender T-shirt and sneakers, Megan wondered what the morning would bring.

She wandered into the kitchen, yawning again, stopping short at the sight of Roarke in a pressed white shirt and trousers.

He finished his coffee, pointed to the counter. "Made breakfast, you can pop it into the microwave. Didn't want to disturb the sleeping princess."

"Where's Rigor?"

"Outside, terrorizing squirrels."

She poured a cup of coffee. "I have errands to run, but I wanted to drop off that money at Chet and Nancy's first. Want to come with? They'd love to see you."

"Send them my regrets. I have errands and an appointment downtown."

"I can drop you off, save you a car ride. Their house is on the way. Where's your appointment?"

Curiosity filled her. Roarke had expressed such disdain for the town; she wondered who was worth his time.

His expression turned guarded. "I'm not sure how long I'll be. See you, princess."

He dropped a quick kiss on her cheek.

None of her business. She had no right to pry, yet his reticence to share information bothered her. It was as if he'd never taken her into his arms last night and shown her a desire she hadn't experienced in years.

When she finished breakfast, she went outside to find Rigor. Maybe a walk would clear her mind.

The dog happily accommodated her as she strolled toward the woods where the body had been found. So many secrets on this property and Roarke seemed to harbor the newest one.

Not that she should care, but she did. Last night's passionate lovemaking had left her with a delicious afterglow, but daylight and his departure had been a slap of reality. Why did Livi have to die and throw them together like this? So much simpler to merely leave her a stipend in the will, and let her move on. But the dangling carrot had been the hope she could accumulate enough money by selling Livi's possessions to save the bookstore and the apartment.

Now she was being evicted, and the bookstore was teetering on the edge of shutting down as well. Roarke's life wasn't here. He didn't care about the town or what happened here. As soon as he secured money for Holly, he could leave town and never look back, same as he had years ago when he'd roared off on his motorcycle.

She walked to the lakefront and sat in one of the chairs on the beachfront, staring at the vastness of the water. Her mind skipped to an image she'd conjured in her mind of Roarke, naked beneath the shower spray this morning, strong throat muscles exposed while he closed his eyes to enjoy the hot water…water cascading down his bare muscles in little rivers…

Meg glanced at Rigor, who nosed in the sand for interesting smells.

"I need to quit daydreaming and get to work. You ready for some breakfast?"

Rigor wagged his tail in agreement.

After feeding Roarke she left him outside with a bowl of fresh water so he could continue his merry chasing of squirrels. Megan took her time driving to Chet and Nancy's house, enjoying the cool breeze through the open Jeep windows. When she arrived, Holly came out to see her. Meg hugged her, painfully aware of how thin the little girl was, and pale.

"I've missed you, Meg." Holly buried her face against her. "I wanted Mom and Dad to bring me to see you, I even wanted to help you pack yesterday, but I haven't been feeling well."

Tears welled up. She fought them, struggling to keep a smile. For Holly's sake, she could muster a smile. They had to save Holly. Only money stood in the way of the transplant operation.

"I'm here now, pumpkin. Let's go inside. It's too chilly out here for you."

Chet and Nancy were stunned and happy at the cash she offered, and not surprised when she explained it came from Roarke through his inheritance.

They invited her to stay and have lunch. She agreed, checking her watch and wondering how long Roarke would be. It was a lovely clear Sunday in Michigan, leaves beginning to turn, and she wished he would spend more time with his stepniece.

They spent the afternoon in the park after Chet and Nancy went to the bank's ATM to deposit the money. Holly was too tired to walk, but had a wheelchair. Megan wheeled her on the pathway, stopping to pick up gold and red leaves Holly wanted to collect.

By late afternoon, Holly was worn out. Megan returned to their house, kissed her goodbye and left.

Surely Roarke would have returned from downtown by now.

As she pulled into the gravel drive up to the manor, she was surprised to see the front door open and Rigor lying next to it. Several boxes were piled on the rickety porch. Roarke came outside, carting a large box and setting it down.

His expression was guarded as she mounted the steps.

"What's going on?" She indicated the cartons.

Her stomach tightened. This couldn't be good. Last night had stirred all her emotions and desires. The former passion was still there.

But she didn't want to get hurt again. She'd already suffered too many losses, people leaving her without much of a goodbye. Involvement with Roarke only meant another heartache.

He fished into his jeans and handed her a set of keys. "Every single inch of this house has been checked and rechecked. It's safe to go through it."

"So you decided to start clearing out some things."

"Thought you wouldn't mind, but I started packing up stuff here in the manor that belonged to me. It should make cleaning out everything go faster. I secured a storage unit and I'll leave them there until I decide what to do with my things."

She leaned against the banister as he set the box down near the front door, near several others. Her heart sank. Losing her father's apartment, and now this, made her feel like someone had pulled out the rug beneath her wobbly feet. Bad enough he was distancing himself after they'd made love.

This felt like a slap in the face.

"Forgot how much I had in here." He folded his arms and regarded her. "Look, I know you wanted to inventory every single item in this house and sell it individually, but it would be easier simply to hire an estate company. You could get a nice bit of cash for all the stuff, and it wouldn't take as long."

"Why the rush?" she blurted out.

Roarke's gaze clouded over. "Chet told me Holly's getting worse. She's running out of time."

After seeing Holly she had to agree with him.

"What about the treasure Livi mentioned? You want me to sell everything without even looking further?"

He sighed. "Livi adored mysteries and secrets. Hell, her whole family was filled with them. But I can't see her hiding ten-million dollars' worth of treasure. She was eccentric, but cautious. And we've already combed through the entire house."

"It's worth a try to keep looking. The money will come in handy."

"Meg, why are you so concerned about money? Chasing a mythical ten-million-dollar treasure when you can sell all the antiques and everything in here and get a flat fee? I already found an estate agent if you're interested."

Everything was moving too fast. She pressed fingers

against her temples. He seemed determined on a course of action. In the past, that course had included her. Now he was in a hurry. Insight hit her. "You want to get rid of everything and leave town."

Bingo. The look on his face assured her she'd nailed her target.

"Holly comes first. She needs that operation. And yeah, I have to get back to work, Megan. I can't stay here forever." His mouth compressed.

Struggling with her pride, she decided on a partial truth. "I was hoping to start selling some of the contents in the library. I can find a buyer in Grand Rapids, a man I've worked with before on book acquisitions. But he's out of town until next week. He would give me the best price for some of the books and other items."

"Then store the books. You do own a bookstore."

She thought quickly. "I could move some of the contents to the cottage to get them out of the manor house."

He stared down at her hand, his expression inscrutable. "I'm afraid you can't leave them there long. You'll also need to find another place to stay. I've got someone representing the historical society coming in five days to do a property inspection on the manor and the cottage and the grounds. The society gave me a deposit and I've accepted their offer."

Chapter 16

He felt like the worst kind of jerk as Megan stared as if he'd punched her. In a way he supposed he had. "You did what? You're selling to the historical society? What about the treasure?"

He looked away, his jaw tight. "I doubt there's a ten-million-dollar treasure here in this house, Megan, and it could take months to find it even if we did. Holly doesn't have that kind of time. The attorney for the society made an offer. Four hundred thousand. They have a generous sponsor who wants to restore the manor. They made a separate offer for the contents, with all those proceeds going to you. Cash."

"How much?"

"Fifty thousand. Pretty generous. I negotiated with them for you to keep the books and anything else you want. You can put the books in your store or to sell them to your contact."

He thought the amount would please her, but she only looked more dismayed. Sensing the sudden tension, Rigor whined.

"I don't understand, Roarke. You've willing to sacrifice ten-million dollars?"

He folded his arms across his chest. "There's no proof a family treasure of that magnitude exists. We've searched the entire house. What's the point? It's best for both of us that we settle this business. This place needs work, Megan. Too much work and it's basically a white elephant. I'm lucky the society offered as much as they did. No one else would touch it. Costs could run well over six figures for repairs."

Even as he said the words, he knew he was making excuses.

"And if the historical society happens to find a ten-million-dollar valuable? What are you going to do, Roarke? Live with the regret?" Her voice rose.

"Even if it is, then if they find it, it would fund the society nicely. Maybe they can erect a shrine to Aunt Livi. I don't give a damn. I have to get back to DC. My life is there. Not here."

Her mouth, ah, her perfect mouth, wobbled. He hated seeing the fear and worry in her big eyes, even more, knowing he had put it there.

"Meg, fifty-thousand dollars is generous for all Livi's things. It's a nice nest egg. But I can't waste any more time here. I have to clear things up and move on."

"I see." Her voice was quiet. "And who made the offer, Roarke? Was it Amanda?"

"Does it matter?"

"It was Amanda. I'm sure of it. Amanda's always wanted this house and Livi's things. She has the connections. She's been working with Deke to redevelop Main Street. I bet he put up the money to buy this place in exchange for her influence with the town council."

Irritation bit him, along with guilt. "Maybe, but Livi is

gone now and if the historical society can fix this place and make it into a showcase museum, let them. No one else in town is remotely interested in this place. I checked with the building department and the chances of anyone getting the land rezoned for multi-family or commercial use is pretty damn remote. Without that, the property isn't worth much."

He exhaled sharply. "Chet and Nancy need to move quickly to get their daughter the transplant surgery."

"I know." Meg bent down and patted Rigor, whose tail thumped against the worn porch boards. "I saw how sick she's gotten. Even in a few weeks."

"Then you agree this is for the best."

"No, I don't agree, but the will clearly states the house and grounds are yours to do with as you wish. And since you're adamant about leaving as quickly as possible, I need to comb through the manor and remove books and other items I wish to sell on my own."

The cool look she gave him told him whatever they'd shared had evaporated like snow on a hot day. He wanted this distance. Why did it make him feel so bereft?

"Take all the time you need," he said quietly.

A slight laugh. "Not that I have much. How much time do I have? When's the closing?"

Roarke drew in a breath. "Two weeks. I planned to tell Chet and Nancy tomorrow night after Chet gets home from work. I was going to order in for dinner for all of us. I was hoping you would come with me."

She didn't meet his gaze. "Excuse me, Roarke. I have work to do."

"Meg, I can help you…"

"I don't need your help and it's obvious you don't need mine."

The door banged behind her. Rigor whined with apparent disapproval.

"Aw, hell," he muttered, sinking onto the steps.

Chet and Nancy could finally relax a little, knowing their daughter's life would be saved. He wouldn't take a damn penny of the money.

And he could leave, never looking back. Never having to see Meg again, or the town. Wipe away the memories and the pain and get back to the work that meant everything to him. Megan was the anchor that could tie him here to the town he no longer called home.

Making love with her last night had reminded him of all they had shared, only this time it roared forth with a life of its own. All the desires and longings and passion he'd felt for her had surged as if they'd stepped back into yesterday when they were young, careless and thought they ruled the world.

He wanted that again, but he *didn't* want it. He was headed toward a future of tumbling her into his bed once more, stripping her naked and losing himself in the soft warmth of her body, a connection as if they were two halves of the same whole.

What they had shared was a perfect cocoon where they'd both felt safe and alive. Yet his jaded self knew that you couldn't recreate the past. He'd moved on, and Meg was stuck in the same town with the same people who detested him and thought he'd caused a fire a wealthy teen had actually set.

There were too many ties to a life he no longer wanted but Meg craved. She was a small-town girl, who deserved a nice man to marry, a family of her own.

Yet thinking about Meg living with another man, wearing his ring on her finger, going to bed with him each night, her gurgling laugh as she entwined her long slender arms around his neck...

The thought nauseated him. He needed to move on, get

away from this place before he lost his focus on what was really important. His job. His career. Ensuring Holly's needs were met.

Roarke sat on the top step, wincing as it creaked beneath his weight. Rigor came over and sat next to him, the dog's big eyes seeming to beseech him.

"What?" He threw up his hands. "You're judging me as well? You'll have a good home. I'll make sure of it before I leave. I promise you'll be well cared for with people who love you." He petted Rigor's head, feeling his guts squeeze. "Not a jerk like me who comes and goes and leaves everyone behind because he doesn't want to get involved again."

The dog whined again.

"This place has too many bad memories," he muttered, stroking Rigor's head. "She wants me to give the town a chance again. I can't do it."

The town would always regard him as Bad Boy Calhoun. With Livi gone there was nothing here for him anymore. Megan was like the yawning jaws of a trap. If he surrendered to his feelings for her, feelings he thought he'd buried, he'd become ensnared once more in Cooper Falls.

The door opened behind him. "Roarke?"

He rubbed the heel of his hand against his weary eyes, forced back from the past to the harsh reality of the present. "Yeah? Need help?"

"No. I wanted to know if I could move my things to a guest bedroom upstairs for the rest of the time I have here. I have some things to do today but wanted to get everything here settled first."

Guilt pricked him. "What's wrong with the cottage?"

Silence.

Okay, he wasn't stupid. "Meg, stay. If you're uncomfortable sleeping in the cottage, I'll move out to the manor."

She pushed at the long fall of her hair, the move lifting

her breasts. He steeled himself against the familiar desire. This was business. Pure and simple.

When had anything with Megan been simple?

He hated the shadow of hurt in her eyes, eyes he had stared into last night as they moved together. Once they had shared so much, their dreams and hopes. Life got in the way. He wondered if it always would.

For years he'd focused on his career and making something of himself. For the first time since leaving his hometown, he wondered if he should have given the town another chance, only because Megan was here. Drawn to her, the smoothness of her skin, the lush curve of her mouth he remembered kissing long into the night, he reached up to touch her, make that connection once more.

Megan drew back as if burned. "No, the property is yours. You should stay there if you wish."

He didn't like her sleeping and unprotected alone in the manor, but knew her stubborn streak. "Take Rigor to stay with you. He'll alert you to danger."

She nodded.

Roarke felt another pang of regret and stood, dusting off his jeans. He had to make up for being such a heel. "Where are you going? Need help?"

"You've done enough."

The rejection didn't surprise him, but his reaction to it did. He didn't care about anything in this town anymore and he'd made arrangements to ensure Megan got a healthy amount of money for Livi's belongings. It was the gallant thing to do to help her out. They had nothing in common anymore. Megan belonged to Cooper Falls and his life was back in DC with the Bureau.

Why then, did he feel like he'd lost everything?

Megan couldn't stay in the cottage. Too many memories of Roarke taking her into his arms, sparking old memories

of when they had their future unwinding as a bright roadway stretching before them.

Deke would demand the keys bright and early first thing
tomorrow and she didn't want to be there when he dangled
them in front of her face, making more sly suggestions. Best
to return to the apartment one last time, awash in memories and regrets.

Slowly she trudged up the stairs to her apartment. The
door was slightly ajar. Frowning, she pushed it open. Did
she forget to lock it?

Not that it mattered. Nothing much of value here anymore, except her clothing packed into a suitcase, along with
her mother's jewelry.

She didn't even care if thieves stole it. Everything around
her was collapsing. Just as she thought she could rely on
Roarke, he backed off and looked to the future without her.

Flipping on the overhead light, she inhaled the air. Musty
and stale. Perhaps she should have opened a window.

*Not my problem anymore. Deke can afford plenty of
air freshener.*

As she walked into the living room, the bareness and the
dust didn't affect her as much as she'd dreaded.

The body on the floor did.

Near her suitcase and the bottle of expensive Scotch
whiskey she'd left behind, Deke Kinkaid lay motionless
on the carpeting. Even from this distance she could see
he was dead.

His mouth was open, his eyes staring sightlessly at the
recessed ceiling her father had loved.

Chapter 17

Emotions never helped in a crisis. He'd been through enough of them to know how to corral his feelings, analyze the sitch and then act.

But hearing the absolute panic and fear in Megan's voice threw all his hard-core training out the window. He could barely breathe. Roarke heard his lungs expand. Contract. Heard the sounds of his breath thundering in his ears, his heart pounding, but it made no sense. He felt as if he were underwater, all sound muffled except for the screams in his head.

He'd felt like this before, during the war. After he'd roared off on his motorcycle, leaving Megan behind, hoping desperately she would follow him after boot camp.

He'd never wanted to feel like this again. Meg was doing it to him all over. Life had a funny way of giving him what he least expected, and wanted.

He was bounding to the driveway to his rental as her quavering voice told him about finding Deke Kinkaid's body in her apartment.

"Give me the address," he told her, gravel spitting beneath his tires as he raced the sedan out of the driveway.

She did, stammering she had to call the sheriff.

Roarke arrived before the sheriff's deputies did. His heart racing, he squatted down by the corpse of Deke Kinkaid. Sitting on the floor near the door, Meg hugged her knees, her eyes wide and terrified.

Much as he wanted to comfort her, hold her tight, professionalism kicked in. He examined the scene. Empty apartment, dead body by the wall lying supine.

"Did you touch anything?" Roarke asked.

No answer. Using the corner of his shirt, he picked up the half-filled whiskey bottle, smelled it and inhaled the scent of bitter almonds. He'd bet his career the guy was poisoned by cyanide.

He set the bottle down carefully. Judging by the body's rigor, Kinkaid was dead less than eight hours.

Roarke went to her, sitting beside her. "Meg, talk to me. Did you touch anything?"

Headshake. Shivering, her gaze blank, she seemed unresponsive. Roarke shrugged out of his jacket and put it around her, rubbing her shoulders.

"You're in shock. Does that fridge have any pop in it?" The sugar would help her.

A short laugh. "It's empty."

He kept rubbing her arms, his gaze scanning the apartment. "Why was Deke here? And where's all the furniture?"

Megan turned her head. "In storage. I guess he came here to get the keys early."

"The keys to what?"

Refusing to look at him, she stared at the floor. "To my apartment. I owe back rent and Deke was evicting me for nonpayment of rent."

His chest tightened. She'd been going through all that

and never shared one word of her own troubles. How could he be so blind?

"Damn, Meg, wish you would have told me."

"I didn't want to trouble you. You have enough on your mind."

Roarke kept rubbing her back. This didn't bode well for her. She had a clear motivation for killing Kinkaid. Yet it made little sense, killing him in her own apartment by poisoning Scotch she couldn't know the man would steal.

Doyle arrived, followed by two deputies. The sheriff scanned the room, saw them.

"Calhoun, when did you get here? Did you touch anything?" The man's voice was calm and professional.

Against his will, Roarke's admiration for the sheriff kicked up a notch. Only a notch.

"I arrived a few minutes ago. I know about working crime scenes. You'll find the murder weapon is the Scotch. Kinkaid was poisoned. I left no prints when I picked up the bottle."

The sheriff walked over to the body, crouched down, seemed to analyze the situation. His nose wrinkled as he picked up the bottle of Scotch using gloves he'd snapped on. Doyle sniffed it. "Whose whiskey is this?"

"The Scotch is mine. I returned here today to get it, and a couple of personal items I packed and couldn't take with me," Megan told him.

The sheriff began rapid firing questions at Meg while the two deputies began processing the crime scene. Meg answered in a monotone voice. No, she hadn't spent the night here or seen Kinkaid since he stopped by the apartment when she cleared it out Saturday with her friends. She had called 9-11 upon seeing the body. Yes, she had an alibi. She had been with Chet and Nancy all day, and with Roarke all night.

Roarke glared at the man. "She didn't do this. Got it, Doyle?"

Doyle pursed his flat lips. "Looks mighty suspicious, Meg. Whole town knows Kinkaid was evicting you. You have the motive to kill him."

Roarke realized how out of touch he'd truly been with everyone in Cooper Falls. He'd suspected she was in financial trouble, but not this much.

How could he not have known the difficulties Meg faced?

You didn't want to get involved.

Meg thrust out her hands as if pushing the entire ugly scene away from her. "With my own bottle of Scotch that I drank out of only yesterday? That makes no sense!"

His heart squeezed as understanding shot through him. "Sheriff, she's right. I don't think this was a case of someone murdering Kinkaid. They wanted to kill Meg. Whoever poisoned the whiskey intended for Meg to drink it, since it was her liquor. Kinkaid stole the whiskey, or planned to, before Meg arrived, and had a drink of it."

She blinked, as if realizing the weight of his words. "I told people yesterday when they helped me move out that I was going to drink a toast to Dad before I took the rest of my things and this bottle. Deke expressed interest in the liquor when he stopped by Saturday to check on the apartment and see if I was moving everything out. He offered me cash for the Scotch."

The sheriff looked around the empty apartment. "Why would someone want to kill you, Megan?"

"I don't know! Must I provide my own motivation for someone to kill me?" she snapped.

"Calm down," he said in a mild voice. "I'm on your side."

"I haven't threatened anyone or evicted anyone like Deke

did. I can't think of any reason why someone would want me dead." Meg hugged herself.

I can... I can think of ten-million reasons. Roarke's blood ran cold. Someone knew about the treasure and the house. They'd heard Livi talk about it and believed it was true. They knew with Meg dead, he wouldn't have a reason to stall on selling the manor.

Everyone in town knew Roarke detested Cooper Falls and wanted to leave in a hurry, as soon as Holly's transplant money was secured. It was Meg who planned to stay.

Meg who stood to inherit all the contents of the mansion.

Roarke stood and pulled Meg to her feet. Trusting this sheriff with her life was like trusting a thief to guard a priceless diamond necklace.

Meg's more priceless than a lousy necklace.

At the question in her eyes, he said brusquely, "We're leaving."

Doyle's head whipped around. "You're not going anywhere."

"Is she under arrest?" Roarke asked.

"No, but…"

"You know where to find her if you have more questions. She's in shock and needs to get the hell out of here." He herded Megan out of the apartment and downstairs to his rental car.

The faster he got her out of here the safer she'd be.

Everything was happening too fast. Megan felt as if someone had put her on a merry-go-round and powered it on turbo. Seeing Deke's lifeless body had made her sick. She balked as Roarke tried to help her into his car.

"Wait a minute. Just wait. I've got my Jeep."

His jaw tightened and his green eyes grew stormy. She'd

seen that look before, when his pure stubborn streak rose up. "No. Leave your vehicle here until I can check it out."

"Check it out? For what?"

"Everything. Loose brakes, someone tampering with the steering wheel, hoping you'll get into an accident since they failed the first time to kill you."

Hearing him speak so bluntly made her legs weak. She accepted his hand as he helped her into the car. When they were buckled up and he started the engine, she turned to him.

"What you said to Doyle back there, you weren't trying to divert his attention and throw suspicion off me. You really believe I was the intended victim."

Roarke nodded, his expression grim as he drove off. "Yes. You have an alibi. You were with Chet and Nancy all day and me all night, and if you wanted to kill Deke, you wouldn't use your father's bottle of Scotch."

She pressed two fingers to her head. "True. I could have used a roll of dollar bills with poison on them. Deke could never resist money."

A flash of his old smile, and then Roarke turned serious again. "Meg, tell me every single thing about Deke and your interaction with him."

She drew in a breath, still feeling shaky and anxious. This was Roarke. He had her back and in a crisis he was better than any lawman. She began with the bookstore and the apartment and the back rent owed on both, and her suspicions that Deke was trying to evict her because he wanted to sell the building.

"My guess is he wanted to steal the Scotch. It's rare, and was a gift to Dad. Deke offered to buy it from me for one-hundred dollars. I refused."

Roarke pulled into the parking lot of Park Place Diner.

He helped her out of the car. She felt wobbly as they walked toward the restaurant.

"Why are we here?" She doubted she could eat a single bite. Not after seeing Deke's body…

"You've had a tremendous shock and need sugar and food in you. And this is the best place for it, where I can look at others to gauge their reaction."

"Their reaction to what?"

"To you being alive."

His grip on her arm steadied her as they walked into the nearly full café. Roarke told the counter waitress to bring over a cold cola right away to their table. She and Roarke scanned the diners' faces. No real surprised looks or dawning shock. Only the ordinary curiosity of people looking up to see the newcomers.

Except one person, who did a double take and then looked away and then looked again at them as if she couldn't believe what she saw.

Amanda. Quite odd. Why would the president of the Chamber of Commerce be surprised at their arrival? Could she… Her stomach tightened as the hostess brought them over to a newly emptied booth and wiped the table. *Amanda couldn't want me dead. Or did she?*

"Did you see Amanda's face?" he asked quietly. "Surprised."

"Amanda could never kill anyone. It's absurd to think so."

"I've seen plenty of horrible absurdities in my career, princess. One of them almost got me killed in Afghanistan."

Sally the waitress scurried over, a glass of soda in hand and set it down. Her eyes were bright with curiosity. "We heard about Deke." Sally lowered her voice. "Everyone has. Dear Lord, Megan, are you okay? It must have been horrible to find the body."

"But not horrible that it was Deke Kinkaid." This from Michelle, taking a break and sliding into a chair at the next table.

"Michelle!" Sally hissed.

"Well, it's true. Ask anyone here and they'll agree. Sooner or later that cad was gonna get his. Half the town was in debt to him and his daddy's business. Yesterday he was in here bragging he got you good, Megan. He said he was going to clean you out."

Roarke pushed the soda toward Megan. As she sipped, he gave Sally their orders. When the waitress walked away, he turned to Michelle. "Tell me about it."

The woman nodded. "Deke came in here late last night, right before closing. He was a little drunk. He was complaining because the liquor store was closed and the bar had shut down for a private event. He ordered a ham and cheese on rye, toasted, ate it in a hurry and then said he had to go check on Megan's apartment. Wasn't supposed to visit until tomorrow but he needed to make sure you had cleaned out everything because he had plans for the place."

Michelle came over and patted Megan's shoulder. "I'm so sorry, honey. Don't worry. No one in this room believes you did it."

But did anyone believe I would inherit a fortune if we found the treasure? Who would know about the treasure?

Amanda was president of the historical society. Amanda had expressed interest in the history of the manor and the Carlson family. Amanda might have heard rumors about the family hiding a priceless valuable. Her stomach turned.

Roarke turned to Megan. "Tell me all about your financial troubles," he urged her.

"There's nothing to it." A slight humorless laugh. "Literally. Dad died in debt. The bookstore's been losing money for a while, the rent and expenses have everything in the red and, oh, Deke Kinkaid tossed me out of the apartment as of Monday. I had to move everything into storage, which I have, thanks to Amanda. I thought about living in the Jeep except I need a bathroom and a shower. Ladies should shower every day, right?"

She laughed again. "I'm homeless now. And a murder suspect."

His jaw tightened as he glanced around at the inquisitive gazes glancing their way. He lowered his voice and covered her hand with his. "You're not homeless, Meg. Livi adored you and wouldn't want you in this position. I'll make sure you're taken care of."

"I suppose a jail cell can be comfortable."

"You're not going to jail, I promise." He looked around, glaring at everyone.

"That bottle of whiskey wasn't intended to kill Deke. Someone poisoned it and left it for you."

A bout of nausea gripped her. Megan sipped more of her pop. "Why would someone want to kill me?"

Roarke shook his head as Sally brought over their orders. "I'll tell you later. Right now we eat," he advised.

When she finally pushed back her half-finished plate, he paid the bill and ushered her out of the diner. Outside, she dragged in a deep breath of the pure, clear air. If only everything else could be as clear.

Nothing would ever be the same again.

Roarke knew they were running out of time. As they returned to the cottage, he felt a renewed determination to find out if there was a family treasure. His grandmother might have answers.

But when he called her and asked if she knew of a family heirloom worth a great deal of money, not only did she deny it, but Abigail hung up on him.

Considering the way he'd all but thrown them out of the house last time, he supposed he deserved it.

Megan's face grew taut as he sat next to her in the living room. "I guess your grandmother doesn't have answers. If the treasure exists, there has to be something in the family history that talks about it. If only we could find Geraldine's journals. I have the feeling Livi didn't want to find her mother's diaries because she was afraid to read them and find out the pedestal she'd put Geraldine on was cracked. Oscar had already been tarnished with his rum-running. Maybe Livi suspected her father was having an affair and didn't want evidence of it."

Roarke nodded. "I can understand that. No one likes to think their parents could be involved in illegal activities."

"I found some ledgers that she kept, but it was all about household expenses and activities and hired help, but maybe there's a clue in there. Livi kept the ledgers upstairs in the closet."

Soon they were sitting in the living room, scanning the ledgers. It was tedious work. Two hours later they still hadn't read over everything. But then Megan brightened.

"Listen to this!" She read aloud a brief mention of JB, who was the family chauffeur. The man had to be replaced after he took off one night and never returned. Geraldine had made a notation that JB had been fond of the drink.

Meg tapped the page. "JB, the same man Kitten mentioned in her letters! I wonder if he ran off or something else happened?"

He shut a ledger. "We won't find answers here, but I'd bet my job that someone believes there is a ten-million-dollar treasure in the manor if whoever poisoned Deke wanted you dead. Someone who would have access to the manor and needed time to search it before I sold it to the historical society."

Before they could discuss it, the doorbell rang. They both went to the front door. Chet stood outside, carrying a red-checked casserole carrier and looking uncomfortable.

"Come on in." Roarke opened the door. "Everything okay?"

"I'm not sure." Chet frowned and went into the kitchen, setting the carrier on the table. "This is from our grand-mother. She thought you would like a hot meal. I went to visit them because Abigail called and asked me to come get an heirloom doll they thought Holly would like."

Food, after she'd rudely hung up on him? Maybe this was an apology. A strange one. "What doll?" Roarke asked.

"Some old rag doll. Hardly looks valuable. She did sound a little confused."

Megan's gaze sharpened. "May I see the doll?"

After Chet fetched it from the car, she examined it. It looked to Roarke like an ordinary rag doll, a little dirty and torn. Not worth much.

She removed the polka-dotted dress and prodded the doll's back. Then she stuck her hand inside and pulled out a large wad of cash.

Chet whistled. "Wow. She was hiding money in there?"

After counting the bills, she handed them over to Chet, along with the doll. "Two-thousand dollars."

"You think she wanted me to have this?" Chet shook his head. "I should tell her there was money inside it."

Roarke studied one of the bills. "No. Take the money and the doll home. Don't say a word to the grandparents. Use the money as you need it. These bills are new. She must have known about it."

"But why the subterfuge? Why not give me the money outright?" Chet looked bewildered.

"I don't know." Roarke glanced at the casserole dish.

"Same reason she sent us a casserole. This is a little pedestrian for our grandmother."

"Is Abigail getting forgetful? She is in her eighties," Megan said.

"Maybe. She did act stressed. You can see for yourself tomorrow when you return the casserole dish. She insisted on having it back by tomorrow."

Strange request. "You know her better than me, Chet. What did you notice?" he asked.

Chet fingered the doll. "I asked if everything was okay and she said she was fine, just a little tired lately. It was hard to hold a conversation with her because their employee, that guy Benson who drives them? He kept hovering, asking Abigail if she needed anything."

His guard went up. "Elderly theft is a big problem. He could be exploiting them."

Chet shook his head. "I didn't get that vibe from Benson. He's a little crude, but he helped out with Holly a couple of times. You might want to check him out, though, with your FBI connections, Roarke."

"I will."

When Chet left, Roarke turned to Meg. "Let's see what's inside this casserole holder."

"It smells great."

"Yeah, and I've never known my grandmother to cook in all her life."

"I don't want to eat it," she admitted.

"You're not touching it. Like I said, my grandmother never cooks and she knows I know that."

Roarke found a fork and scraped the casserole into the trash.

Megan unzipped the carrier and pulled out a folded paper. "Maybe this is the reason she sent you food."

She began reading. "Roarke, I didn't want to say anything on the phone, but you are correct. There is a family treasure, worth a great deal of money. Come to the house tomorrow on the pretext of returning the dish, but be discreet."

The note was signed *Abigail*.

Hope flared on Megan's face. "There is a treasure, I knew it! But why go to such lengths to tell you?"

He felt deeply troubled. "Maybe she's being watched and this was the only way to get a message to me."

Roarke had a bad feeling his grandparents didn't only know the treasure existed, but could be in trouble as a result.

After a restless sleep in which Roarke didn't leave her side, he and Megan drove to his grandparents' house the next day.

Benson ushered them into the house, took the casserole carrier and sat them in the formal living room. Roarke gazed around the room. Nothing seemed out of place.

But when William and Abigail entered the room and sat on the sofa, Benson hovered.

"That will be all, Benson," Abigail said tightly.

"I can fetch tea or coffee, stay here in case you need me."

Irritated, Roarke glared at him. "My grandmother told you to leave."

Abigail shook her head. "It's fine, Roarke. Benson may stay."

Roarke stood up. "It's not fine. I wish to have a private conversation with my grandparents." He strode over to Benson. "Get out."

After he all but pushed the man out of the room, he closed the doors.

Megan joined his grandparents on the sofa. "We received your note."

Abigail twisted her hands in her lap. She glanced over her shoulder. "What note?"

Not good. He began to pace. "The note you left about the existence of the treasure. The note asking me to visit you today and return the casserole container."

William took his wife's hand. "She wrote you no note, Roarke."

A prickle of unease raced down his spine. "It was in the casserole carrier."

"I don't remember." Abigail yanked her hand from her husband's, pressed two fingers to her temple. "I've been so tired lately. And that horrible news about Deke Kinkaid. I don't believe you are guilty, Megan."

"Thank you," she said quietly, looking as troubled as he felt.

His irritation flared. "Of course she didn't, because the bottle of Scotch was poisoned, and Meg planned to drink it if Deke hadn't touched it first."

Both Abigail and William paled.

He continued, his gaze never leaving them. "With Meg gone, whoever bought the house would legally own the contents that weren't sold…"

Abigail kept looking to the hallway. Roarke turned, saw a shadow outside the door as Benson knocked.

The man opened the door. "I made fresh coffee."

"Fine. Go drink it. But first…" Roarke took out his cell phone and snapped a photo of the man. Benson's jaw dropped. Roarke closed the door, shutting the man out.

When he turned back to them, his grandparents looked tight-lipped.

He lowered his voice. "I think someone wants Meg dead to go through the house and get the treasure Livi mentioned leaving there. You said there is a family heirloom. Do you know where it is?"

Leaning forward, he locked his gaze on them like a laser. "I need to know because someone tried to kill Megan and her life is in danger. Is there a treasure or is it a myth?"

"I don't know what you are talking about. I know nothing. Do you hear me? Absolutely nothing." Abigail's voice rose. "I'm sorry."

"Please, can you help us?" Megan pleaded.

"I can't. I'm tired. I need you to leave now," Abigail said.

He stepped back, willing himself not to jump to conclusions.

For as he searched their faces, their stiff postures and the sweat beading on their temples, he realized something else was going on.

They were terrified.

He looked at his grandmother's hands and wrists, always delicate and pale, now sporting bruises. "Who's threatening you? Who hurt you, Grandma?"

Abigail shook her head.

"You have to tell us. Or the sheriff," Megan said gently.

Megan hadn't changed. Always more concerned for others than herself.

William put an arm around his wife's shoulders. "Nothing is wrong. No one is threatening her."

He tried another tack. "The statue of Cupid and Psyche... you wanted it because the treasure was hidden inside."

The slight nod from his grandmother could have been nothing, but he knew Abigail agreed with him.

William shook his head. "The statue did hide something."

"Who is after it?" he snapped. "What aren't you telling me?"

He tried persuading them to talk more, and realized they wouldn't say another word.

"Please, keep Megan safe. That's all I can tell you. It's best you leave now." Abigail stood. "I'll walk you out."

They were all but throwing them out. He took Megan's hand. As he walked down the steps, he thought his grandmother whispered, "Our family is counting on you."

But he couldn't be certain.

Chapter 18

As they drove back to the manor, Megan felt as if someone had punched her. His grandparents' fear was as real as the treasure Roarke thought was a myth.

Now she felt certain someone else knew and could have caused Deke's murder.

Her murder, had her landlord not been greedy and drank the valuable Scotch.

Rigor came around the corner, barked happily to see them as they parked the car and got out. Roarke let the dog inside the house first and headed for the living room.

"We know they wanted the statue because it hid the treasure," Megan mused. "But that base could only hold something small…"

His expression changed. "Something as small as a few coins. That's got to be it. The treasure is old coins."

Roarke palmed his cell phone. "I sent that photo I took of Benson Miller to the FBI to run in our facial recognition program. I'm calling Sheriff Doyle and asking him to do a welfare check on the grands. I don't like how terrified they seem."

Relief filled her. She hadn't liked leaving them alone like that. "While you're doing that, I'll start checking the library."

Knowing they searched for something as small as a coin proved to be daunting, but at least she knew what they needed. She'd already begun to inventory the books.

Roarke joined her a short time later. "Doyle promised to send a deputy out to check on Abigail and William, and he promised to do a little digging on Benson while we wait to hear back from my boss on that facial recognition software match."

An hour later, they had torn through every single book in the library. Roarke sank onto a chair by the window. "Livi said in her letter we knew her hobbies and that would lead us to the treasure. Can you think of anything other than reading where she would hide a coin?"

Megan sighed. "She had a lot of hobbies. Traveling, collecting artifacts. But I can't think of one hobby she liked that would be a good hiding place for a coin."

His phone buzzed. Roarke glanced at it and frowned. "I'll be damned. My grandmother joined this century. She actually texted me."

His frown deepened. "Abigail said she needs to tell me what she knows and needs to meet with me at their house. Alone. She requested you don't come with me."

Odd behavior, but perhaps they'd had a change of heart. "Go, Roarke. Find out what is going on and what they know."

He shook his head and called instead. Finally he hung up. "No answer. I don't like this. I think someone is threatening her."

"You have to go over there, Roarke."

"Why doesn't she want you there, Meg? Doesn't make sense."

Megan studied her hands, the short-clipped nails. "You're her grandson. I'm a suspect still in Deke's murder. Maybe she's nervous around me and that's why she didn't want to talk. Don't worry. I'll be fine. Maybe you can convince them to talk to the sheriff's deputy when he arrives."

"I don't like this. It won't take me long. I'll be back soon. Rigor will stay with you for protection." Roarke dropped a kiss on her cheek. "If you see anything suspicious or you get afraid, call me. Deal? And don't stay here in the house. Go to the cottage. It's safer there. Make sure you have Rigor with you at all times."

After he left, she wandered around the cottage, opening drawers and looking on shelves. The cottage, unlike the manor, was homey and relaxed. She could see Livi staying here, entertaining friends with her tall tales.

Maybe Livi hid the treasure here instead of the manor. She glanced down at Rigor, lying on the carpet before the brick fireplace.

"What do you think, buddy? Is the treasure here?"

Suddenly her cell phone pinged a text. Bob, texting from the library.

I remember Livi saying something about the old newspapers she kept in the woodshed. She'd found something that deeply troubled her. If you bring me the edition with the missing pages, I can check for you. I don't have copies at the library, but Vivi has some at the shop she saved for people who collect newspapers.

She'd wait for Roarke to return, but first, at least she could do this small thing. Megan changed into a forest green button-down shirt, her favorite jeans and hiking boots.

Somehow she knew the old bones were connected to everything disquieting Livi before she died. Before the body was discovered, Livi had been enthusiastic about discussing her family's history and everything about Greystone Manor.

Afterward Livi put a halt to her family's historical biography and seemed distracted. She also hadn't been interested in who had been buried on her family's land. Roarke's great-aunt had been agitated every time Megan brought up the topic and wondered who the poor soul was.

Certainly Livi couldn't be responsible for the man's death. Meg picked up the pocket watch, still sitting on the end table where Roarke had left it in the living room. Grabbing a magnifying glass from the junk drawer, she closely examined the faint initials on the watch.

That wasn't a letter *i*. She barely could make it out, but the letter hooked at the end. *J.*

Her heart skipped a beat. Now she could see the name after the initial. *Beaumont.*

JB. The man mentioned in Kitten's letters!

Bob might know more. He seemed to be up on the town's history more than anyone, except Amanda. She itched to find out.

Dead leaves crunched beneath her feet as she strolled along the sun-dappled path leading into the woods, Rigor bounding ahead of her to check out interesting smells. Today was a splendid Michigan day, the temperatures in the sixties and the sun warming her skin.

The air smelled of autumn and woodsmoke from someone burning a fire in the distance. Megan paused before an opening in the trees giving a splendid view of the dark blue lake waters mirrored by bright sunshine. Bright yellow and brilliant red leaves adorned the branches.

Sharp regret keeled through her. Holly loved this time

of year. How long did Holly have? Nancy told Megan every day she seemed to grow more fragile.

Silently she vowed no matter what it took she would help Holly get the operation. Roarke was even more dedicated.

Suddenly she realized the birds in the trees had fallen silent and she couldn't hear Rigor racing ahead of her. No, that was him barking, right? Her heart skipped a beat as she realized his barking carried a frantic tone.

The dog was in trouble.

Remembering Roarke's admonition to call him if anything odd happened, she fished her cell phone out of her jeans pocket. Dismay shot through her as she saw there was no signal. She'd forgotten the coverage in this section of forest was poor.

Her heart lurched as the barking grew louder and more frantic. Meg ran toward the woodshed. Rigor was locked inside.

She texted Roarke that she was at the woodshed because Rigor was locked inside and pressed Send, hoping the text would go through.

Panicked barking sounded inside the old wood shack. Megan raced toward the sound, her heart thudding against her chest. Dead leaves crunched beneath her boots as she ran, tree branches scratching her face as she broke through the forest.

Reaching the shack, she jiggled the knob. It stuck. Always had. She'd meant to tell Livi to hire someone to oil it, or burn the shed down because it was so dilapidated. Fumbling with the rusty doorknob, she finally managed to partly open the door, but no dog emerged.

Light from the small square window showed the interior cluttered with stacks of firewood Livi never used, the old newspapers and some rusty tools. Rope ringed the dog's neck, the length trailing down to the ground and tied to the rusty potbellied stove in the corner. Rigor jumped up and down, barking now with obvious joy to see her. Megan threw her arms around the pup.

"It's okay, buddy. It's going to be okay now. I'll get you out of here."

"Stupid girl," a deep voice hissed outside. "Burn in hell."

Too late she turned for the door. It creaked shut behind her. She threw her entire weight at it. It did not budge. The hinges were rusty, but strong.

The oily smell of gasoline filled the shed. Meg's breath came in panicked gasps. She'd walked straight into a trap. Now she was locked inside with the dog, and whoever had done this remained outside and wanted them to burn to death.

Chapter 19

Roarke raced to his grandparents' house, his instinct tingling. Why hadn't his grandmother talked previously? She'd seemed nervous and he'd attributed it to their strained relationship. Now he wondered if something else was going on.

When he reached the stately mansion, he parked out front and ran to the front door, pounding on it. His grandmother opened the door.

"Roarke, what are you doing here?"

"You texted me, asking me to return, and said you were ready to talk. Alone, without Meg." Cold dread rushed down his spine. He should have listened to his gut feeling, but he'd ignored it, hoping for once his grandmother would do the right thing.

"Oh, dear heavens." Abigail buried her face into her hands. "He has my cell phone. He sent that message."

"Who?"

No answer, but for a soft sobbing. Roarke reminded himself he was dealing with an elderly and obviously terrified woman. He swallowed impatience and brought her over to sit in the parlor, then knelt before her, wrapping his fingers around her wrists and pulling her hands away. She felt cold, like death.

"Grandmother, what is it? Who is threatening you?"

Eyes wet, she stared at him, but he could tell her focus wasn't on him. It was in the distance. Hearing a noise behind him, he glanced over his shoulder. His grandfather, looking worried.

"Don't tell him, Gabby. You know what will happen!"

"What will happen, Grandfather?" Roarke asked, centering his attention on his grandmother. "Why are you both so scared?"

"He threatened to kill us both. We're old, Roarke. We can't fight him."

He drew in an impatient breath. "And you have a grandson in the FBI who can protect you. I know we haven't had the best relationship, but I won't let anything or anyone harm you."

"You have no idea how dangerous he is," Abigail cried out. "You can't protect us."

In his gentlest tone he reserved for parents of missing children, he told her, "Trust me. I can. Tell me what's going on. Who is threatening you?"

William came into the room and sat next to his wife. For the first time Roarke saw them as they really were—not two wealthy and aloof relatives who had shunned him as a child, but two elderly people who struggled to cope with a problem much bigger than themselves.

He took a seat in the wing chair near the sofa.

Abigail twisted her hands in her lap. William took her right hand, squeezed it. Finally he nodded. "She threatened Livi, but he's the one behind everything."

His blood ran cold. "Who?"

Abigail sagged against the seat. "Vivian. Benson is her nephew. I only found out two days ago they were related when I overhead him on the phone speaking to her. Bob recommended him after Andy retired earlier this year. I had no idea he was related to them. I think he's been stealing from us. We couldn't say anything, couldn't tell you..."

He blinked. Certainly not the answer he'd expected. "Vivian and Bob? That nice elderly couple?"

"Vivian is my sister," Abigail blurted out. "My illegitimate half sister. We never knew... Benson threatened to kill William and me."

Roarke swore loudly. "Benson texted me from your phone to lure me here. Where's Bob and Vivian?"

She wrung her hands. "I don't know where they are, Roarke. They want everything that belongs to Lavinia. Benson found my mother's private diaries and he found out everything."

Suddenly his phone beeped a text from Megan. I'm headed for the woodshed. Rigor's locked inside.

Roarke swore and stood, checking his sidearm. "Call the sheriff. Have him send two deputies here to arrest Benson and meet me at Livi's house at the woodshed. Tell him to bring all the first responders."

As he tore off in the car, he prayed he'd be there in time.

The stench of gasoline grew stronger. Megan's eyesight adjusted to the gloom as she stumbled toward Rigor, looking for a way to set him free. The rope around his neck was knotted loosely and she managed to untie it. He jumped up, licking her face.

She hugged the dog as the person outside moved around the woodshed. She heard ominous splashing and tried to stay calm.

Maybe reasoning with whoever this was…

"Hello? I assure you, I mean you no harm," Meg called out.

"I'm not scared of you. But you should be," the voice told her.

She knew that voice, a woman's voice, but couldn't identify her. "Why are you doing this?"

"You should have stayed out of it, Megan. You should have stayed away from Lavinia. You and your eagerness to buddy up to her, get in her will to save that failing bookstore. Your father was a loser and so are you."

Another chuckle, this time from a man. "Then again, antiques aren't selling so well, either. Right, Aunt Vivi?"

Megan's heart skipped a beat and her palms went cold. "Vivian?"

The man laughed again. "I did you a favor, Megan. Meant that poison for you, after Aunt Vivi said you were drinking the Scotch on your last day in the apartment. No more greedy landlord for you. Then again, you won't live long enough to enjoy it."

"Benson, enough talking. You know I intended that for Deke, after I called him and told him Megan left the Scotch for him. I only wanted to make him sick enough for the hospital. That man tried to destroy my business." This from Vivian, who sounded a little shrill.

The news fed Megan hope. Maybe she could reason with her.

"Why are you doing this, Vivi? You were my friend."

"You had to stick your damn nose into business that wasn't yours. You should have left Lavinia to rot in peace."

"You were her friend!"

"Her sister, dammit, I was her sister! Her sister from the wrong side of the sheets."

The woman's face appeared in the tiny window. Twisted

with rage and anger, it looked like a pale ghost returning for revenge.

"My mother was in love with Oscar Carlson. He adored her. Gave her the world. He called her his kitten. And then she fell pregnant with me and Livi's mother found out and threatened to divorce him. Oscar gave my mother money and sent her away and threatened to ruin her if she ever returned."

Megan sank against the wall. "Vivi, I didn't know. I found the love letters. Your mother wrote them?"

Somehow she had to buy time. As she spoke, she gazed around the woodshed. Not much in the way of weapons. An old axe used for chopping wood had seen better days. Piles of newspapers. An old-fashioned fire extinguisher!

Knowing Vivian couldn't see much inside the dark shed, she moved toward the fire extinguisher as Rigor growled at the window.

"I should have had the same privilege and wealth Livi and Abigail had! I'm a Carlson as well! Greystone Manor and the treasure belong rightfully to me. I would have had all the access I needed to the manor and all the time I needed to search every single item for the treasure if you hadn't interfered." Vivian was shrieking now, clearly furious. "You, with your so-called expertise on the town's history and knowledge. You know nothing!"

As she moved closer to the fire extinguisher, Megan thought of the old boards on the shed and how quickly a fire could spread. She had to act fast. "Vivi, you're wrong. There is no treasure."

"Of course there is! My mother told me everything on her deathbed. Oscar told my mother he had secured the future of his family with something worth millions. We set up my nephew Benson at Abigail and William's house to spy on them to get more information. But we needed money in the meantime, and Benson has connections, so he planned to sell all the items he stole from Lavinia. Then he found old letters in Abigail's house that Oscar had written to a coin dealer, asking for an appraisal of a rare coin. He was hiding it in the manor house."

The fire extinguisher was within reach. Crouching down, Megan depressed the handle, hoping it would work.

A trickle of water pumped out. Her heart sank. Not enough. Rigor whined as the ominous odor of gasoline grew stronger. She removed her shirt and used the remaining water from the extinguisher to wet it.

"Vivi, why are you doing this to me? I never threatened you."

Megan pressed against the boards opposite the window. One creaked and bowed outward. She kept pressing on it, loosening it.

"Benson, maybe we shouldn't do this," Vivian said, sounding uneasy. "I never wanted anyone to die, except Lavinia."

"Aunt Vivi, you know what must be done."

"Vivian, don't listen to him! You know me, you were friends with my dad, you're not a killer."

"Shut up, you bitch," Benson shouted. "You're the holdup in all of this. Everyone knows the contents belong to you. The historical society already has an offer on the house and property. Aunt Vivian is the vice president and will have full access to the house. With you dead, Aunt Vivian can search thoroughly and find the treasure. She will finally get the inheritance she should have gotten."

"Benson, I don't want her to die a painful death."

Megan recognized Bob's voice and her heart sank. He was in on this as well.

"Can't you simply shoot her?" Vivian asked.

"No. It has to look like an accident. This shed is a tinder-box," Benson yelled. "Give me the damn matches."

"Please, release the dog at least. He doesn't deserve to die. He's just a dog," she pleaded.

"That dog!" This from Benson. "He's a menace. Bit me when we used the secret tunnel to enter the house. Tied him to the railroad tracks but damn Roarke set him free."

As she listened, Megan kept working at the loose board. Most of the gasoline was poured near the door. Maybe Benson figured she'd try the door, not the back of the shed.

"Aunt Vivi, what are you doing? Give me that phone."

She heard a hard slap and the elderly woman cried out.

She heard the whoosh of something igniting, saw black smoke from the window.

"Let's go," Benson shouted. "Let her burn."

The crackle of flames and the acrid stench of smoke filled the air. Megan took the fire extinguisher and broke the tiny window. It wasn't big enough for her to wriggle through. Using the axe, she quickly cleared the glass shards away and then lifted Rigor, pushing him through.

"Run, boy! Get away," she screamed.

At least the dog would live.

Tying the wet shirt around her mouth and nose, Megan sucked down a breath, striving for calm as she took the old axe and began chopping at the loose board. Smoke filled the shed now, making her cough. Outside, frantic barking ensued. Bless loyal Rigor—he wasn't leaving her alone to die.

She kept swinging the axe, the smoke making her eyes tear. Panic threatened to suffocate her. Through the tiny now-broken window, she saw orange flames licking at the shed. Chopping harder, with all her might, she loosened one board and kicked. Smoke poured into the shed. The roof was burning now. With every ounce of strength, Megan threw her weight against the boards.

They cracked and splintered outward, leaving a gap three feet wide. Megan swung again and then dropped the axe. Lungs straining for air, she pushed herself through the gap, wriggling frantically as the flames came closer. A portion of wood scraped her stomach, but she kept working her body through.

Finally! As she nearly cleared the shed, someone kicked at the remaining boards and a strong hand pulled her outside, into fresh air and freedom.

He kept pulling, yanking at her and dragging her far from the woodshed as water hissed on the flames. Roarke had brought the cavalry, and the fire department. Nearby, Rigor barked and barked, and then he came up to her, licking her face.

She doubled over, coughing violently. Someone thrust a mask at her face and she breathed deeply, grateful for the flow of oxygen.

Pain flared on her hands. Megan blinked, seeing her palms laced with blood. She'd cut herself trying to free Rigor. Roarke knelt by her side, taking a first-aid kit from an emergency medical technician. He dabbed ointment on the cuts. She winced, started to protest. He gently pushed the mask back on her face.

"Keep breathing that O_2. You probably inhaled smoke." Roarke nodded at the fire, now extinguished by the firefighters.

Megan removed the mask. "Vivi… Bob… Benson…did this. Benson… Your grandparents are in trouble."

His touch was gentle as he replaced the mask. "Keep this on and keep breathing. Doyle captured Vivian and Bob as they were trying to leave. Benson escaped. But my grandparents are fine. Two deputies are with them now."

The news relieved and alarmed her. Benson was a clear threat.

An EMT cleaned the wounds on her stomach and bandaged them. "The cuts aren't deep. Just scrapes," the man assured her.

Roarke shrugged out of his jacket and put it around her, his touch reassuring. He brushed a lock of hair from her face. "You okay?"

At her nod, he dragged in a deep breath and then hugged her. "I got your text and saw the smoke, and my grandparents alerted the sheriff as I drove here. Then I got a text from Vivian, saying there was a fire in the woodshed. Doyle had the fire department here in record time. Meg, when I saw the fire, realized you were trapped inside…"

He pulled away, his hands trembling. Roarke touched her face again with shaky fingers. "I wanted to die. I can't lose you. Not again."

Having come so close to dying painfully, she knew what was most important. Megan pulled off her mask, framed his face with her hands. "You're not going to lose me, Roarke."

Roarke touched her face, and his fingertips came away with soot.

"You should go to the hospital."

"I'm okay. I didn't inhale that much smoke."

Sheriff Doyle came over, hat in his hands. He didn't meet her gaze. "I'm sorry, Megan. I didn't know you were in danger or I would have told…"

Shaking his head, he pulled out his radio, rattled off instructions and then lowered the instrument. "Vivian and Bob confessed everything after we read them their rights. They had a change of heart after realizing her nephew wanted to burn you alive. We'll find Benson. But I want to assign you an armed deputy to watch over both of you."

Roarke's expression turned grim. "No one can protect her better than I can, Doyle. But I'd appreciate it if you had someone watch the manor house."

Doyle barked out orders over the radio. As the sheriff walked away, Megan tried to make sense of everything. Roarke helped Megan shrug into his jacket. "Okay, Megan Robinson, I'm driving you to the hospital to get checked out."

"I'm fine. I need a shower first. I smell terrible."

"You smell pretty great to me."

"Smoke?" She sniffed.

His expression softened. "Life."

She had no words, because of the lump forming in her throat. Megan took his hand and didn't protest as he hoisted her onto an ATV left by one of the deputies. Roarke whistled for the dog and Rigor climbed into the basket in the back.

They roared off for the cottage.

Inside she all but ran for the bathroom, then sponged off the dirt and ash. When she emerged and dressed, the cottage was silent.

She went into the living room, where Roarke sat on the sofa, checking his weapon. At his frown she asked what was wrong.

Roarke slid the pistol into the holder at his side and pulled his shirt over it. He glanced around the cottage living room. "We know now there's a valuable coin in the family. What if she didn't leave it in the manor house, but here?"

Megan's excitement flourished. "It makes sense. She wrote in her letter to you that we knew her hobbies. Could it be hidden in plain sight?"

"You grew closer to her. What was she doing in the last few months of her life?"

"She was always painting…" Her voice trailed off. Megan stared at the large wall painting of boxes. "I always thought that painting was so ugly. I mean, if you're going to paint, why boxes? So boring."

The chunky painting method was one Livi had taken up before her death. Megan had never liked it, but her friend was obsessed with the oil painting and slathering paint on the boxes.

Livi told her it was her *Picasso mimicry*.

"Help me get this off the wall," she told Roarke as she reached the painting.

The canvas was large, and bulky. They set it on the sofa. Megan examined the back and ripped off the paper covering it. Nothing. Disappointment filled her.

"Hold on a minute. Turn it over to the front." His gaze sharpened. "There's an awful lot of paint here."

"It's the method of painting."

"Or...something else." He glanced up with a rueful expression. "Forgive me, Livi, for ruining your masterpiece."

Roarke flipped open his knife and began picking apart the smaller boxes. He carefully inserted the knife's tip between a smaller painted box and the canvas.

As he moved the blade, something popped and fell onto the sofa. Megan's excitement flowered. "Is this it?"

Roarke carefully scraped the paint from the object, revealing a hard plastic coin capsule. She gasped as he scraped off more paint, showing a flash of gold in the container.

With extreme care, he opened the container and lifted the object. A wide grin lifted his mouth as he examined it. "I'll be a son of a biscuit... Livi, you clever girl."

He searched the internet on his cell phone and whistled. "A 1933 uncirculated double eagle gold coin. These were minted by the government but never released."

His grin widened. "Livi was wrong about one thing. I bet this is worth more than ten-million dollars. Maybe worth eighteen million."

Her legs suddenly couldn't support her. "Eight...eighteen-million dollars?"

A low growling alerted her to trouble near the staircase. Before she could react, Rigor leaped toward the stairs, only to yelp in pain as someone kicked him.

Hard.

"You've found it. Put your hands in the air and put the coin case down. I've been listening this whole time."

Benson, holding a handgun. Megan knew there was no escape now. Biting back a juicy curse, she went to Rigor, examining the dog as he lay there.

"Stupid mutt," Benson said. "Should have killed him when I had the chance."

The man sneered at them. "You thought you were so smart, nailing the manor secret entrance shut. You never found the cottage secret entrance beneath the stairway, you fools. You pride yourself on knowing so much of Greystone Manor's history, Megan, but you didn't have Geraldine's journals."

Benson laughed. "That antique bookcase hid them."

Megan's heart skipped a beat. "The Queen Anne secretary and bookcase with all the junk in it?"

"You're so stupid. I used to sell pieces stashed in old furniture found in hidden drawers. You pull out the bottom left-hand drawer and there's a secret compartment in the back. You'd never know unless removing the entire drawer."

Roarke said nothing, but Megan knew he held the coin in his left hand. Not his shooting hand. He wasn't next to the end table, but she knew him, knew how fast he could move and retrieve his weapon...

"Give me the coin and you won't get hurt," Benson demanded.

"Your aunt and uncle are in custody," Megan told him.

"You won't get far. And you won't be able to sell that coin anywhere."

He laughed, riveting his attention to her as she'd hoped. "Who cares about them? More money for me. I know someone who won't pay top dollar for that coin, it's too hot, but I'll get a few million for it."

"Catch," Roarke yelled.

Roarke threw the coin at Benson as Megan dropped to the ground. Sure enough, the man lowered the gun to catch it. Roarke fired his pistol. Benson screamed as the bullet hit his shoulder.

"Hands up," Roarke said calmly. "Drop it or I'll put a bullet in your head."

With shaking hands, blood streaming down his arm, Benson put the pistol on the floor. He reached for the coin. "Just let me look at it."

Roarke kicked the coin out of reach. "Not a chance."

"I've got this, Roarke," Sheriff Doyle called out.

Roarke helped Megan to her feet. Doyle stood at the doorway as deputies ran forward and cuffed Benson. But it wasn't the sheriff's response nor his presence that sent Megan stumbling backward in abject shock.

It was the woman pushing her way past the sheriff, who surveyed the scene with a look of satisfaction on her care-worn but still attractive face.

Lavinia Carlson Tremaine Walker.

Roarke's dead great-aunt.

Chapter 20

It was the strangest family reunion Roarke had ever attended. He couldn't stop hugging Lavinia, who cried upon embracing him. Abigail and William arrived at the cottage shortly after, looking equally shocked to see his great-aunt.

Roarke sat on the sofa next to the discarded painting. He gripped Megan's cold hand. She kept staring at Lavinia as if seeing a ghost, which in a way was true.

"How did…" His voice became clogged with emotion.

"It wasn't easy, dear boy," Livi declared in her strong voice. "Toby Doyle arranged everything at my request, along with my attorney. I'm sorry, but the only way I could prevent someone from killing me was to pretend I was already dead."

She turned to her sister. "I didn't want you or William to know, either. I thought if everyone believed I had died, it would lessen the danger to you both, especially since I left everything to Roarke and Megan."

He didn't know whether to be furious with her for lying, or overjoyed to see her again. Roarke frowned.

"Livi, why did you do it? Why didn't you simply call me and tell me what was going on? Do you realize what danger you put Megan into?"

A sheepish look came over his beloved great-aunt's face. "Bother you at work, dear boy? When you were out saving lives and bringing those lost children home? What was more important?"

He glanced at Megan, who still looked pale. "Family is more important. My family. You."

Megan, he wanted to add, but focused on Livi. "You could have saved us a lot of time and grief by simply telling me what happened and that someone was trying to kill you."

"Hold on, Roarke." This from his grandmother. "You have no idea how terrifying it is to grow older and think you are going senile because odd things are happening. Or worry because your heart medication goes missing and then turns up. Every time I asked Benson about missing items, he told me I was growing forgetful. He would turn on the oven and then tell me that I did it. He made me think I was going mad."

"He was gaslighting you," Roarke said slowly.

Abigail's voice quavered. "I noticed little things went missing around the house, but thought I had misplaced them. Two months ago I found my father's irrevocable trust papers had been rifled through in the desk. Benson must have discovered that the family trust was worth only one hundred thousand a quarter."

His grandmother's expression crumbled as her husband gripped her hand. "I told Livi and she advised me to keep quiet and she would handle everything. My big sister, always looking out for me."

Livi sighed. "I always will, Gabby. I knew something was terribly wrong. I just couldn't figure out what was going on or who was doing it, so I did tell the sheriff. That's when the threats to me started getting worse."

"I suppose you're the one who wrote that message on the attic window," Roarke told Livi.

"Yes. I thought to leave a warning. I didn't dare say more because Vivian watched the house constantly. But she never touched the attic because it was the only safe place she couldn't access. I had no idea who kept coming into the house. I suspected there was a secret entrance, but never did find it."

"That day we came to visit you, Roarke, William hoped to find the Psyche and Cupid statue because we knew the family treasure had been hidden there at one point. We wanted to make sure it was safe with Livi's things." Abigail gripped her husband's hand.

"I moved it," Lavinia said. She heaved a dramatic sigh, flapping a hand. "I suppose I should apologize for my deception and pretending I was dead."

"You'd damn well better," Megan burst out. "Do you know how hard it was, grieving my father and then you? I felt as if my world had fallen apart."

Roarke's mouth twitched at Livi's shocked expression. Megan had found her voice at last. He placed his hand over hers. "The sheriff knew all along."

"Toby's a dear friend. He wanted to help me, but worried something would happen before we found out who was the real threat. So we arranged to fake my death. The funeral director was splendid in helping with the ruse."

Roarke exhaled. "There's a matter of that will you left, pairing us together."

Livi sighed. "I trusted both of you would work together and find who was trying to kill me and steal the estate's valuables. I also knew you would protect Megan with every fiber of your being, Roarke. I couldn't do anything to erase the mistakes I made in the past, but I could give you the chance to find the love you lost. I knew you still loved her, Roarke, and for you, Meg, I know you never stopped loving him as well. After you left, Roarke, I did nothing to change Albert's mind about you. I thought it was for the best that you and Megan remained apart until you both grew older. I didn't realize how determined Albert was to keep you apart until right before he died and Albert confessed destroying all your letters, Roarke, and sending that email that ended your relationship. I should have known and should have done something and I failed you both… Can you forgive an old lady?"

She gave them a sly look. "Especially one recently returned from the dead?"

Much as he remained angry at her deception, he understood the reasons for it. Always Livi, interfering in affairs of the heart while proclaiming she never wanted to interfere in his life.

"You're forgiven." He glanced at Megan. "Right?"

Megan rolled her eyes. "I suppose. We should talk about the gold coin and what your plans are for it. Now that you're alive and we have no claim on it."

"Oh, but you do," Abigail exclaimed. "It was our plan all along."

"I have a prospective buyer for the coin." Livi winked at Megan. "We didn't work out the details before I disappeared, but I called him yesterday and he will now purchase it at a considerable sum, and avoid any government red tape, since I'm not quite certain my family was supposed to have it. He's agreed to pay ten million, the sum I mentioned in my letter. Holly will have her surgery."

Megan's mouth wobbled as Roarke felt sheer relief. Holly's life would be saved. The thought of that precious little girl finally able to ride her bike, run and play like a normal child made all her previous anger dissolve. "That's quite generous."

"Fifty percent of the money will go to Chet and Nancy to fund Holly's operation, set aside a healthy nest egg for them, and pay for Holly's medical bills and hopefully her college tuition. The rest will be divided between you and Roarke."

Roarke looked at his grandparents. "What about Abigail? It was her father's treasure, too."

William shook his head. "We only want our grandchild to be healthy once more. We talked it over with Livi before all this happened when we all agreed to sell the coin. We did contribute to Holly's fund, as much as we could from our cash accounts. Unfortunately, it wasn't enough."

"You were the ones who contributed the one-hundred-thousand dollars!" Megan exclaimed.

His grandmother blushed, the pale pink spreading on her paper-thin cheeks. "We didn't want a fuss. We wanted to help Holly, but thought it best to make the donation anonymous."

Lavinia beamed. "Now that it is settled, Roarke dear boy, would you loan me that preposterous phone of yours? I have a call to make to an eager coin collector. The sooner the money is transferred the faster Holly will get her surgery."

He shook his head. "Before you do, I'd better call Chet and Nancy and tell them the news. Chet needs to stay healthy to donate his kidney, and if he sees you're alive like we did, he might have a heart attack."

Two days later Megan was at the cottage, packing all her things. Doyle had told them that Vivian and Bob had confessed everything, in hopes of avoiding charges of attempted murder. Because Vivian had tried to warn Roarke, chances were they would get a reduced sentence.

Benson, who had changed his name to avoid Abigail and William discovering he had a criminal record, faced much more serious charges, including the murder of Deke Kinkaid.

Megan felt sad to know the identity of the body found on the estate. JB—otherwise known as James—had been the Carlson family chauffeur who wanted to marry Rose, Vivian's mother, who worked as a secretary to Oscar Carlson. When JB discovered she was having an affair with Oscar, James threatened to tell Oscar's wife.

On her deathbed, Rose had confessed to striking James and accidentally killing him during an argument. Oscar had had him buried on the grounds since the man was an orphan without any family. Rose also revealed to her illegitimate daughter, Vivian, who her birth father was.

Vivian admitted to smashing the gravestones at the family cemetery. She'd always been ashamed of not having a father and hated Oscar and the family for failing to acknowledge her birthright.

In some good news, Holly was at the hospital in Detroit for the operation. Money was no object. Even with the sale of the gold coin and half of the money going to Holly, both Megan and Roarke had trust funds of two-and-a-half-million dollars.

It was time to make some tough decisions about her life.

On one hand there were all the years she'd spent in Cooper Falls, the tender memories and the sad ones. She wasn't a fan of change. She'd lived in the same small town her entire life, loved only one boy turned man, called the same bedroom home, had the same friends, the same job.

Too much sameness.

Change wasn't something she easily embraced. Now she had the funny feeling it had snuck up on her, like her father's cancer had overtaken his body. It stared her in the face, a fact she could no longer ignore. She could no longer hide behind routine. The ordinary.

Ahead of her lay a long winding and exciting road to the unknown. Her world had transformed, but she had the power to shape it into her dreams.

She picked up the framed photo of her father on the nightstand. In his favorite jacket, book in hand, he looked studious and distant, yet she saw the familiar spark in his eyes he always had for his work. All his accomplishments had impressed everyone in town, making him a hard act for her to follow.

Change was hard. Not as painful as remaining stuck in a place and a job where you no longer belonged. Staying there to carry on a legacy that wasn't her dream, only her father's.

"You had your life and your dreams, Dad," she told the photo. "I need to make my own way in the world. I'll always love you. Maybe your legacy was the bookstore, but like Roarke said, mine isn't. There's potential inside of me waiting to be fulfilled."

Meg put the photo into the suitcase, facedown.

A knock came at her door. She glanced up and beckoned Livi to enter. Roarke's aunt swept inside, her loose lime-and-neon-pink blazer floating around her in a swirl of silk. Never afraid to be bold and different, Livi had paired the outfit with cobalt blue silk trousers and a white silk top. Livi touched her short white hair.

"Are you settling in fine, dear? Have you made up your mind about your life?"

"Yes." She thought about the challenges ahead of her, and instead of feeling familiar apprehension and fear, she felt excited.

Livi sat on the bed and patted it. Meg joined her. "I'm so glad you're moving on with your life, Meg. It's what your father would have wanted for you. He often told me in our late-night discourses."

Aghast, she stared at Roarke's great-aunt. "He did? Why didn't he ever tell me?"

Livi sighed. "Because it's one thing for the father bird to want the chick to leave the nest, another to push her out himself. He kept hoping you would work up the courage to find what you truly desire."

"He acted like he couldn't bear to lose me."

"When you were seventeen and too young to forge your way into the world, yes. He told me before he died he always regretted intercepting your letters and emails from Roarke, but he feared you were like him, headstrong and determined, and would run after my great-nephew. Only after you both went to Washington did he express concern that you needed to break free of this town and seek your own path. Then the cancer struck and he needed you with him."

"He never told me." So many lost opportunities and regrets. All she could do was push forward with her life and look to the future.

Livi nodded. "Now you do. What are your plans, Megan?"

She touched the suitcase. "I'm leaving Cooper Falls. I contacted the professor in DC who wanted to hire me five years ago and he needs my help to write another book."

Livi beamed. "I know a certain young man who would be happy to accompany you to Washington."

Perhaps. For once, she wanted to let things happen as they unfolded instead of planning every moment of her life. "We'll see. What about you and your life, now that you have one again?"

"The dear boy has finally forgiven me." Livi heaved a dramatic sigh and put her hand across her forehead. "My life can now go on."

"After you convinced everyone you were dead." The irony wasn't lost on her.

Livi had the grace to look guilty. "I had to do what I must."

"What about the house?" She looked around the bedroom at all the antiques, thought of all the memories made in this place.

"I've deeded it over to the historical society. My attorney drafted the deed to allow me to live in the caretaker's cottage for as long as I shall like. Besides, I don't need much room, not when I plan to tour Europe and meet up with Ralph." She leaned forward, her gaze twinkling. "He's the sexy guitar player I met in Spain two years ago. He recently got divorced and invited me to stay at his villa in Greece."

Meg felt a great weight lift. "So you're not staying in town."

"Me? I've been given a second chance at life and I have no intention of wasting it." Livi patted her hand. "Speaking of second chances, my great-nephew is waiting for you at the lake. I do believe he has a question to ask you before he catches his flight later today. I hope your answer is yes."

She couldn't answer Livi, for the emotion clogging her throat. So many times she'd envisioned a life with Roarke. So much had changed since she was sixteen and looked at him with starry-eyed worship.

Could they regain what they both had lost the day he stormed off, out of her life?

Roarke paced the sand by the lake water. The ring that had belonged to his mother burned a hole in his trouser pocket.

"Hey, stranger," a soft voice said.

Glancing up, he saw the one woman whom he wanted for the rest of his life. The woman he'd lost and, by a miracle, found again.

Rigor, recovered from the hard kick Benson had given him, accompanied Megan as she joined him on the beach. She sat on a lounge chair and he joined her as Rigor sniffed at the water.

He'd never fully appreciated the serene view, or the legacy of his birth. Living on the fringes of society, he'd been an outcast and blamed the town for all his problems.

Now he saw the truth—maybe he had never been happy here, but fundamentally small-town life wasn't for him.

He needed to know if Megan felt the same way.

For a few minutes they sat in companionable silence, gazing at the clear lake waters, the docks put away for the winter, the houses dotting the lakeside. Most boat owners had already secured their watercraft for the season, but for a lone pontoon boat anchored a distance away. Finally he spoke.

"Now that Holly's future is secure and Livi is busy with her plans, I'm returning to DC. I need to know what you want to do with your life, Megan. Are you planning to stay here in Cooper Falls?"

Her expression, always so readable before, turned inscrutable. "I've worked out a deal with the Kinkaids. They're donating the bookstore to the university, and leasing my apartment to a retiring professor, a friend of my father's, for a low rent for two years. In exchange I'll drop any legal action against their development firm for Deke trying to blackmail me."

Roarke waited. He'd learned to be patient.

"I need to move on. I called the professor who wanted to hire me in DC and he needs an assistant to help write another history book. I've agreed to accept the position."

He dared to hope. "You'll be in the same town as me. Meg, I don't want to lose you again."

Meg said nothing for a moment, gazing out at the water.

Finally she took his hand and squeezed it. "What are you asking, Roarke?"

"I'm asking you, ah." He fished out the ring box he'd carried around for two days, since he'd found it in the safety deposit box his mother had left him years ago. His hand trembled as he opened it and held out the square cut ruby encircled with tiny diamonds. "Will you marry me?"

She stared at the ring, and then lifted her face. "No."

His heart fell to his stomach. Guess it was too late. Maybe if he'd tried years ago to contact her, tried harder...

"I won't marry you now, Roarke. It's too much, too soon. I can only handle so much change at once. But I will move in with you and if everything works out after six months, ask me again." Her gaze twinkled. "I think the answer will be different."

Roarke swept her into his arms for a long drugging kiss. Her mouth opened beneath his and he allowed himself to get lost in the softness of her body, the passion they shared. When they finally parted, he gazed down at her smiling face and brushed a lock of hair from her face.

"All these years I've felt like my life was empty, Megan. Never knew what I really wanted until the day I returned to Cooper Falls and saw you standing outside the bathroom with that spear."

His voice turned husky as his chest tightened with all the emotions he'd kept inside. "I never planned for it to be like this, but life has a strange habit of changing direction into the unknown."

"As long as we're headed there together, then I know we'll be fine," she said, and kissed him again.

* * * * *

WE HOPE YOU ENJOYED
THIS BOOK FROM

Danger. Passion. Drama.

These heart-racing page-turners will keep you guessing
to the very end. Experience the thrill of unexpected
plot twists and irresistible chemistry.

4 NEW BOOKS AVAILABLE EVERY MONTH!

SPECIAL EXCERPT FROM

ⒽHARLEQUIN

ROMANTIC SUSPENSE

*Ex-SEAL and holiday hater Nicholas Kane is no saint.
But he and sexy CIA agent Alexander Creed must find
a priceless nativity crèche his boss stole and return it
before Christmas. Between double-crossings, rogue
agents and their own guarded hearts, these spies will
need a holiday miracle to find love—and survive!*

Read on for a sneak preview of
His Christmas Guardian,
the newest in the Runaway Ranch miniseries from
New York Times *bestselling author Cindy Dees!*

Alex blinked, startled. This man had already done
80 percent of his job for him? Cool. All that was left
now, then, was for him to finish investigating Gray and
kill him.

Nick was speaking. "...got to New York City, I got
lucky. I texted a guy who was brought in for some training
with me about a year back. He was being groomed to
take a spot on the personal security team. At any rate, he
didn't answer my text, but his phone pinged as being in
Manhattan. I tracked it to a restaurant and spotted Gray
having supper there. I've been on his tail ever since. At
least, until you knocked me off him."

"In other words," Alex said, "we need to hightail it over to wherever Gray is bunking down tonight and pick him up before he leaves in the morning."

"If we were working together, it would go something like that," Nick said cautiously.

"Seems to me we're both working toward the same goal. We both want to know what Gray stole. Why not cooperate?" In his own mind, Alex added silently, *And it would have the added benefit of me keeping an eye on you until I figure out just what your role in all of this is.*

Nick nodded readily enough and said a shade too enthusiastically, "That's not a half-bad idea."

Alex snorted to himself. Nick had obviously had the exact same thought—that by running around together, he could keep an eye on Alex, too.

If Nick had, in fact, been pulling a one-man surveillance op for the past week, he had to be dead tired. With nobody to trade off shifts with him, he'd undoubtedly been operating on only short catnaps and practically no sleep for seven days. Which made the fight he'd put up when they met that much more impressive. Alex made a mental note never to tangle with this man in a dark alley when he was fully rested.

Don't miss
His Christmas Guardian *by Cindy Dees,*
available November 2022 wherever
Harlequin Romantic Suspense books and
ebooks are sold.

Harlequin.com

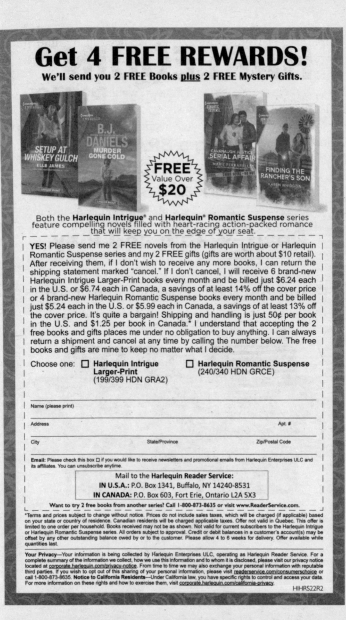

HARLEQUIN
PLUS

Announcing a **BRAND-NEW**
multimedia subscription service
for romance fans like you!

Read, Watch and Play.

Experience the easiest way to get
the romance content you crave.

Start your **FREE 7 DAY TRIAL** at
www.harlequinplus.com/freetrial.